Falling Apart Beautifully

Falling Apart Beautifully

Tilda Carrow

First paperback edition published 2024

This is a work of fiction.
Names, characters, places and incidents are either the
product of the author's imagination or are used fictitiously.
Any resemblance to actual persons, living or dead,
events or locales is entirely coincidental.

Text copyright © Tilda Carrow 2024

Cover art copyright © Tilda Carrow 2024

ISBN:9798322493228

All rights reserved.
No part of this book may be reproduced in any form, or
by any electronic or mechanical means, including information
storage and retrieval systems, without prior permission in writing
from the publisher, except by a reviewer who may
quote brief passages in a review.

To My Husband
*For every moment of encouragement
and support and for weekends
looking at fonts*
xxx

One

THE ONLY THING I know about Ivy Edwards is that she died two days ago at the Royal Victoria General Hospital. Ironically, just three floors below the very ward where she was born, seventy-nine years ago. If life is a circle, then for Ivy it began and ended on the far side of town in the draughty, red brick, Victorian buildings of the Royal General. Everything else that happened to her between those two momentous occasions, I'm about to discover for myself.

I open the door to her flat with a key from the housing association manager and pause, hit by the robust scent of lavender. There are other less identifiable smells, stale cooking fat perhaps: the kind that clings to your curtains and then leaches back into your house making everything, including the air, seem stale. There's also a hint of damp but it's an undertone if anything, mostly obliterated by the lavender. I pull a mask out of my pocket and attach it securely over my nose and mouth. There's no point taking any chances.

I push the front door closed and move slowly down the hallway. The green and brown carpet is partially hidden beneath stacks of old telephone directories, which are piled high against one wall, pages facing outwards like a flutter of off-white birds. Strangely, Ivy also had a collection of bowler hats, brushed and shiny. Some sit on top of the telephone directories, others hang on their own hooks, as if a convention of bankers visited her flat, sometime in the 1960s, and left without their head wear. The coat stand is much more conventional, with one raincoat in faded lavender, two knitted scarves and a warm-looking winter coat. But normal coat stand notwithstanding, Ivy Edwards is already an enigma. The last remnants of the life she lived, and everything that proved her existence, is contained within this flat, at number nine Starcross Crescent. It's my job to sort through all of it and dispose of Ivy's possessions, deciding what needs to be donated to charity, thrown out or sold.

I don't like the term house clearance, although technically that's exactly what I'm here to do. Every last toothpick, hairbrush and tin of beans has to go. But I prefer to look at it differently. I'm more like a niece or a trusted friend who has come over to help you have a good sort through and a clear-out. I'm here to recycle and repurpose, not for clearance. Ivy had no family left to carry out that kindness for her, someone who could take their time, reminiscing over photos and letters, living her life over again through their memories. On occasions like this, I'm grateful that the manager uses us and not one of the cheaper companies – the fishing dredgers of the clearance world – who scoop up everything in their nets, skimming off only the most valuable items to sell. Everything else gets dumped like a stinking pile of fish heads and gizzards. People like Ivy, and their belongings, deserve more respect than that.

My phone pings with a message before I can let myself through one of the doors at the end of the hall. It's from my almost sister-in-law, Poppy.

> *Juliette, fancy meeting me for a drink tonight, at the old Toad and Fiddle? I'll throw in a packet of cheese and onion crisps, if you're lucky.*

I hesitate before replying, wondering how to play this.

> *Sorry, I can't. I'm meeting Vanessa.*

> *Again? Didn't you see her last week for some stupid basket weaving class?*

> *It wasn't basket weaving it was beginner's macramé, and it was excellent. You should try it. It helps calm the mind.*

> *Never going to happen, macramé is for grannies and internet weirdoes. So, that's a definite no for tonight?*

I pause, feeling guilty.

Sorry, maybe Friday instead?

I'll think about it. But I'm feeling very wounded by your constant rejection of my friendship.

I'll pay.

Friday sounds perfect! Looking forward to it already!

You're such a fake.

I'm not a fake. I'm just easily bought xxxx

I set a reminder on my phone for Friday evening. I hate saying no to Poppy, but sometimes she's so pushy she leaves me with no other choice. That's why I'm grateful for my laid-back friend, Vanessa. Vanessa isn't on social media. She's old-fashioned that way. She's the same age as me, forty-five, although so far, she has fared much better in the aging lottery. The collagen in her jowls is still hanging on by a thread, whereas mine has recently developed a looseness that suggests a big silent defeat in the fight against gravity. Anyone who sees us together can't help but notice the wide gulf in our physical natures. Vanessa is statuesque, of Amazonian splendour, whereas I am firmly rooted in the earthly realms of ordinary, with dullish brown hair and slightly muddy-green eyes. She lives in Leeds, half an hour in the opposite direction to everyone else I know. She likes football, which all my other friends detest, so none of them have expressed any desire to meet her. She loves 1990s pop bands and she's also completely fictitious. I invented her one desperate Friday afternoon, when I could think of no other way of getting myself out of a weekend of engagement celebrations with another friend. The funny thing is, I kind of like Vanessa. I even caught myself thinking about what to buy for her birthday once. She's not the only friend I've invented either. There's also Angelique, a stylish French seamstress. I'm more than a little jealous of Angelique and the life she lives in a beautiful old apartment building, close to the Eiffel Tower, in the upmarket 7th arrondissement area of Paris. She conveniently asks me over to stay whenever I need an excuse that spans anywhere from a weekend to a fortnight. And then there's Natalia, who often needs me to support her through yet another tumultuous episode in her love life. But she's a bit of a drain emotionally, if I'm being honest. I may have to cut her loose. Every time she breaks up with Damian, her idiot boyfriend, she swears blind she's never talking to him again. But then about a week later, she inevitably takes him back, avoiding my calls for ages, and the whole sorry cycle starts all over again.

I adjust my face mask wondering if everyone else – over the age of ten – has a whole gang of imaginary friends they use to keep their real friends at a safe distance. But I also know I'm not about to abandon Vanessa, Angelique and Natalia anytime soon. The alternative is still too difficult. I'm not ready to engage in what most people consider to be normal levels of real human contact yet.

I pick the left-hand door at the end of the entrance hall and let myself into Ivy Edward's sitting room. It's a decent size, big enough for a sofa, two armchairs and two tall cabinets that show telltale signs of bursting at the seams. An open archway leads to a compact kitchen at the back of the property, with just enough room for a small table and two chairs. I always start in the sitting room when I'm on a house clearance job. The bedrooms are too personal and prone to delivering a variety of unwanted surprises: surgical supports, bottled gallstones, ill-advised photos of an extremely personal nature. The kitchen is too functional to get any real sense of who I'm dealing with: preferences in pickle variety won't tell you much about a person, other than the state of their digestion. But the sitting room is the perfect blend of the public and the private, and it's the ideal room to get to know someone. Everything that's on display for everyone to see – the scatter cushions and cosy blanket throws, the blue and white salt and pepper shakers bought on holiday in Portugal – that's only part of the story. It's the cupboards and drawers that fill in the details. Drawers are where real life happens. But I always do a quick tour of the whole property before diving into any drawers. Experience has taught me that this is wise, just in case there are any fish that desperately need feeding, or any smells that desperately need ventilating. Sometimes food has been left out on a counter and it has to be double bagged and disposed of before ripe skins burst, releasing mouldy spores into the air, like a puffball mushroom ready to explode. Kitchens can be hazardous. I double mask for those.

I start my tour in Ivy's kitchen, which is reminiscent of the 1970s with shiny olive-green cupboard fronts, a tiny melamine table and two matching chairs in blue. The whole kitchen has clearly been scrubbed on a regular basis. There are none of the sticky countertops or little crescents of ancient crumbs that I usually find around the base of ovens and bread bins. Ivy was a house-proud woman. I take a quick peek inside the cupboards, but there's not much that can be salvaged and most of it will be heading to the tip.

When I take a closer look at the sitting room, it's more interesting than I first realised. Two tall cabinets, placed either side of a gas fire, have obviously been handmade from beautiful, warm, honeyed oak. Mice and wildflowers, skilfully carved into every door panel, add a whimsical woodland feel. Every handle has a mouse's tail wrapped around it and they're so realistic, I have to prod one with the end of my pen, just to double-check. Long trails of ivy have been carved through the hinges and along the sides of the first cabinet, winding themselves into the shape of a heart close to the base. It's a private message, almost hidden from view. Someone made these cabinets for Ivy; they only exist because she did. These beautiful pieces of furniture are completely at odds with an ugly purple sofa, and two matching armchairs, which must have been bought in the 1980s, judging by their faded velour coverings. They will end their days in a skip, to the relief of all humanity.

On the inside, the first cabinet is split into open shelves at the top and drawers at the bottom and every inch of space has been crammed full, as I suspected. The second cabinet, decorated with equally exquisite carvings of wrens, blackbirds and painted lady butterflies, is also filled to capacity and beyond. I feel a familiar pull of anxiety as I close the door again. I already like Ivy. I want to find things in these cabinets that prove she had a life well lived. But it doesn't always go that way. Some people's cabinets – the people who die alone because they've alienated their families, or have a long history of being emotionally or physically abusive – are nothing like Ivy's. I can sense the ugliness of their lives long before I start opening any doors. Stuff is never just stuff: the things you buy, the mementos you choose to keep, the way you store them, it speaks whole languages about who you are and the life you've lived. Cupboards are gateways to the soul. Poppy laughs at me whenever I tell her this, then she accuses me of taking my job too seriously. But if I've been brought in to clean out a house then I am the only witness left, the last person who will ever touch, see, or sense the evidence of a life lived. I am the only person left to admire and appreciate a lifetime of treasures gathered. Poppy would hire a skip and chuck everything in it without opening a single envelope, studying a single photograph or piecing together any of the human puzzle. Maybe it's because I love solving the puzzle that I'm so well suited to my job. Poppy also regularly accuses me of spending more time with dead people than with the living, and she's not wrong. But for the time being at least, that's the way I want it.

I move quickly onto the bathroom, which is a bit utilitarian, with a simple white suite. There are three floor-to-ceiling cupboards at one end of the room, and a cursory rummage inside reveals that Ivy never threw a single old duvet cover away if she could help it. There's a solitary shoe box carefully concealed behind a heavy patchwork quilt, but I don't investigate the contents yet.

Ivy's bedroom is an homage to her obvious love of the softer shades of pink, and it takes my eyes a moment to adjust to the happy, rosy glow. Bedrooms are usually where I find the most personal of possessions: secrets kept close to heart and under lock and key, letters and tokens from lost loves, the ones that were never meant to be but were also never quite forgotten. And Ivy had plenty of space to hide her secrets. There are two chests of drawers, a bedside cabinet and a large built-in wardrobe, with three sliding doors.

I'm just about to see if all of Ivy's clothes are as pink as her pillow cases, when I'm interrupted by my phone again. This time it's Loretta calling from the office, she doesn't believe in messaging.

'Loretta,' I say, attempting to slide one of the wardrobe doors open with my free hand, but it's snagged on something inside and even a good tug won't free it.

'The boss wants to know if you're coming into the office this week, you've got some paperwork to file.'

Loretta, queen of her office kingdom, doesn't waste time on small talk. She's a one-woman miracle of efficiency and organisation. If Nigel, the boss, sneezes, then Loretta swoops in with a well-pressed handkerchief to entrap the speeding sputum, before it can splatter across her neatly ordered paperwork. Other than the fact that Nigel owns the company and pays our wages, Loretta has very little need for him. She's the main reason I avoid the office whenever possible.

'I'm coming in for an hour or two on Friday,' I tell her reluctantly, and I know that before the words have fully reached her ears, she'll have me marked in on her digital calendar.

'Will you be finished at Starcross Crescent by Monday?' she asks. I can almost sense her finger hovering over her keyboard.

'Tuesday at the earliest, I'm afraid,' I say, wondering if I can extend the job at Ivy's until next Wednesday, just to mess with her dates.

'I'll inform Nigel.' And Loretta hangs up. No questions about my health and well-being, no snippets of gossip about my co-workers. If Poppy and Loretta teamed up and took over my job, they'd be finished with a house clearance like Ivy's in under four hours, in a hurricane of chucking, dumping and discarding.

I give up on Ivy's reluctant wardrobe doors and head into the second bedroom to finish my initial assessment of her flat. From everything I've seen so far, I know it will take a minimum of three or four days to clear out Ivy's possessions and deal with her furniture, unless the second bedroom contains a lifetime collection of novelty belt buckles or antique pincushions. I inch my way over to the closed curtains to let in some light. This room is more of a study in green with delicate leaf-print curtains. The textured carpet comes from roughly the same era as the kitchen cabinets, with worn spots by the sliding wardrobe doors, which are a mirror image of those in Ivy's room. It's not until I turn to face the bed, pushed up against the far wall, that I realise someone's sleeping in it.

I manage to stifle ninety percent of a yelp with my hand but an odd strangled sound still escapes from between my fingers. I grab a lamp from the bedside table and take several hasty steps backwards. This has never happened before. In nearly ten years of clearing houses, I've never had to deal with an unexpected living person. The closest I've ever come to it was when a life-sized cardboard cut-out of a reindeer (with a red nose) fell out of a cupboard, and hit me on the head.

The person in the bed has their back turned towards me. A white head of hair pokes out from beneath a duvet, which is pulled so far up I can't see any facial features. But the general size and shape of the human lump looks more masculine than feminine. The covers slide up and down with the man's rhythmic breathing, which suggests he's still asleep. A hearing aid sits on the bedside table, next to a glass of water containing a set of dentures. I lower the lamp a little. This is no housebreaking-ne'er-do-well situation. It's more of an old age pensioner squatter conundrum. Or did Ivy have a companion? Surely, if that was the case, the housing association manager, Mr Thurston, would have warned me. This kind of house clearance does not happen when there are living occupants, someone to take care of the deceased's belongings, deal with affairs and tie up loose ends.

'Um, excuse me,' I whisper, not sure how to proceed. Is it rude to wake someone up if they're technically trespassing?

There's no sign that the man has heard me, no change in his breathing or stirring of limbs. His clothes have been neatly folded on a chair beside the window, I notice, his shoes tucked under the seat.

'I'm sorry to disturb you,' I say, a little more loudly this time. 'I'm Juliette from Hobson's House Clearance, Juliette Jones.'

This is getting me nowhere. Without his hearing aid, the man is oblivious to my presence. But I can't proceed with anything until I understand what's going on. I turn on the lamp that I'm holding and wave it over my head, hoping the flickering of light will register in some part of the man's sleeping brain. Nothing. I approach the bed cautiously, just in case he's faking it, and catch a faint whiff of something medicinal, a pungent herby rub for aching muscles perhaps? Touching his shoulder seems too personal. I don't even know his name. So I switch the lamp off and turn it around in my hands, gently prodding him in the shoulder region with the wooden base. This time, there's a definite shift in his breathing.

'Hello?' I say, edging backwards again so I can make a quick exit if it turns out he's not the Father Christmas type after all.

The man turns slowly onto his back and blinks up at the ceiling, scratching something in the buttock region of his body with his right hand. It takes him several seconds to realise he's not alone. He sits up smartly, reaching hastily for his hearing aid first and then his teeth.

'Who the bloody hell are you?' he says, before his dentures are properly settled in, and his words come out sounding slurred. His eyes widen as he takes in the lamp that I'm still clutching at shoulder height. I lower it slowly. 'I haven't got any money, if that's what you're after. You'd be doing me a favour if you found any.'

'No, I'm not a burglar,' I say, in my most reassuring, non-housebreaking voice. 'I'm Juliette Jones, from Hobson's House Clearance. I've been sent by Mr Thurston, the housing association manager, to clean out Ivy's stuff.'

'Oh.' The old man deflates and crumples forward slightly. He attempts to clear some kind of blockage in his left ear with his little finger, and then shakes his head like a cocker spaniel trying to dislodge a grass seed. 'What's your name again?'

'Juliette Jones.'

'Well, Juliette Jones, I'm Alfie Evans, Ivy's brother.'

'Brother?' This puts a whole new slant on the situation. 'I'm so sorry, Mr Evans, I had no idea you were staying with your sister. I never would have let myself into the property if I'd known you were here. Mr Thurston never mentioned—'

'That weasel doesn't know I'm here,' he grunts, wiping sleep out of his eyes. 'And I'll thank you not to tell him.'

Mr Thurston, Adrian, is undeniably a weasel, not generally prone to spontaneous displays of human kindness, compassion or understanding. I've been dealing with him for years now and there's something about his smirking demeanour that makes my skin crawl. He also has a way of looking at women that ought to land him on some kind of register. The only reason he doesn't use one of the very cheapest house clearance companies is because he's a distant cousin of Nigel's, and Nigel gives him a generous friends and family discount. If I go straight to Thurston's office, like I probably should do, and tell him about Alfie Evans, he'll have Alfie dressed and marched off the property in under thirty minutes. Maybe all Alfie needs is a little time to gather his things together and organise another place to stay? And then I won't have to alert anyone to his presence.

'I can see this isn't a good time,' I say. 'So I'll call back on Friday morning, and we can have a proper chat about things then, if that's okay with you, Mr Evans?'

'I suppose,' Alfie says, sounding less than thrilled at the prospect of our reunion.

I place the lamp on the bedside table and back out of the room, closing the door quietly behind me.

House clearance – never dull.

Two

'WE ARE GATHERED HERE today to commemorate the life of Robert Butler. An avid football fan, and a lifelong Leeds United supporter, he is being cremated today in his most treasured possession, a number seven shirt from the Peter Lorimer era.'

The minister pauses to read his notes, and I shuffle in my hard seat trying to ease the ache in my lower back. Amos Stickythorn has a voice that could put a coop full of chickens to sleep in under a minute. He has perfected this ministerial drone until his words cease to have any real meaning, and simply hover in the pointed ceiling space above us, like a dark and spiritually menacing cloud. He is my least favourite of all the ministers that perform public health funerals. And in my job, I see a lot of public health funerals. These are carried out when the deceased has nothing set aside to pay for their own cremation or burial. No savings, no assets to sell, no hoard of Saxon coins stashed under the bed for a rainy day. Under these circumstances – when there's also no family to pay for the service, or none that are willing to come forward and chip in – the local authority is bound by law to pick up the cost of a no-frills funeral. Some authorities also pay for a service to be performed, and along with that comes a no-frills minister. Some of them I like, they are decent, hard-working, respectful people. But this minister, Amos Stickythorn, is none of those things. And I often find myself planning the service I would give if I was ever called upon to officiate at his funeral – it would involve singing something doom-laden and filled with references to fire, brimstone and getting your comeuppance.

I come to as many of the funerals as I can. If I'm being sent in to clear someone's life away, it usually means there are no parents, partners, children, sisters, brothers, friends, cousins, nieces or nephews, which also means there are no mourners at the funeral. It happens more than you'd think. Not everyone is lucky enough to have a family, or a wife, husband or partner. Some people live longer than everyone else they know, the last survivor of their little clan to die. Others walk a lonely path through life, through no fault of their own, unable to make lasting connections with their fellow human beings. Having no mourners at a funeral doesn't always say something bad about the person in the coffin. Sometimes, it's just a poignant reflection of the way things turned out.

When I clear out the last of someone's belongings, I always get a sense of whether I would have liked that person in life. And that's why I'm here today, at the funeral of Robert Butler. His life simply took a series of sad and fateful turns, and someone other than Amos Stickythorn should be here to listen to his final send-off.

This crematorium, The Cedar Trees of Peaceful Rest, is decent enough. There's a generous space for mourners, a lofty peaked ceiling that lifts any singing to a higher plane, and a suitably sombre colour palette running through the curtains, carpets and pictures. But peaceful isn't always an accurate description. The crematorium sits right next to a major road and sometimes, when a particularly large truck thunders past, the candlesticks rattle on the alter like a collection of old bones. More than one mourner has been freaked out by this apparently timely judgement from the Almighty.

It's impossible not to think about Jamie, of course, and the day we brought him to this place too. Although that was a very different occasion, both sides of the aisle were packed with family and friends, with standing room only at the back. It's the only time I've ever had a front row seat at any service and I would have given anything to sit anonymously in the middle, a second-tier mourner. The details of that service have faded so quickly, I often question whether it really happened at all. But I have a portion of Jamie's ashes to prove it, the contents of his casket split three ways between me, his parents and my almost sister-in-law, Poppy. My third of his ashes sits in the airing cupboard at home, wrapped in a blanket. Putting him on the mantelpiece, between the clock and a vase of dried flowers, felt wrong, like he'd somehow been demoted to the status of a fireside ornament. Sitting him next to my bed made it impossible to sleep, the kitchen cabinets felt too disrespectful. The only place I could think of putting him was in the airing cupboard. At least it's nice and warm.

'Robert Butler lived his whole life in the town of Sholtsbury, and spent many years as a welder at the local shipyard,' Amos Stickythorn says, continuing with the service.

He wouldn't know anything personal about Robert Butler, if I hadn't supplied him with some details. I was the one who cleaned out his flat three weeks ago. It was small, reasonably well kept, homely in its own way and full of Robert Butler's life. That's how I know that a football signed by the entire Leeds United team, from 1975, was given pride of place in a glass cabinet. It's also how I know that he did crossword puzzles every day, and that a chiming clock – presented to him on his retirement from the shipyard – meant more to him than anyone could have guessed. It was one of the only things in his flat that was dust free, a treasured possession. Robert Butler loved chocolate digestives, bought his clothes at the supermarket and once owned a dog called Rusty – a collar bearing that name had been kept in a drawer along with a single clipping of reddish-brown fur, sealed lovingly inside an envelope.

If I had any say in the matter, I would make it compulsory for all funeral officiates to visit the home of the deceased, if there was no one left to mourn them. So that when they came to deliver the service, they could do so with a modicum of authenticity. Stickythorn doesn't do authenticity. The man checks his watch in the middle of reciting "The Lord's Prayer." I have considered using a well-aimed catapult to bring his attention into sharper focus. But I'm already on thin ice with the manager of the crematorium, after the good minister put in a complaint about me for heckling. Normally, I'm not a heckler, but on this occasion, when Stickythorn kept calling the deceased Archie Lambolt, I couldn't stop myself.

'His name's Gerald Archibald,' I said, clearly and loudly into the empty crematorium, my words soaring into the space above us and reverberating around the room. At least Stickythorn had the decency to look shocked.

The minister moves onto a different part of the service, and I close my eyes, bow my head and remember the details I've learned about Robert Butler. This is my way of honouring the life he lived, the personal and private things I've discovered about him. This feels like the right place to leave those memories. If I bring them to mind, here in the crematorium, maybe they will be reunited with Robert Butler and then they'll both be sent into the great cosmic beyond together, whatever that means.

The minister begins to wrap things up, the coffin taking its final journey behind the curtain. Stickythorn is already heading for the exit before the coffin has finished its slow slide beyond the veil. I make a point of sitting in my seat until Robert Butler has disappeared completely, and the velvet curtain has fallen back into place, like the end of an eternal magic trick. And then it's just me, sitting in an empty crematorium. The words *deathly quiet* seem appropriate. Somewhere in the building a door slams, and I catch an almost inaudible burst of laughter before it's gone. And that's how it ends for Robert Butler, with a velvet curtain and some anonymous laughter.

I stand up and stretch my stiff back before following the route marked out for those departing the departed. Nothing sours a funeral more quickly than a bottleneck of mourners. I can already see the next group gathering outside the main front doors. The whole thing seems indecently hasty, thirty minutes and your time is up. Even in death, you don't always get good value for money.

I shift into autopilot on the drive home, changing gears and checking mirrors without really registering what I'm doing, thinking about Robert Butler and his life. By the time I pull up outside my house, it's already dark. I turn off the engine, lean my head back against the seat and close my eyes with a mounting sense of anticipation. If I wait just a few seconds more, breathe very quietly and say his name, speaking softly – 'Jamie?'

I can suddenly sense that he's sitting in the seat beside me, and I open my eyes again. I'm not going crazy. I know he's dead. I know this glorious vision isn't real. I'm painfully aware that it's just some bizarre figment of my imagination throwing me a bone, but I don't care about the mechanics. I'm just grateful that Jamie's here at all. It's the only place I ever see him, in the passenger seat of my car when I pull up outside my house. It doesn't happen every time, and I never know how long he's going to stay. There are occasions when I catch nothing but a brief glimpse of his soft, soft smile before he fades away to nothing. Other times, I've been lucky enough to sit with him for several hours as we chat about life, love and memories. There's always something slightly wrong with his appearance – either his ears are too small, his hair is too brown or his smile is a little too crooked – and I cannot make it right. It's as if some part of my brain disapproves of these apparitions and won't let me have a whole and perfect version of Jamie. It's trying to remind me – with a tweak of his nose or a piercing of his eyebrow – that Jamie is dead, and shouldn't be sitting in my car at all. Once or twice, he's even appeared as an unsettling blend of himself and a rock star, with full sideburns, an impressive quiff of hair and a curled lip. A handful of times, he's been a bizarre combination of himself and a scientist, with crazy eyebrows, white hair and a desire to talk about nothing but molecules.

Thankfully, there's no hint of the scientist about him today. In fact, he's a pretty good copy of the man I loved for five years. His chin looks a little too narrow, perhaps. A faint golden glow has also wrapped itself around his body, and it sparkles in the headlights every time a car drives past. He appears to be wearing a small green earring shaped like a palm tree, which he never would have worn to anything but a pirate-themed fancy dress party, when he was alive. I'm just grateful there's no accompanying eye patch.

I turn my body towards his. He reaches out and goes through the motions of brushing my hair behind my ears. But I can't feel the touch of his fingers or the warmth of his skin, and my hair stays exactly where it was. I try not to let it bother me. This is the first time I've seen him in fifteen days, three hours and thirty-seven minutes, and it has felt like a lifetime.

'Where have you been?' he asks, the warm tones of his voice filling me up like an empty battery on charge.

'To Robert Butler's funeral,' I tell him.

He nods as if he knows, as if we sat next to each other in the crematorium and whispered jokes about Amos Stickythorn, and his horrible habit of picking his nose and inspecting his finger under the alter lights.

'Was Robert Butler the Leeds United fan? Did he get a good send-off?'

'It was just me and Stickythorn.'

'They shouldn't let old Bogie Face conduct those services. He gives death a bad name.'

Jamie shakes his head until his hair tumbles into his eyes. That's one of the things I miss the most, the way his hair used to fall across his face and annoy him. Not that he ever dreamed of getting it trimmed. Jamie's hair – and the fact that he still had plenty of it at the age of forty-six – was his pride and joy.

'So, tell me about Robert Butler.' He wriggles himself into his seat, settling in for the long haul. 'Did he have a good life?'

I tell him about the football-shaped toothbrush mug that I found in the bathroom, the old match programmes stuffed down the side of an armchair, and the donations he made to a local dementia charity over the years. I tell him about the family photos, from long ago, and the brother who died in his twenties. Robert Butler's life never quite got back on track. Jamie listens without interruption. He lets me get all the details out in the open and off my chest, where they can sometimes sit for weeks, if I'm not paying attention, with the crushing power of a curling stone. And then we get to my favourite part, the part I've been looking forward to since I pulled up outside the house and sensed his presence settling in beside me.

'Robert Butler sounds like a decent sort of bloke,' Jamie says, playing with his palm tree earring. 'But now I want you to reimagine everything you've just told me, and describe his life as a musical.'

Jamie invented this game when he was still alive. If I'd had a particularly upsetting house to sort through, or discovered that the person's life had been touched by more tragedy than most, he'd get me to describe that life as a West End musical and the gloom would slowly lift. Rock concerts were perfect for those who'd lived a life of high drama. Operas seemed a good match for the people who'd done something unusual, exciting or brave. There was never anything disrespectful about it. Jamie just figured that everyone had wondered what their life would be like as a musical, and we were simply adding some colour to that vision.

'And I want to hear everything about Robert Butler's life, mind, no skimping on the details,' he says, pretending to be stern. 'So, tell me how the musical of his life starts.'

I close my eyes for a second and the visions start to come. I've had years of practice at this so I know how to create a good, catchy, opening number.

'It all starts with the number seven shirt he was cremated in today.

I can hear thousands of football fans crammed together on the terraces at the Elland Road Stadium in Leeds, they're all chanting Robert's name.'

Jamie nods as he pictures the scene. 'I can definitely hear it too. It's loud enough to raise the rafters on any roof. So, what happens next?'

'Robert Butler's running out onto the pitch, he looks like he did in his younger days. He was quite handsome in his early twenties. He looked a bit like an old-fashioned Hollywood star.'

'I looked more like a Boreham Wood star in my early twenties, but that's the way the cookie crumbles.'

'Robert is carrying a football,' I say, imagining the noisy, happy scenes. 'He runs around the entire pitch with the ball held above his head, waving it at the crowd. They clap and stamp their feet in response, flapping their scarves like a football salute. That's when the line judges and referee appear to the sound of Bobby Bo Steward.'

'He was one of Robert's favourite singers?' Jamie asks, interested in all the details.

'He had almost every Bobby Bo record ever released.' I know because I've seen the same records in dozens of other homes. And it's the perfect soundtrack to celebrate Robert Butler's life. I can hear the first strains of one of Bobby Bo's most famous songs as I picture everything unfolding before me. 'The line judges perform a synchronized dance routine, using their whistles and flags. Robert looks on, smiling, tapping his football boots. As the song reaches its crescendo, fireworks begin to shoot upwards into a suddenly darkened sky, and it's a real crowd-pleasing moment. Everyone stops to watch the pretty reds and greens and bright trails of orange. Robert tilts his head in wonder, and I see the last of the rockets fade in the reflection of his eye. Now the scene shifts.'

'I was wondering if it might.' Jamie fidgets in his seat, impatient for the next part in the musical I'm creating.

'The stadium dissolves and we are transported to a shipyard, where it's dusk. It's very atmospheric. The sound of riveters and welders forms a musical backdrop this time. They're working on a huge ship, a great hulking chunk of metal that looms high above everyone, the lights from the welding torches look like little bursts of starlight.'

'I already like where you're going with this,' Jamie grins. 'I can practically see the blue welding flames from here. Go on.'

'Robert is now kitted out in overalls and steel toecap boots. Welders turn from their work and he shakes them by the hand as he passes by. No, wait, I can do better than that.' I rewind the action a few seconds in my head, and start again from that point. Jamie always had a more inventive imagination than me. He would have given this shipyard scene some real pizzazz, brought in some elephants, or acrobats on unicycles tossing flaming torches wildly through the air. But I'm doing my best.

'The shipyard welders form an archway with their torches, welding masks down, and they look like an honour guard of medieval jousting knights. Robert walks proudly beneath the blue blaze of flames until he reaches a winch. It lifts him all the way up the side of the ship and deposits him on the deck, where a cute dog rushes towards him.'

'This is much better. You've really got it nailed down now.'

'Robert bends on one knee and scoops up the animal into his arms, as Rusty, his beloved dog, licks his face.' And now for the grand finale, the show-stopping number that I've been building up to. 'There's a band, they're wearing crisp white dress-uniforms, and they look like a cross between a Royal Navy band and something out of a romcom.'

'You always did have a thing about those films.'

'Shush! I'm concentrating.' I close my eyes so I can picture all the details and ignore Jamie's smirking face. 'They stream onto the deck of the ship, coming from all directions, playing trumpets, drums, trombones and tambourines. The sound is incredible. Robert can feel the drum beats thumping through the soles of his boots. It's at rib-cracking volume as they circle around him, filling the night air with the big brassy sound. And then the trumpet players are moving aside, leaving a clear path through the centre of the band, and a woman runs towards him.'

Geraldine Richards was his wife of fifteen years, until she died of cancer at the age of forty. Robert had photos of her all over his flat. The one he kept next to his bed stood out the most. Geraldine was in her twenties, happy, laughing, sitting on a garden swing in a delicate floral-patterned dress, with her hair trailing loosely behind her in the breeze. She had her whole life ahead of her. That's the way Robert chose to remember her every night when he went to bed, and every morning when he woke up. This is where I almost lose control. It reminds me so much of the photo I have of Jamie, the one that sits next to my bed, where he's midway through telling a terrible joke. And I have to put the band in a holding pattern for several minutes before I'm able to carry on again. Jamie waits patiently, as I attempt to stop the tears from sliding down my face but it's hopeless, and all I can do is wait for them to stop.

'Geraldine glides towards Robert across the deck of the ship,' I say, when I've finally pulled it together again. 'She's dressed in the same floral print from the photo, the one that Robert treasured, her hair trails behind her with just a trace of sparkle. He runs to embrace her and lifts her off the deck, swinging her around, and it's such a joyful reunion that even the tuba player and the trumpeters are sobbing into their sheet music. The sound of noses being blown mixes easily with the dying notes of the tune,' I say, adding my own blown nose to the imagined symphony that's filling the car around us. 'And that's when the music stops and the image slowly fades to darkness.'

'That was your best one yet.' Jamie gives me a round of applause, as I wipe my eyes. 'I particularly liked the scene on the deck of the ship at the end, but I think I would have gone with more of a Celtic vibe for the music,' he says, thoughtfully. 'I like the image of the military band, but Robert and his wife needed something softer, more romantic.'

I can't help replaying the final section of Robert's life musical in my head. Celtic music is the perfect contrast to the cold steel deck of the ship. The soulful tones of the violin give it a much more personal touch than the ceremonial sounding trumpets and drums.

'No elephants this time?' I ask.

'The elephants have been retired to a sanctuary, but I might bring in some hippos the next time you get a bit stuck with one of your musical numbers. Not that you needed any help, love, you did a grand job with Robert Butler's life.'

Reimagining his life has also helped to ease some of the sadness I've been feeling. I'm thankful for Jamie's intervention.

I smile and reach for his hands, trying to remember what they used to feel like – the hard skin on the outer edges of his fingers, the way they were always warm, even in the middle of a snowstorm his hands were impossibly toasty.

'So, where are you working at the moment?' he asks.

'I'm at Ivy Edward's flat in Starcross Crescent. You'd like her. She's got a collection of bowler hats in her hallway.'

'A collection, you say? And just the bowler hats, no top hats or ladies' wedding hats, or woolly hats?'

He's teasing me with his gentle humour, but I can tell he's intrigued by the hats, that he'll be back to hear more about them.

'She's also got a brother, I found him asleep in her spare room. He's got to move out next week.'

'That must have given you quite a shock.'

'I threatened him with a table lamp.'

'Well, that would have terrified me. The hospitals must be filled with people who've been sent into shock at the sight of a threatening table lamp. Does he have somewhere else to go?'

I pause, considering the question again. But I don't want to think about Alfie Evans now and run the risk of having his white hair and false teeth blend in with Jamie's face, the next time he makes an appearance in my car.

'I see you've been spending quite a lot of time with Vanessa again.' It's a gentle chide. He knows all about my host of imaginary friends and the reasons why I use them. But it's still enough to leave me feeling shamefaced and prickly hot inside my coat. 'How about spending a bit more time with my sister, I know she'd love to have you round for dinner.'

'I will. Soon,' I add, in case he's expecting me to rush over to her house tomorrow.

'And have you been through those boxes of my stuff yet, like I told you to?' he asks, giving me his firm look now.

He used to save that same look for the times I refused to search for cheaper car insurance, because I was tired and all I wanted to do was watch TV. He's already told me, on numerous occasions, that I need to go through his belongings, the ones I've got stuffed into boxes in my spare room and cannot bear to look at. This is the only thing I don't like about his visitations. Why is a figment of my own imagination harassing me about things I don't want to face?

'I haven't had any time,' I tell him, shifting guiltily in my seat. 'I've been really busy.'

'Juliette, love, you know you can't hang onto all of that stuff forever.'

That's exactly what I *was* planning to do.

'I understand if you want to keep some of the more important things.'

'Like your favourite T-shirt, you mean,' I say, trying to distract him. I picture him wearing it, his most treasured possession in the entire world: an old, scrappy T-shirt with more holes than a cheese grater, bearing the name of his favourite band, The Eighteen.

'If you ever get rid of *that* we'll be having words,' Jamie warns. 'That cost me twenty quid in 1993, it's probably worth an absolute fortune now, a collector's piece. But you don't need to hold onto everything else. I know for a fact that there's some old deodorant mouldering away in those boxes.'

It makes the whole box smell like him, a warm herbal mixture of scents that I won't be discarding in this lifetime.

'And I won't need any of those old electricity bills or credit card statements any time soon either.'

Each bill and statement has his name and address printed in bold letters at the top, like he still has a place in this world.

'And there's no sane reason to hold onto that scabby old pair of trainers that smell so rotten they're stinking up the whole spare room. Juliette, love, please just dump them in the bin before the environmental people call round to give you a warning.'

His trainers are the most precious of all the relics, with their smudged, grubby imprints of his toes. It's like he pulled them on just yesterday and ambled down to the corner shop for the Sunday papers, or a bag of my favourite muffins – the ones with chocolate *and* blueberries. Getting rid of the trainers or the deodorants or the bills would be like discarding little pieces of Jamie, and I won't do it. Not when I know they'll end up at a landfill site mixed with tonnes of actual rubbish, destroyed, defiled, dead.

'You've got to treat my belongings like you're going to treat Ivy Edward's stuff,' Jamie says, trying to appeal to my sensible side. 'Keep the things that have real meaning, real memories, and get rid of the rest.'

'I can't,' I tell him truthfully. 'I can't let any of it go, not yet, it's too soon.'

'I've been gone for eighteen months now, love. Don't you think it's time to throw my old trainers away?'

Most of the time, eighteen months feels like eighteen minutes, eighteen hours, eighteen days – the actual number is meaningless. The world and its orderly passing of time stopped making any sense the day Jamie died. Some things have got easier. I no longer stare at the glow of the streetlamp outside my bedroom window, into the early hours of the morning, unable to close my eyes. I stopped eating packets of biscuits for dinner about ten months ago, and reintroduced a few portions of fruits and vegetables, some of the time. But he cannot make me forget him, he cannot make me move on or get over him before I'm ready. And I'm not ready for any of it yet, maybe I never will be. Jamie Matthews was the absolute love of my life, the man I was six weeks away from marrying when he carelessly died. He was the man I was going to renovate a house with. The man who had vowed to sit by my side through every compulsory family gathering, and through every weepy film I promised him he'd enjoy. And no one can make me get rid of his stinky, old, falling-to-pieces trainers, not even a bizarre apparition of the man himself.

I turn towards him again and he's smiling at me, like he knows he's pushed that particularly thorny subject far enough for one visitation.

'Do you remember the time we tried to take the train to Brighton,' he says, 'and somehow ended up in Eastbourne instead?'

I can't help smiling. I love it when he does this, reminds me of all the great memories we share, and I take it as a sign that he's just as keen as I am to keep them alive.

'We had lunch in that strange little cafe,' I say, picking up the story, 'burnt cheese on cremated toast. The tables were pushed so close together that when you tried to reach into your jacket, to get your wallet, you accidentally put your hand inside that woman's bag instead, and pulled out a packet of her tampons.'

'She was so angry and embarrassed I thought she was going to ram one of the tampons up my nose.'

'What was the name of that place again?' I ask.

I already know what it was called. I just want to hear him say it.

'It was The Cloud-Cuckoo-Land Cafe. And then we walked along the seafront and got attacked by seagulls because they wanted my chips.'

'And I sat in a pool of cola on a bench.'

'Call it cola, if it makes you feel any better, but it looked a lot like something else from where I was standing.'

'We finished the day off by going to a tea dance at the Winter Gardens, and you got your shoe caught in the hem of that woman's dress and caused a pile-up on the dance floor.'

'You know that wasn't my fault.' Jamie is chuckling quietly now. 'You backed me straight into her because you were trying to steer. You kept saying it wasn't fair that men got to lead all of the dances and you wanted to take a turn.'

'It was a good day,' I say, 'one of the best.'

Jamie nods in agreement. 'Now imagine that day as a rock opera. And I want the full headbanging version, so don't go all soft on me now.'

I rest my head back against my seat and smile, and for a fleeting moment I feel fully whole again. I have to consider his request carefully and give it the treatment it deserves. He can always tell when I'm not committed.

'Well, first I'd have to decide on a song for the train journey,' I say, turning my gaze momentarily as a set of ridiculously bright headlights catches my eye. And when I look for Jamie again, he's gone. I'm sitting in the car by myself. This visitation is over.

Three

IT TAKES ME ANOTHER fifteen minutes to peel myself out of the car seat, lock the door and go inside. Since Jamie died, our small Victorian terrace hasn't felt much like a home. I no longer take any joy in settling down by the fire with the curtains drawn, reading a book or watching a box set. The dining room used to be my haven. A peaceful, sunny nook where I could sit with a cup of tea and watch as the birds picked their favourite seeds from the feeder outside the window, or talk to my collection of struggling plants. Jamie always managed to coax the plants back to life, even when I'd given them too much water or placed them perilously close to the radiator. My bedraggled assortment of ferns, Madagascar Dragon Trees and ficus plants always flourished under his green-fingered care. But they've now suffered a terrible relapse, terminal in some cases, and I fear the rest are not long for this potted world. It doesn't matter what I do, the plants don't respond. It seems I'm not the only one who has withered since Jamie died.

I trudge towards the kitchen flinging my coat and bag over my neglected sewing machine, in the corner of the dining room. There's nothing in the fridge but a jar of ancient apricot chutney and some old Double Gloucester cheese, which has developed a hard crust. I grill some toast and let the cheese bubble up under the heat of the element until it's almost edible again. It's very reminiscent of the lunch we had at The Cloud-Cuckoo-Land Cafe. I add some cherry tomatoes and a banana to the side of my plate and take it up to the bedroom, climbing carefully under the quilt so the toast doesn't slide off my plate. Then I relive every word Jamie said to me in the car. Sometimes,

I write out as much of the conversation as I can remember, so I can read it whenever I want, trying to prolong the life we lived together. But even I can sense the desperation of such an act, and most of the time I keep the notes hidden away in a drawer.

*

By Friday morning, I can't avoid the office any longer. I have to file all my paperwork for Robert Butler, so that invoices can be sent and bills paid. Going into the office requires a careful selection of clothes and the applying of just enough make-up to give the impression that I am coping fine: that I'm taking care of myself, my health, my appearance, my home, and that me and my plants don't require any kind of well-meaning intervention. I choose a soft green shirt that always makes me look healthy, even when I've been living off chips. I steer clear of the perfumes on top of my chest of drawers, however. Each one has the power to summon up a memory that I don't want to revisit before going into the office. My fingernails are clean, my shoes are decent enough. I grab a cardigan, coat and bag, and head for the door with my battle armour firmly in place.

Hobson's House Clearance has a small fourth-floor office in an ugly building on the outskirts of town. And I'm fortunate that I only have to visit once a week, twice on rare occasions. It was built in the days before air conditioning, insulation and wall-to-wall carpets. So it's unbearably hot in the summer, freezing cold in the winter and just plain uncomfortable at every other time of the year. Decorated with a mishmash of furniture, from the first house clearance jobs undertaken by the Hobson family, it has the atmosphere of a junkyard in the final days of a massive, bargain-basement, everything-must-go sale. Some might call it vintage, or even atmospheric, and Jamie and I used to love buying quirky second-hand tables and chairs for our home. But this furniture is fit for nothing but a good bonfire. I've often wondered if Nigel's home is decorated with the same kind of house clearance finds – rag-and-bone chic.

I've never felt comfortable spending much time in the office. After half an hour, it always takes on the feel of an airless coffin, with the lid screwed tightly down. And I have to wedge plenty of doors and windows open, just to fight off the panic-inducing sensation that I've been buried alive. Today, I'm pleased to see that Alan and Carmel, my fellow house clearers, are already sitting at their desks. They're much easier to talk to than Loretta, who is positioned like a spider in her web at the dark end of the room. She lifts a single eyebrow as I sit down.

'It's nice of you to join us.' Her voice has a tone, like paint stripper for the soul. 'It's been so long I'd almost forgotten what you looked like.'

'I was here last Wednesday, Loretta.'

She shrugs, like it's just one interpretation of the facts.

I sit down and swivel in my chair so I'm facing away from her. My desk is a 1960s artefact with protruding drawers that catch my knees, every time I turn to the left. It also smells strongly of aniseed, which gives all my paperwork a liquorice allsorts aroma.

'How's it going?' Alan asks, leaning back in his chair with a cat stretch.

As the longest serving member of the team, he has adopted the air of my superior and never misses an opportunity to pass on his so-called wisdom. For the last few months, he's also been growing sideburns because he's convinced that they'll give him a more distinguished air, now that he's reached the male menopause. Unfortunately, the sideburns resemble two strips of hairy carpet that have somehow attached themselves to his face. And I have to stifle an urge to shout 'shag pile!' whenever I'm in his presence.

'It's going fine, thanks,' I say, swallowing down my shag-pile shout. I smile at Carmel, who is sweet, chatty and uncomplicated.

'I see you got the job at Starcross Crescent,' Alan says. 'My aunt used to live in the same complex. I always liked visiting her flat. What kind of a state is it in?'

House clearers love to trade stories about the most horrible jobs they've done: bathrooms with mushrooms growing out from behind the sink, and enough hair clogging plugholes to knit fireside rugs. Kitchens are also a favourite room for comparison, and Alan usually has enough stories about what he's found festering inside fridges and pantries, over the years, to fill any gap in office conversation.

'It's a lovely little flat, actually,' I tell him quickly, before he can regale us all with the familiar tale of the time he found a freshly hatched infestation of blue bottles, behind a pantry door. 'Ivy

Edwards was house-proud. I can't see this one giving me any problems.' Apart from the fact that her brother is currently living in her spare room.

This would have been the perfect time to tell everyone about the moment I discovered Alfie Evans in his pyjamas – the hearing aid and false teeth would have lent a nice accent of humour to the whole tale. I know that Alan would have been impressed, despite himself. Loretta would have been on the phone to the housing association manager, before I'd finished describing the moment I prodded Alfie awake with a bedside lamp. Instead, I hear myself telling them about the bowler hats and the beautiful handmade cabinets in the sitting room. Alan looks disappointed. Carmel listens intently from behind her computer screen, her fingers suspended above her keyboard. Loretta is quickly bored and drifts over to a grey bank of filing cabinets with a handful of folders. And Alfie's name remains unspoken.

'How's your friend, Juliette?' Carmel suddenly asks, leaning across her desk to offer me a jaffa cake. 'The one who had her house broken into on the night of our office Christmas party, she's the reason you couldn't come, remember?'

'Oh, yeah, Lauren,' I nod, not quite meeting anyone's eye.

Lauren is another of my imaginary friends. I invented her specifically to get me out of attending any office function that extends beyond a slice of birthday cake, eaten at Nigel's desk. She's a highly strung friend who I've known since high school. And even though our lives have taken very different paths, and we no longer have much in common, I still feel a sense of loyalty towards her. In the past, I've used distressing arguments between Lauren and her neighbours to get me out of attending a karaoke night and a summer picnic in the park. On the night of the Hobson's Christmas dinner, Lauren's life took another turn for the worse and her flat was broken into. I tell Carmel that Lauren's still feeling a bit jumpy but is doing much better now. Then I get my head down guiltily, making a start on the paperwork for Robert Butler's house clearance. This office visit has already gone on for too long.

It takes some time to fill out all the boxes on the standard forms we use. I have to add a note explaining that I took Robert Butler's Leeds United memorabilia to a football charity, where they run free summer clubs for struggling families. It's always good publicity for

Hobson's, and Nigel gives us some agency over charitable donations, as long as it doesn't eat into the company profits too much. All reports are kept on file in case anyone comes forward claiming to be a long-lost brother, cousin or child, demanding to know what happened to the family silver. It's happened more than once. I always add a personal note saying something nice about the deceased's home, and when I've finally finished, I send a copy to Nigel and another to Loretta.

I have to listen to Alan describing the house he's been cleaning out for the past two days, where he discovered dozens of empty washing-powder boxes stacked under one of the beds. It opens up a lively, office-wide discussion about hoarding. Loretta doesn't have any time for hoarders and thinks it's just an excuse, used by some lazy people, to live in a pigsty. Carmel agrees with my brief comments about it being part of a broader mental health issue. And Alan doesn't care either way, as long as he gets to clear it out. I take the time to notice that Carmel's wearing a new top, and she goes into great detail about how she almost didn't buy it because the lights in the changing room made it look a funny colour against her skin. And with one final jaffa cake, I manage to escape the office in just under an hour and a half. At least this time, I didn't have to examine the cut on Alan's leg. Or explain to Loretta why I go through twice as many bin bags and boxes as any of my fellow co-workers – no, it's not because I've got a secret stall on the Monday market in town, and it's not because my brother sells house removal products on the internet. The only thing I've got to deal with now is Alfie Evans.

I stop at a petrol station for a coffee on the way to Starcross Crescent. I need a few minutes to get Alan and his washing-powder boxes out of my system before I can face the problems awaiting me in Ivy Edward's flat. I wonder again why I didn't mention Alfie to anyone in the office, and how I'm going to explain it to Loretta when it takes me five days to clear out Ivy's home, instead of the usual three or four. I'm already behind schedule and I haven't filled a single bin bag yet.

I reach Starcross Crescent at 10.56 a.m., and I'm glad to see that the curtains at number nine have been opened. I'm also very relieved that Alfie's fully dressed (and not wearing his pyjamas) when he answers the door. His hair is neatly combed, his dentures gleaming, and the unmistakeable smell of English Crab Apple surrounds him like a fine haze of sea spray, on a summer's day at the beach. I am very familiar with English Crab Apple, Boot Leather and Country Gentleman, the aftershaves of choice for men of a certain vintage. A small part of me had been hoping that Alfie might have taken off to stay with a friend, after our first encounter, and that I wouldn't have to deal with him. It's not a part I'm especially proud of.

I follow him down the hallway to the sitting room, where we stand facing each other, awkwardly.

'Mr Evans, let me say again how very sorry I am for barging in on you the other day. I was under the impression, well, Mr Thurston was under the impression that this flat was empty. And you say Ivy Edwards was your sister?'

'I'm her little brother.'

'Oh,' I say, not quite sure how to continue.

'Thurston doesn't know I've been staying here with Ivy for the last couple of months. She thought it best not to tell him, she said it would only complicate matters.'

Complicated is the perfect word.

'Mr Evans, I—'

'You'd better call me Alfie, since you've already caught a sneaky peek of me in my pyjamas.'

Alfie winks at me, which, for some unaccountable reason, makes me blush. Alfie chuckles as he sits in the nearest armchair, one leg crossed elegantly over the other. He's wearing a black jumper over a white shirt with a neatly ironed collar, and smart-looking trousers with sharp creases down the front. Alfie Evans has style. His hair has been cut recently and still has plenty of volume. His fingernails are manicured, and in a better state than mine. I thrust my hands into the pockets of my jeans.

'Juliette, I think a cup of hot tea might help grease this conversation,' he says, 'if you wouldn't mind doing the honours?'

I bustle into the kitchen and fill the kettle, adding a packet of rich tea biscuits and some teacups to a tray as I wait for it to boil. I'm sure Ivy wouldn't mind me using her best china, under the circumstances. By the time I return to the sitting room, Alfie has placed a small side table between his armchair and the sofa, and I sink into the cushions gratefully.

'Mr Evans, Alfie,' I correct myself, as he wags an arthritic finger at me, 'as I mentioned yesterday, I've come here to clean out your sister's belongings. The housing association hires us when there's no family left to do it themselves.'

Alfie nods, giving every appearance of understanding.

'But as you're her brother, if you'd like to do it yourself, Mr Thurston needs the house cleared by next Wednesday, at the latest.'

'Next Wednesday? That's a bit speedy, isn't it? Ivy only died five days ago.'

'Because this is a housing association property, it can be rented out again relatively quickly. And with waiting lists being so long...'

Alfie frowns into his tea. 'So, you want me out of here by next Wednesday too?'

'It's not my decision, I'm afraid. But, yes, by next Wednesday.'

I suddenly understand why Alfie might have been staying with his sister in the first place. He's got nowhere else to go.

'How does this work then?' Alfie dunks a biscuit into his tea and sits back in his chair, suddenly looking smaller.

'I usually spend three or four days sorting through the deceased's, I mean through Ivy's possessions. I pick out anything that can be donated to charity or sold, and the rest of her belongings are then disposed of by our team.' It all sounds very professional, but I'm not used to explaining the process to a member of the dead person's family. 'Do you know if your sister ever made a will?'

'She never told me about it if she did.'

'Do you think Ivy wanted you to have any of her possessions?' I ask, seeing layers of impediments unfolding before me.

'I don't know what to do with my own stuff, never mind taking on a load of Ivy's things as well.'

'Do you have anywhere else you can go?' I ask.

Alfie shakes his head. 'I'm on the waiting list for one of those sheltered housing schemes, that's why I've been staying with Ivy. I couldn't manage the stairs at my old place anymore with my dodgy knee. It kept giving way on me.'

I stare at his knees, as if they might provide some answers. But they're just knees.

'I have an acquaintance, Jaya, who works in the Council Housing Department. I can have a word with her, if you'd like, check on the situation with your new home.'

Alfie nods wearily. 'That wouldn't be the worst idea, seeing as how I'll be out on my ear in under a week.'

I take my phone and move swiftly into the kitchen, already dialling Jaya's number. The most logical thing to do at this moment would be to tell Thurston about Alfie, hand the problem over to somebody else, so I can get on with my job. But Jaya once helped me rehouse a litter of kittens that I discovered in a cardboard box, when I was clearing out an old house, which wasn't part of her job description either. And Alfie has the same helpless look on his face. He disguises it well with smiles and jokes, but I know that Jaya is the right person to call. Thurston would have thrown the kittens out onto the street, or sent them straight to the bottom of the canal in a bin bag.

'Hello, Jaya? I don't know if you remember me,' I begin, when she finally answers her phone, already sounding harassed and worn down at 11.12 a.m. 'But you once helped me re-house—'

'Some kittens! You're the kitten lady,' she says, her tone brightening just a touch. 'Don't tell me, you've found a basket full of Dalmatian puppies this time, and they need rescuing from a horrible woman who wants to make them into a coat?'

'You're not that far from the truth.' I look at Alfie and the way his white shirt cuffs poke out the end of his jumper sleeves, wondering if that's exactly what I've found. 'I have an elderly gentleman who might need some help with accommodation.'

'I'm not that old, Juliette!' Alfie shouts from the sitting room. 'I've still got all my own hair and that's more than you can say for some blokes who haven't even broken sixty yet.'

Jaya laughs quietly. 'Sounds like you've got a lively one there.'

'You have no idea,' I say, peering around the side of the arch and into the sitting room. Alfie is shaking his head at my use of the word *elderly*. 'He says he's on the waiting list for a place at a sheltered housing scheme, if you wouldn't mind checking. His name's Alfie Evans.'

There's a pause on the other end of the phone as she logs onto her computer. 'Do you know the name of the housing scheme?'

I ask Alfie. 'I can't remember the name, but it's got some grand-looking gardens and all the flats have got the same blue carpets.'

'It sounds like it could be Orton Lodge, or West Lake Gardens,'

Jaya says, slowly, as she looks it up. 'I've got an Alfred Douglas Evans on my system, born on 2nd January 1947?'

'I'm pretty sure that's him.' I decide not to ask Alfie to confirm his date of birth, in case he's still smarting at the idea of being old.

'His current address is number nine, Starcross Crescent, Sholtsbury.'

'Only until next Wednesday,' I say.

'That's a shame,' Jaya sighs, 'because it looks like he's down for a place at the Orton Lodge Sheltered Housing Scheme, but it could be another couple of months until that becomes available, I'm sorry to say. I'll have to find Mr Evans some temporary accommodation in the meantime.'

'Temporary accommodation?'

'Best-case scenario is a B&B in the town somewhere, shared facilities, I'm afraid. But it shouldn't be for too long.'

I'm too much of a chicken to ask about the worst-case scenario.

'Is there any possibility that Mr Evans can stay at Starcross Crescent until his Orton Lodge flat becomes available?' Jaya asks.

'Not unless your friend can bring Ivy back from the dead,' Alfie mumbles. There's nothing wrong with the hearing in his right ear, apparently.

'Leave it with me and I'll see what I can do,' Jaya says. 'I've already got all his documentation from his sheltered housing application. I might need a letter from someone saying his current living arrangements are coming to an end.'

'I can send you a letter from the housing association about the termination of Ivy's tenancy.'

'Good, that should help speed things up. Do you have a contact number for Mr Evans?'

I glance over at Alfie suspecting he doesn't have a phone, and Ivy's landline has already been disconnected. I tell her to contact me instead and then thank her sincerely for her help. Alfie's staring morosely into his teacup when I return to the sitting room, all the banter suddenly gone.

'This is a rough old business, Juliette, and I've had some rough times before,' he says. 'I've been hit by a car and had my ribs broken, and I once spent a night in the police cells. But I never thought I'd have nowhere to live.'

Alfie takes himself off to his bedroom, and I have to make a start on Ivy's possessions. Normally, I work alone in the unique kind of stillness that always settles over the home of the recently deceased. It's like the chairs and the cupboards and all the pots and pans can sense that the person who sat in them, or opened their doors, or made dinner in them every night, has now gone. Any last traces of the life force they left behind dissipated, turning the air to stone. Ivy's house should have the undisturbed feel of the dead about it, but Alfie has changed all of that.

I bring a kit in from my car – black bin bags, flat-pack boxes, industrial strength cleaning supplies for things that need to be sanitised before I can handle them safely – and decide to start with the cabinets in the sitting room. The actual pieces of furniture themselves will be sold. I take several photos with my phone and then scroll through my list of work contacts, choosing Claudette Hawkins, who sells high quality second-hand furniture. I send her the photos asking for a price and a pick-up date. Ivy's cupboards deserve to go to a good home, have another life beyond the one that has just ended. Now I have to tackle the contents. This is going to take some time. Ivy wasn't exactly a hoarder, but when it came to organising her photos and documents, she clearly didn't believe in filing systems either. And it looks like I've got several decades worth of papers to sort through. I know most people find this a chore, as dull as a slow-witted Saturday afternoon doing their taxes, but I love the whole process. This is where I really start to learn who Ivy was, what kind of life she lived.

I move one of the armchairs to make more space on the floor for sorting, place a black bin bag at my feet, and begin. But the first thing I pull out of the cupboard is a stack of old dressmaker's patterns. Squashed and crumpled, it takes me some time to lay all forty-two of them out on the floor. Some are clearly from Ivy's later years, with comfy, elasticated waistbands and pleats that cover a multitude of post-menopausal bumps. They can de donated. But the patterns that really catch my eye come from a much earlier era in Ivy's life. There are skirt suits, A-line dresses and little fitted jackets, all very flattering to the form. Patterns for cute sleeveless dresses hark back to the 1950s, with full knee-length skirts. Ivy was a dressmaker, a home-sewing fan, just like me.

'Ivy always loved making her own clothes.'

Alfie has wandered into the room behind me; he's surprisingly quiet in his loose-fitting slippers. He picks up one of the 1960s patterns for a slimline skirt.

'I almost can't remember a time when Ivy wasn't laying some pattern out on the floor, with a mouthful of pins, smoothing out the corners or snipping away with her pinking shears. She was always nicely turned out, our Ivy.' Alfie smiles to himself, inspecting the pattern in his hands. 'She had a way with her sewing machine, even made her own wedding dress. She bought the material from the Haberdashery Department at Shimming's, saved up for it herself.'

Shimming's is a Sholtsbury institution. A five-storey Edwardian emporium of delights, with dark wooden floors and a solid, dependable feel. The Haberdashery Department is as popular now as it's ever been. I've spent many an hour at Shimming's choosing material for my own sewing projects: summer skirts, corduroy trousers and a very ambitious posh dress that never sat correctly on my shoulders, making me look like I had an abnormally short neck.

Me and Ivy have a connection, we both love Shimming's.

Alfie places the pattern back on the floor and inspects the inside of Ivy's cupboard. 'And you've got to go through all of this stuff?'

'Do you... is there anything of Ivy's you want to keep?' I ask, in uncharted territory again.

Alfie simply shrugs his shoulders. 'I haven't got much use for dress patterns.'

'But what about some family photos, perhaps?'

'I'll take a look at those, I suppose. But I could tell you some stories about our Ivy you won't find in any photos,' he adds. 'A proper little tearaway, she was.'

'Ivy was a tearaway?'

'She was always climbing over the walls at the vicarage, in the summer, to pick plums, apples and pears. The vicar almost caught her a dozen times or more, but Ivy was as slippery as an eel swimming through a barrel of oil back in those days.'

I glance at the pattern for comfy stretchy trousers at my feet, finding it hard to imagine. Clearly, there is much to learn about Alfie's big sister. She was more than the elasticated waistbands of her later years. Alfie has managed to maintain a slender shape himself, his clothes look like they're hanging off his frame a little, if anything.

'Do you know why Ivy had a collection of bowler hats in the hallway?' I ask, as Alfie picks up two more of the patterns and studies the pictures on the front.

'Ivy loved hats. She used to wear them all the time, when she was younger, said they made her feel like a bit of a film star. But then they fell out of fashion and she stopped buying them.'

'And the bowler hats, do you know why she had so many?' I prompt.

'No idea about those. I don't remember Stanley, her husband, ever wearing anything on his head until he started losing his hair. And then he knotted a handkerchief over his bald patch, while he was mowing the lawn at their old house on Quince Road. He was a good man, Stan, decent, hard-working sort. But he looked like a proper idiot with that hankie on his head.'

Alfie drifts away to the other end of the sitting room. He sits on the sofa, turns on the TV and starts watching a programme about auction houses. I try to concentrate on a stack of old electricity bills from Ivy's cupboard, but Alfie likes to offer up a running commentary on the people taking part in the programme, and the purchases they've made. And keeps saying things like, "You paid how much for that? What a piece of junk, you'll be lucky to get a spit in the eye for it at the auction." Alfie also likes to channel surf, I quickly discover. He watches half an hour of an old black and white film, followed by a programme about a famous trumpet player. And then a vintage comedy that's offensive on so many levels, I have to retreat to my car for twenty minutes, while he roars with laughter. Alfie occupies a lot of space, and a different time in history.

When I risk a return to the sitting room, a much gentler programme about English country gardens is on the screen. But the excitement has clearly been too much for Alfie, and he's now snoring heartily in his chair. I marvel at the decibels, hands over my ears, amazed that the china cups in Ivy's cupboards remain unaffected. By rights, they should be rattling like a tea trolley hurtling over a cattle grid. I have to fight a very strong urge to poke Alfie in the ribs with a broom handle – probably not the smartest idea, given the high risk of broken bones at his age. I settle for dropping a pile of old magazines onto the floor instead. Alfie sits bolt-upright, startled by the sudden noise.

'Sorry,' I say, feeling no guilt whatsoever.

There are certain conditions that make it impossible for any house clearer to carry out their job: hazardous levels of mould, unsafe floorboards and collapsed ceilings. I add intrusive snoring to my own personal list.

Alfie adjusts his teeth and settles down again, but thankfully, this sleep is silent and peaceful.

By 1.34 p.m., I've managed to clear out most of the first cupboard and have two large bin bags full of rubbish. There are lottery tickets, a stack of Christmas club saving books (dating back to 1991), and a collection of building society statements and old bills that need to be shredded. The donations pile is growing too: with old patterns, a magnifying lamp for reading, a sewing box with an impressive supply of quality needles, scissors, thimbles and threads and some sherry glasses that were buried behind a box of unused envelopes. I've also had a decent offer on the cupboards themselves, and Claudette will be picking them up on Wednesday.

Normally, at lunchtime, I sit quietly and read a book or listen to a podcast on my phone, but none of that's going to happen today. Alfie heats up some soup for his lunch – I have my own pasta salad from Boots – and sits at the table, slurping his way through the bowl. I'm forced to make conversation just to drown out the disconcerting noise.

'So, Alfie, tell me about yourself,' I say, just as the spoon makes its way up to his mouth again.

'There's not much to tell really. I've had an ordinary sort of life.'

One of the many things I've learned from my job is that no life is ordinary.

'Were you ever married?' I ask, hoping it's not too personal a question to lead with.

'Not once,' Alfie says with a nostalgic smile, resting his spoon on the side of the bowl, 'but I've been engaged a dozen times. There was Betty Arbuckle, she was my first and a real bonnie lass. We had a lot of laughs together. Then there was Rita Richards, Annie Richards and their youngest sister, Sylvie Richards.' Alfie counts them off on his fingers.

'You were engaged to three sisters from the same family?' I ask, not sure if he's pulling my leg, or if I'm sitting in the presence of a consummate heartbreaker.

'Ivy wasn't impressed. She said I must have had rocks in my head, and it caused a fair few arguments between Rita, Annie and Sylvie, I can tell you,' Alfie shakes his head. 'But I was young and thoughtless back then. Getting engaged felt about as serious as planning a Saturday night out at the cinema. It was like playing at being an adult. After Sylvie, I was engaged to Susan Smith for a whole year, until she got fed up waiting around for me to commit to a wedding date. She ran off with my best friend, Arthur.'

I study Alfie's face for any signs of tale-telling, but he appears to be giving me a truthful account of his love life, or the truth as he remembers it anyway.

'Then there was another Rita, Bonville this time, and her best friend, Margery Mavers. Me and Margery were pretty serious, I'd grown up a bit by then and even got as far as buying her a ring. After Margery, there was Valerie Peach, Margot Walters, Pamela Johnson, Yvette Pearson and Hillary McSweeny.' He thinks for a second. 'And I almost forgot about little Jane Chubb. Her dad owned a sweet shop in town, so we used to sit by the river with a bag of mint humbugs, making up silly poems about frogs. So, that's thirteen, all told.'

'You've been engaged thirteen times?' I ask, still having trouble with the numbers involved.

'Pamela Johnson was my fiancée for a grand total of four hours, and then her father found out, and he put a stop to our engagement pretty sharpish. I had something of a reputation, by that point, for being a ladies' man. I dread to think what they'd call it these days,' he chuckles, picking up his spoon, and the slurping resumes.

I haven't got the heart to mention some of the names he might be called today, but dangerous flirt and commitment phobic are two of the more polite terms that spring to mind.

'I suppose I'm not really the marrying kind. But they were all lovely lasses, and I stayed friends with most of them, even after they found themselves some decent chaps to marry. Sylvie never spoke to me again though.'

I'm starting to wonder if Alfie has a tendency towards exaggeration. Thirteen fiancées, even assuming most of them weren't concurrent with each other, would have been a full-time job. There must have been very little time for anything else in his life.

'I haven't been engaged for a good forty years now, so I think my romancing days are over. But then again, you never know who you might meet down the Dog and Duck on a Saturday afternoon.'

There's a genuine look of optimism on his face. I wonder if I should issue a warning to the women of Sholtsbury, anyone over the age of sixty is at risk of being added to Alfie's list of fiancées. I've only managed one engagement, and I'm not sure I'll ever do it again.

After lunch, Alfie takes himself out for a walk, and for the first time since entering Ivy's home I can relax into the house clearing process. The second of the tall cupboards in the living room is crammed with old photograph albums and packets of loose snaps. Photos can be dangerous. It's easy to get lost in somebody else's world, their history and memories, so I have to set myself a time limit. Sort quickly and efficiently and put aside any particularly good snaps that might be wanted. Normally, I leave them in a small box at the office along with any other special sentimental items, in case someone comes to claim them. If they're still sitting in the same box several months later, however, Loretta swoops in and clears them out. I've never asked what she does with them. But, on this occasion, I need to run everything past Alfie first, I realise.

Ivy took plenty of photos in her life. There's not enough time to go through them properly now, so I decide to take the pictures home with me and tackle them at the weekend. Maybe I can claw back some of the time I've already lost to Alfie? Strictly speaking, I'm not supposed to remove any of the deceased's possessions from the property, unless it's to dispose of them. And I only ever take things home in exceptional circumstances, but Alfie Evans definitely falls under that heading. I also feel like I know more about Alfie's life than I do about Ivy's, and I need to redress that balance. I leave a note telling him I'll return on Monday, at 9.00 a.m., underlining the time. I'm keen to avoid any more encounters with Alfie's pyjamas.

Instead of heading home, I drive into town and try to put all thoughts of Alfie to one side. A reminder pings on my phone telling me I'm supposed to be meeting Poppy at the Toad and Fiddle in half an hour. But I'm already driving into the car park at the back of the pub, and I set my phone to silent. Meeting with Poppy usually requires my full attention.

Four

THE TOAD AND FIDDLE is one of the most insipid-looking pubs I've ever visited, decorated in shades of city centre sandwich-bar beige, it has all the personality of an off-licence. But it's large and convenient, and it's already filling up fast with people meeting for post-work drinks. Poppy has bagged us a table in a quiet corner, away from the bar, and waves me over with a waiting glass of wine. She stands up and gives me a big hug, her standard greeting for everyone: family and friends, dentists, bank managers and any person who happens to deliver her pizza. As usual, I am hit by her remarkable resemblance to Jamie. This is both the best and worst part about meeting up with Poppy. She looks so much like Jamie that it's as if a small part of him is still living and breathing and sitting right in front of me. I've never shared this particular observation with Poppy. I don't want her to think that's the only reason I'm meeting up with her, when the truth is she's my best friend. But her resemblance to Jamie still knocks me sideways every time I see her, and it takes me a few moments of slow breathing to gather myself together again.

As she sits down and turns her phone to silent, I sneak a glance at her face in profile. This is when she looks like Jamie the most. Her hair is the exact same shade of shiny hazelnut brown, and she has the same expression of thoughtful concentration. If she had a square jaw and the ability to grow stubble, they'd be almost identical.

'So, how was your friend?' she asks.

I have to trawl through my scrambled thoughts quickly, trying to remember exactly what falsehood I've told her, which imaginary friend she's referring to.

'You said you were going to a macramé class with Vanessa?' she says, seeing the confused look on my face.

Why couldn't I have picked something less difficult to describe? A quiet dinner at Vanessa's would have been far easier to lie about. I wasn't even sure what macramé was until I looked it up on the internet. If Alan from the office had told me it was an ancient form of French football, I would have been none the wiser.

'It was okay,' I say, taking off my coat and draping it over the back of my chair, 'but I'm not sure I'd do it again. I think Vanessa enjoyed it more than I did, and she wants to try a pottery course next. There's a class on at the college on Wednesday evenings. She's keen to try throwing a pot for her spider plant.'

'Well, it's good that you're getting out and about and into the world,' Poppy says, 'even if Vanessa has got you messing about with bits of string and clay.'

I smile and shake my head at the thought of Vanessa at the potter's wheel, she'd be hopeless, all fingers and thumbs and smears of clay wiped across her face. 'Honestly, I never know what she's going to suggest next, I'm half expecting her to sign us up for potholing.'

I stop talking abruptly, embarrassed by the lengths my imagination will go to just to make a story believable. Sometimes, even I have trouble remembering that Vanessa's not real, recognising where the lines have blurred. But Poppy just nods like she understands and then raises her pint glass.

'To Jamie,' she toasts. 'My annoying, irritating, pain-in-the-arse big brother, who would not stop pinching my arm for a whole year when he was ten, but I miss him anyway.'

We clink glasses and I take a few sips of wine. Now that our opening rituals are completed, we can get down to the good stuff. Poppy misses Jamie almost as much as I do. It was hard to say which one of us was more devastated by his death. We were already good friends by the time it happened, and would have been close even if we'd met under different circumstances. She is, and will always be, one of my favourite people. But one of the absolute best things about her is she lets me talk about Jamie, as much as I want to. She never gives me *the judgemental look*, the one that my family and friends all started to adopt about a year after Jamie's death. The one that said I should be just a little bit better at pulling myself together after a whole twelve months in mourning. The one that said I should be moving on, no matter how much I loved Jamie, that I should be ready to start engaging with the world again and embracing the green shoots of my own life recovering.

Poppy has never looked at me that way. She understands that getting over the death of Jamie isn't really an option for me, and that I want to keep him close and present and involved in my life. I never have to explain to her how I'm feeling. She's the one person who I still meet on a semi-regular basis, and I am so grateful to have her in my life.

'I was thinking about Jamie, the other day, and how he always used to sing when he did the washing-up.'

Another thing I love about Poppy, she doesn't waste precious time asking me what I've been doing with myself, or what's been happening with my other (imaginary) friends. We get around to those questions, eventually. But she is just as eager as I am to bring Jamie to the table and into the conversation, like he's a silent witness.

'And it was always some old sea shanty,' I say, picking up the thread, 'like that was the only appropriate song to sing, when he had his hands in a bowl full of soapy water.'

'If he was pulling up weeds in my garden, he'd be singing some ancient folk song about blackbirds and talking trees.'

'If he was in his car, it was always songs about Mustangs or Cadillacs. He used to drive me nuts singing that song about a Corvette when we drove to the supermarket.'

'I *despised* that song.' Poppy holds her head in her hands momentarily. 'He sang it constantly when we were growing up. He only stopped when I pummelled him with a cushion, or when he was laughing so hard he couldn't breathe. But when he got older, he had a lovely singing voice.'

Poppy smiles and I can tell she's enjoying the memory of her brother's smooth tones. That's another one of the things I miss most about him.

'He always knew exactly what song to sing,' she says. 'He should have been in a band.'

'No self-respecting band ever would have taken him on. He could sing the angels out of heaven itself—'

'Which was one of Jamie's favourite sayings, of course.'

'But his guitar playing was embarrassing.'

Whatever talent he had for singing simply refused to translate itself to his fingers. And it wasn't from a lack of trying. He loved his guitar, but the only songs he could play on it were old two-chord country and western ballads about men who had lost their faithful dogs, and then lost the will to live. He never gave up on the hope that one day he would get in touch with his inner guitar legend, and take to the centre stage at Glastonbury for a special guest appearance with The Eighteen. His dreams were nothing if not ambitious.

Poppy takes a few gulps of beer and a new, thoughtful look crosses her face. Usually, we follow up stories of Jamie's mixed musical abilities with some reminiscing about the time he met three members of The Eighteen, at a concert, and almost passed out on the drummer's shoulder. Or about his one-thousand-piece record collection, which contained dozens of albums from the 1960s and 1970s by obscure bands that no one else had ever heard of. And which always had names like End of the Pier, Gibbon Toast and Hobbihoyt. It's a well-trodden path we both like to travel down.

'I've got something to tell you, Juliette,' she says instead, and her face is so serious I almost have a panic attack.

'Oh God, please don't tell me you're moving away, I don't think I could stand it.' My reaction is more honest than I usually allow, but she's taken me by surprise. 'Are you and Zarina splitting up?' I ask, hit by another devastating thought, and then the worst and most terrifying of all possibilities: 'You're not sick, are you?'

But Poppy smiles and takes my hand, giving it a long, reassuring squeeze.

'Stop making everything into such a catastrophe. Nobody's sick, me and Zarina are fine and we're not moving anywhere. Zarina's more married to her job at Jodhpur and Jitney than she is to me, and they're not moving offices any time soon either.'

Zarina is Poppy's long-term partner, and the chief accountant at a fancy law firm in Leeds. By anyone's assessment, they are perfect for each other. Poppy is a children's book illustrator and a total cliché of an artist, practically living in her paint-splattered dungarees – which she was threatening to wear to the wedding that Jamie and I never had. Her hair is permanently teased into a bird's nest arrangement, with beads and actual twigs sometimes woven into the mix. There isn't a single finger or toe on her body that doesn't have its own silver ring, embedded with amethyst, topaz or amber. There are definitely fairies at the bottom of her garden. Zarina, on the other hand, has her own seat at the hairdresser's, a coordinated collection of finely tailored clothes and a strong leaning towards minimalism. She constantly complains about Poppy's paint brushes and how they end up in the kitchen sink, with the dishes, on a daily basis. Somehow, they manage to live a mostly harmonious and deeply connected life with each other. And that is the real reason I insist on meeting Poppy in this faceless, second-rate public house, with its sticky tables and questionable wine. It's just too hard to see them together in their own home, to witness the life they live and the possibilities they have for any kind of future. And I'm getting a strong sense it's the future that Poppy wants to talk about now.

'Do you remember, a couple of years ago, when I said I was tired of doing illustrations for other people's books, and wanted to create artwork for my own stories instead?'

This was before Jamie died. Jamie, in fact, was the one who encouraged her to follow her dreams. He told her, again and again, how talented she was until she started to accept it might be true.

'Well...' Poppy takes a nervous, shallow little breath, 'I've just signed a three-book deal with Rothbury Publishing.'

'Rothbury Publishing? Bloody hell, Poppy, I've actually heard of them. They're like a proper grown-up publisher.'

Poppy's face glows with sudden pride. I pull her out of her chair and give her a long, tight hug, unable to form any coherent words. That's one of the biggest secrets about grief. How it can blast through any roadblocks in your heart, exposing whole new seams of empathy and understanding that you have no idea how to handle. Nobody ever warns the grieving about the dangers presented by the sight of something as innocuous as a solitary teacup, in a charity shop, or a toothpaste poster in a bus shelter. How even a teacup or a toothpaste poster can suddenly knock you off your feet, reviving the memory of a single moment with your beloved, long forgotten and filed away. And through it, show you all the most important truths about life. And the only person who would appreciate all your newly acquired wisdom is gone. Grief is a decongestant for the heart, a terrible, merciless decongestant.

I know this book deal means a lot to Poppy, how she's dreamed of writing her own stories, of creating her own artwork and presenting it to the world. And the world should be eternally grateful. Her illustrations are wonderful, every brushstroke coming straight from her beautiful soul. She and Jamie had that in common too.

'I'm so happy for you,' I eventually manage to say, as we take our seats again. 'Jamie would have been obnoxiously proud of you.'

Poppy nods and wipes her eyes with the frayed cuffs of her sleeves. 'It's being published next autumn. I'm calling it *A Fairy's Guide to Friendship*, I've already done the artwork for the cover and I'm starting work on the second book in the series next week.'

I nod and smile and laugh in all the appropriate places, hoping she cannot detect the other feelings I'm working extremely hard to conceal. Up until now, there has been an unspoken agreement between us that life cannot move on. That if we meet up and share stories about Jamie, our best and most shining of memories, he will never fade. Poppy was the one person I could rely on not to break that code, and now her life has taken a giant leap forward. And Jamie cannot be a part of that. He will never see her book on the shelves of any shop, or have the joy of reading it. He cannot go on this journey with her, and this is how it begins. What next? Will Poppy and Zarina eventually move to a bigger house, despite what Poppy says, one with a proper artist's studio at the bottom of the garden? If they do, it will be a house that Jamie never entered. A place where I won't have a hundred different recollections of him every time I visit: Jamie falling asleep on a stool in the kitchen, or sitting on the sofa strumming his guitar, or teasing Poppy about her new boots with fairy wings painted on the soles.

I let Poppy tell me all the details of her new agent. She describes the signing of her book deal, and the day she met the publishers in London. They took her to a fancy restaurant for lunch, and she was so excited she accidentally tipped half a bowl of chilled beetroot soup down the front of her new shirt. Her face shines with the thrill of it all, and I slowly start to register that she's been keeping this from me for months.

'I was going to tell you,' she says, interpreting the shocked look on my face correctly, 'but there never seemed to be a good time. And then we'd start telling stories about Jamie, and I didn't want to ruin the moment.'

'How can news like this ruin any moment?'

'I don't know.' Poppy twirls a stray strand of hair around the end of her finger, looking uncertain. 'It just felt wrong.'

I raise my glass to her and manage to pull off a fairly convincing smile. I don't want to spoil this wonderful moment for her. 'Congratulations to my very good friend, and future best-selling author/artist, Poppy Matthews, who will promise never to keep such exciting news from me ever again.'

Poppy smiles with obvious relief.

'Okay, I swear.'

She goes to the bar a few minutes later, and I suddenly feel lonelier than at any other time since Jamie died. We order some chips, and I tell her about Vanessa and the fictional new house I've just decided she's going to buy. It's a long way out of town, and she'll probably need a lot of help because it looks like a big renovation project. I warn Poppy I might not be around much for the next few months. Neither of us mentions Jamie again.

Juliette and Jamie
I
The Wise Old Whale

THE WISE OLD WHALE Bookshop wasn't exactly what I'd been looking for. The shop I needed – the one that carried the book I wanted to buy for Hope's birthday – was on the other side of town. But thanks to some roadworks, a closed car park and a baffling new one-way system – that had clearly been designed to make anyone having a slightly challenging Tuesday lose their mind – I had already circled the entire town centre three times. I needed a new plan. When I spotted the empty parking space outside The Wise Old Whale Bookshop, I took it as a sign.

The window display was set out like a scene from an atmospheric 1950s stage play. There was a faded armchair sitting next to an Anglepoise lamp, and a coffee table buried under discarded teacups, crossword puzzles and chewed pencils. Books were hanging from invisible wires overhead, their spines stretched and taut, covers open, pages dangling downwards; they looked like a flock of migrating birds in mid-flight. There were no fairy lights or glossy displays of the latest releases from the book world. There were no quotes painted on the windows designed to lure you inside, to make you question your life choices and encourage you to purchase three hundred pages of questionable help. I liked the crazy flying-books scene, it set a tone.

On the inside, the shop was even more alluring. It was arranged like a maze with different paths leading off to the left and right, and no clear line of sight through to the back of the shop. The books towered over me as I took the left-hand route, grand skyscrapers of poetry, historical fiction, romance and classics. Each shelf of books was punctuated by cactus plants in bloom, trailing ivy, teapots, and photos of other charismatic bookshops in Paris, Rome and Barcelona. The gardening section – where books about growing marrows and cultivating meadow gardens had been stacked between tubs filled with real tomato plants – looked like it had been reclaimed by the wild.

By the time I reached the counter at the centre of the shop, I was equal parts charmed, mystified and disorientated.

'Can I help you?'

I stumbled towards the bookshop guy suddenly remembering that I had a present to buy and a job to get to.

'I'm looking for this, please, if you have it,' I said, handing him a slip of paper with an author's name and book title.

He disappeared into the depths of the shop, returning several moments later with an impressively thick tome.

'I haven't read this particular one in person, but I hear it's a total load of codswallop,' he said, with a kindly smile. 'I hope you're not buying it for yourself,' he added, before I had a chance to respond. 'I'd put money on the fact that it's a shameful waste of printer's ink, and in all conscience, I cannot allow you to buy it.'

'E-excuse me?'

'This is not the book for you.'

'I'm sorry, I don't think I—'

'I've read many books like this before.' He waved the glossy book cover at me. 'It's part of my job. I always like to know what I'm selling to the people who enter my bookshop. And I can tell from the blurb on the back, and the greasy picture of the author, that this book is about as phoney as a sauce bottle shaped like a tomato. It will disappoint your expectations on every page, and leave you feeling like it's your fault for not understanding what it's trying to say. If this author has ever set foot inside a Buddhist temple, as he claims, I'll eat the entire bestseller list for breakfast.'

I stared at the shop guy now standing before me. I was instantly drawn to his eyebrows, the way they moved independently of each other when he talked. His face was a comic book of expressions.

'But it's for a friend,' I managed to say. 'And the reviewer in the paper said—'

'Not a good friend, I hope, because you won't be doing them any favours by giving them this heap of crap. If they're interested in eastern philosophy, I can recommend something really worth reading. It'll blow their socks off. I've read it three times already and I'm still finding new meaning in the words every time I pick it up.'

When he returned again with the recommended book, I was still standing in exactly the same spot, not entirely certain what was happening.

'That'll be £16.99, please. Can I offer you a loyalty card?' he asked, putting the book in a brown paper bag as I handed over some money. And that's when the words that I wanted to say suddenly broke through to the surface, and dissolved the daze I was in.

'If you think the other book is such a waste of time, why have it on your shelves at all?'

'That's a fair point,' the shop guy smiled, like I'd just asked the very question he'd been hoping I would pose. 'Let's just say that for some people, opening the pages of any book is a triumph of self-improvement. You are not one of those people, and I'm guessing the same applies to your friend.'

It wasn't the answer I'd been expecting. But then nothing that had happened since I'd stepped out of my car had been normal.

'I just need your name, for the loyalty card,' he prompted.

'Juliette, I'm Juliette.'

'I don't get many Juliettes in my shop,' he smiled, as he wrote down my name and handed over a card in the shape of an armchair. 'Don't worry, I'm not going to make any corny jokes about Romeo, I bet you got sick of that at school.'

'I didn't go to a very *Romeo and Juliet* kind of school,' I said, still feeling off kilter, 'most of my classmates didn't have a lot of time for Shakespeare.'

'Can you imagine not knowing about *Romeo and Juliet*?' he said, with a shake of his head. 'I'm not sure I'd be who I am today if I hadn't read that play.'

'What do you mean?' I asked, trying to remember the most famous quotes from my A level English lessons with Mrs Archer. The Arch (as she was affectionately known) had also made us watch a very blurry film version of the play, in a classroom that had been so stuffy I could barely breathe, never mind grasp the importance of

Shakespeare's words.

'That play showed me how the power and beauty of a great love can transform molecules, and shorten your lifespan, if you're not careful,' he said, scratching an eyebrow with his knuckle. 'It was an entirely foreign concept to me before *Romeo and Juliet*. It opened my eyes to the possibilities.'

'You want to open yourself up to the possibility of dying in a crypt from a broken heart?'

'That wouldn't be my number one preference, but I can think of worse ways to go. Let's just say I want the full human experience, and a *Romeo and Juliet* kind of love, well that's something I haven't encountered yet. I'm Jamie, by the way,' he said, handing me my change.

I took the coins but it was Jamie's face that held my attention; open and kind, soulful brown eyes framed by an abundance of thick shiny hair. His eyebrows had now taken on an impossibly lopsided quizzical stance. Most people in bookshops didn't tell you how they felt about *Romeo and Juliet*, or throw you off balance so badly with their easy, appealing manner, that you forgot to pocket your change and leave.

'So, is it rude of me to ask, what's your own personal philosophy on love, Juliette?' He sat on a stool behind the counter, hands resting on his knees, fully expecting an answer. 'Or have I already asked too many questions, and made you desperate to get out of my shop?'

I was definitely in uncharted territory, but my feet were firmly planted to the spot and my palms had started perspiring. It was a sure sign that I was intrigued by Jamie, who was already ten times more interesting than the last two men I'd dated, combined. Not that there had been anything wrong with Simon, who had a strong work ethic and a love for his family that was endearing. But when it came to making me laugh, to sharing a moment or understanding the nuances of life, the word that kept leaping to mind was *stodgy*. John, my most recent romantic partner, had been a lot of fun, spontaneous and thoughtful. Unfortunately, it had taken me some time to figure out that his sense of fun sprang from the fact that he was a middle-aged man with the maturity of a twenty-year-old. He literally turned several shades of sage, when I mentioned any kind of future that extended beyond a trip to the pub on a Saturday night. It had been more than a year now since I'd felt any inclination to start dating again. But a man who put flying books in his shop window and who talked about the meaning of love, within the first five minutes of acquaintance, was a man worth getting to know.

'I'm not sure I've got anything like a philosophy on love,' I said, wondering if that was true. And also wondering if Jamie was married, engaged, attached or at all interested in me? Maybe he was just as friendly with everyone who walked through the doors of The Wise Old Whale Bookshop, and I was misreading the signs. 'But when I was twelve, I fell for a boy in my class because he had an ice-cream maker at home, and his mum let him use as many chocolate sprinkles as he wanted,' I said, having a vivid recollection of Tommy Two-Scoops as I told the story – one tooth missing at the front, but his hands were steady and sure. 'I don't know what that says about my philosophy on love, but I think my position on ice cream is pretty clear.'

Jamie laughed out loud, his teeth looked lived in but they suited his face. 'Access to an ice-cream maker at the age of twelve would have been enough to win my affections. I fell in love with my sister's best friend once, because her dad owned a guitar shop and it tugged at more than my heartstrings.'

Even his terrible jokes were better than the average attempt.

'Have you got time for a cup of tea, Juliette? I reckon you've earned yourself a good strong brew, after I insulted the book you came in here wanting to buy for your friend. And I'd like to give you a proper tour of my shop, if you're interested. There's a whole section of books about ice-cream making that I think you might appreciate.'

Two hours later, I finally left the shop with a beautiful present for Hope. I had a phone full of angry voice-mail messages from Loretta at work, asking if I was suffering from amnesia and had forgotten that I was supposed to be clearing a house on Queen Street. But I also had a date with Jamie. He was coming to my house, tomorrow evening, to cook a Bolognese. I was supplying the wine and the kitchen.

I hurried over to my car feeling grateful to the one-way system, and the council, who had decided to ignore the wishes of the townsfolk and build it anyway. I also said a silent thank you to the benevolent gods of fate and chance, who had led me to The Wise Old Whale Bookshop and to Jamie – who had already messed up the wiring in my heart and altered its connections forever.

Five

WHEN I GET UP on Saturday morning, I'm still thinking about Poppy and the news of her picture book. But it's the animated look on her face that has troubled me the most. I cannot remember the last time I saw anything like excitement settle over my own face. And it bothers me. It also bothers me that along with some genuine happiness for Poppy, I also feel a tiny bit resentful that she has broken the Jamie bond between us. It's hard to admit that fact, even to myself. Why can't I just be happy for her? I have no right to hold her a hostage to the past.

By 8.30 a.m., I'm already at the supermarket doing my weekly shop. I like to get in early before anyone can judge the contents of my trolley, which makes me look like I'm shopping for a teenager with a very sweet tooth, or an elderly parent who has given up the fight against diabetes. I'm not proud of my trolley. I grab some apples and a bag of frozen vegetables wondering if I'll actually eat them this time. I also stop at the Butterfly Bakery, on my way home, for a loaf of white bread, a coffee and walnut cake and some warm cheese straws. They're so fresh that I've already eaten half of them by the time I drive into Raglan Road.

I sit with a cup of tea in the dining room, after I've packed my shopping away, and wonder how I'm going to fill the rest of the weekend. Weekends are by far the most difficult chunk of time to deal with. I still haven't figured out any reliable strategies for filling the endless hours between Friday night and Monday morning, even though I've had eighteen months to think about it. Weekends are when I feel Jamie's absence the most.

Jamie and I only moved into our Victorian terrace four months before he died. It was the perfect house for us, the place where we wanted to start our married life together. Jamie was attracted by the potential. He had plans to transform every square inch of wall, floor and attic space. I loved the tiles in the hallway, and the sunlight that streamed into the dining room and made me think of Italian piazzas. But four months was barely enough time to plan a wedding, unpack our boxes and find the stopcock for the water, let alone make the place feel like our own.

I don't have to worry about a mortgage. I'm very lucky, I know that. I made a healthy profit from the sale of the flat that I bought ten years ago. And because Jamie had been living cheaply above the bookshop for some years, his savings account was impressive. But I have no idea how to renovate this house without him. We spent whole mornings together planning attic conversions and kitchen extensions, drawing up elaborate plans on anything that came to hand, too absorbed in the details to stop for a single moment and rummage around for a proper pad of paper. Envelopes, paper bags and doctor's appointment cards became our impromptu drawing boards. But all the excitement has gone out of it now that Jamie is no longer here, and I haven't got the heart to touch anything.

I top-up my tea and toy with the idea of killing a couple of hours by cleaning the house. But lugging the vacuum cleaner out from the cupboard under the stairs seems like too much effort. I've also run out of bathroom cleaner, and the stack of paper plates that I bought, a month after Jamie died, negates the need for doing any real washing-up.

If I'd been born into a life of service as a scullery maid, in the early 1900s, I would have felt the back of the housekeeper's hand as a punishment for my slovenly ways. And just at the moment, I can't find a good enough reason to fight that tendency. I never invite anyone round anymore (see previous statement about my slovenly ways). My mum and dad live an hour away, and never drop by unannounced. They're too busy enjoying life in the Autumn Leaves Retirement Village, where they moved three years ago after selling the family home, and are now gleefully spending my inheritance. They take full advantage of the gym, swimming pool and karaoke nights, none of which they ever showed the slightest interest in before. They have found their nirvana. I speak to them once every couple of weeks and visit once a month, if they can fit me in around the badminton matches and lectures on Japanese gardening. But once a month is more than enough contact for all of us. My older brother, Daniel, lives at the other end of the country, where he claims it's necessary to base himself because of his job. But he's a self-employed software engineer, so he could work from the Outer Hebrides (assuming the internet connection was fast enough) and it wouldn't damage his career prospects. We only see each other at Christmas. Both his kids are at high school and don't have any reason to speak to an aunt they barely know. His wife, Melissa, is concerned that my job puts me in the path of some highly dangerous germs and pathogens – she follows me around with an antiseptic spray whenever we're in the same house together.

As a family, we are barely adequate and not exactly close. So cleaning feels like a waste of time when there's very little prospect of anyone calling round on the off-chance. I allow my poor, slovenly heart a victory today, which is just the latest in a long line of victories, if I'm being completely honest.

At lunch, I make a start on the coffee and walnut cake, adding a thick slice to the cheese sandwiches already on my plate. By 1.45 p.m., I'm really starting to struggle. Sometimes, I meet Poppy and Zarina for lunch, or we have a leisurely wander through a flea market. I help them look for vintage bath taps, picture frames or silver pendants for Poppy's growing collection, but not today. Occasionally, I take myself off to a garden centre or a department store in town, just to be in the presence of other people that I don't have to talk to, or explain myself to. I like the buzz of their voices and the snippets of conversation I catch as they drift by, bags full of shopping, children clutched in hand. There are grave discussions about the importance of bras with serious scaffolding, for those attending Zumba classes. I've heard in-depth, solemn debates about the advantages of homemade sourdough bread over shop bought. And (my personal favourite to date) a lively chat about why aliens would never bother invading planet earth now, because of the pollution. But I can't face that today either.

At 2.17 p.m., I suddenly remember that I've got Ivy Edward's photos in the boot of my car. It's the perfect thing to fill my time until 6.00 p.m., when I can order a chicken chow mein with egg fried rice, and try to watch a box set.

I carry two boxes of photos and albums into the dining room, clearing a space on the table so I can make a start. I decide to work my way forwards from the earliest photos in Ivy's collection, to the last ones she ever took. It takes over an hour to sort them into some kind of chronology, based on Ivy's appearance through the years.

There's an austere-looking portrait of her mum and dad on their wedding day, in 1943. Frances Mary Reed and Joseph Evans standing outside the church. It's nothing like the candid, happy photos of today, with billowing veils and handfuls of confetti clouding the air around the wedding party. Photography was obviously a much more serious business in the 1940s. Or maybe it's a reflection of the fact that neither of Ivy's parents looked certain of the vows they'd just taken.

When I look more closely at the photo, there are no reassuring signs of intimacy, no light touch on the arm or any unconscious leaning towards each other. Ivy's mum looks painfully self-conscious. She's holding a modest bouquet of roses and stands awkwardly in a simple white dress with a sweetheart neckline, her shoulder-length hair set in wartime waves. There is no hint of a bridal glow about her, just a tightly pinched expression that speaks of many things left unsaid beyond the realm of the camera. Her dad has the stocky kind of build that only comes from hard physical labour, his hands clenched at his sides like two hammer heads. Everything about his appearance suggests he'd be much happier in boots and a rough-necked shirt, than the suit and tie he's obviously been wrestled into. There's a story in that photo somewhere.

Ivy makes an appearance a year later, in a frilly white christening gown, with an angelic smile. It's the first photo I've seen of her, I realise. There are no more photos of the family until the birth of Alfie. I study a more relaxed family snap, taken in the garden of what must have been their home. Ivy, now a toddler, squints into the sun. Her mum is in the middle of saying something to whoever was taking the photo, her hand a misshapen blur as she points towards the camera. Ivy's dad has a sombre expression and a cigarette hanging out one side of his mouth. He's resting his hand on a large old-fashioned pram, occupied by Alfie. Alfie's face is indistinct, but it's obvious that he takes after his dad, not his mum. They share the same broad nose.

I lay these photos aside; they belong to Alfie, if he wants them.

Joseph Evans doesn't appear in any more of the pictures, but there's no evidence of a funeral, or of a move to a new address following some kind of big life upheaval. Alfie is captured in various combinations of adorable shorts and shirts, with snot, jam, mud or crayon inevitably smeared across his face. Ivy clearly dotes on her brother and she's always holding onto one of his grubby hands, or trying to plant a kiss on his turned cheek, or attempting to lift him up higher into the frame of the camera lens. In every image the affection between the siblings is obvious. They often look as if they're bursting to laugh at a private joke, only to be shared in the safety of a secret hideaway after the photo was taken. In one cute-as-a-button picture, they're both dressed in smart sailor suits, standing shoulder to shoulder, saluting. I'll never be able to look at Alfie in the same way again. The thought makes me smile, and there isn't much about Alfie Evans that has made me smile until this moment.

I wander into the kitchen and help myself to another slice of cake. When I return to Ivy's lifetime collection of photos, there's a big leap forwards in time. Ivy is no longer a gangly-looking child, wearing ankle socks and sensible sandals with broad straps. She is now a young woman standing outside Shimming's, the biggest department store in town, where we've both spent many happy hours in the Haberdashery Department. She's smiling nervously and carrying what looks like a lunchbox tucked under her arm. Could this be Ivy's first job?

This is where I start to get a real sense of the person Ivy became, as she transforms from a happy-looking child into a young adult. She's still smiling, and dressed in a well-fitted skirt and smart blouse, the loose ends of her hair caught in a slight breeze. I can't help wondering how she felt on her first day at work. Shimming's would have been the perfect place to feed her creative spirit. I can imagine her sneaking between the gorgeous bolts of fabric, in her lunch hour, feeling the fine sheen of a satin, or trying to choose between a cotton blend and a cheesecloth fabric for a new sewing project. The perfect music to accompany such a scene would have to be something bold and cheerful, something with a Big Band kind of sound. I close my eyes and the music instantly finds me, as if it's been waiting patiently, fully formed, in the recesses of my imagination, for this exact moment to arrive. I concentrate on the melody the trumpets and horns are producing, as Ivy twirls around the haberdashery pulling a length of printed silk behind her, like a long flowing cape. The rest of the haberdashery suddenly springs to life and joins in with her joyous dance, in this musical that I'm creating. Large bobbins of cotton roll together across the fabric-cutting table, scissors are pirouetting en pointe in a ballet of precise snips and cuts. Swirling tape measures fall through the air, a ticker-tape parade in centimetres and inches, and a gaggle of dressmaker's manikins waltz each other gracefully across the polished floor. Ivy dances with each of the manikins in turn, a tiara of dressmaker's pins glinting in her hair, a princess at her own haberdashery ball, until the music finally fades and the lights dim. I keep my eyes closed, clinging to this wonderful vision of Ivy for as long as possible, the pins in her hair still gleaming. But the image eventually scatters and fragments until all I'm left with is a fuzzy kind of darkness. The trumpets and horns now unreachable.

I don't usually start reimagining someone's life until I'm sitting in my car with Jamie, after their funeral. But there's something about Ivy Edwards that makes me want to picture her life now, in the boldest of colours and sounds. I just hope I can remember all the details when I tell Jamie later.

For the next two hours, I sort Ivy's photos into eras, seeing the progress of her life like a series of stills from a movie. The day she married her husband at St. Martin's church on the edge of town, with cherry trees in full blossom on the street outside. Her well-trimmed wedding dress in a beautiful white satin, delicate buttons on each sleeve hugging her wrists. A photo of the house Ivy and Stan moved into together, a tiny red-brick terrace with net curtains at the windows. Ivy and Stan standing on the doorstep, arms locked proudly around each other, itching to get on with the business of setting up a home. The first year the pink roses bloomed in their front garden, droopy headed with dew and the weight of their own perfume. The day trips they took with friends to Filey, Scarborough and Bridlington – ice creams and fish and chips eaten on the promenade, hair whipped by the sea breeze. Ivy and Stan huddled together on the beach, laughing at the wind as it tried to steal scarves and hats. Alfie appears in some of these photos, when he's old enough to tag along. There's no snot or jam on his face now. He has a shock of wavy hair and his arm around a laughing girl, the first of his many fiancées, perhaps?

I love the photos of Ivy and Stan on holiday in Spain and Portugal. They're pink cheeked with sunburn and sangria, taking refuge in cafes on Acacia-lined streets, visiting the old quarter of a town. When they moved into a bigger house with its own driveway, Ivy captured each season's change in the garden, and every birthday celebrated at the kitchen table with a flourish of candles and cakes. Thanks to Ivy's diligence with the camera, I can see every wallpaper choice and new carpet fitted. There's an enchanting photo of Ivy, Stan and Alfie all piled together in the backseat of a brand new blue Mini, faces luminous with delight at their purchase. But one glorious image stands out above all others – Ivy on a bicycle, clips around the ankles of her tailored trousers, freewheeling down a hill like she's still a child and reckless with joy.

A whole series of photos shows Ivy at work in the haberdashery, it seems my instinct about Shimming's was right. She's always smiling and sharing a joke with the other women, arms linked together in friendship. Every moment caught by the camera is just a single point in their shared history. In later years, Ivy's smile becomes a little more rigid and less carefree. It's clear that Ivy and her husband never had any children. They stayed in the same house until Ivy moved into Starcross Crescent, and Stan no longer appears in any of the photos. Only a handful of snaps were taken in the last few years of her life. I can still see hints of the same young woman who stood outside Shimming's, with all of life before her, but the years have layered themselves over Ivy and weighed her down. The last photo was taken six months before she died, and it's just her and Alfie again. They're sitting at her kitchen table with a homemade birthday cake between them. Alfie is now the only custodian of those memories.

Based on these photos, I'd guess that Ivy's had been a relatively happy life. There's always something genuine and warm in her smile. When those feelings are forced, or faked for the camera, I inevitably see an unravelling. The truth is always exposed sooner or later, with divorce papers or angry letters hidden at the back of cupboards, abandoned but not forgotten.

I put together a curated collection of photos for Alfie to keep, if he wants them. But the rest have to be disposed of. I hate throwing anyone's memories out with the rubbish, like they're nothing more important than potato peelings, or toenail clippings. Usually, I burn them in my little garden furnace, better for them to go out with a blaze. But I'll have to hold onto Ivy's until I'm sure that Alfie hasn't had a change of heart. I wonder if Alfie's got many photos of his own. I've seen very little evidence of any personal possessions at Ivy's flat, but since he's got nowhere else to go, that's where they must be.

I grab my phone and look up the sheltered housing scheme that Alfie's on the waiting list for. Orton Lodge looks peaceful with well-kept communal areas and garden spaces. If Alfie wants to get to know his neighbours, or sit outside in the spring sunshine, he'll be well catered for. The flats themselves are small and neat, and a little on the institutional side when it comes to decor. But they also look safe and clean. Am I looking at Alfie's final home?

Six

AN UNHAPPY SCENE GREETS me in the kitchen at Starcross Crescent on Monday morning. It's like the devastation left by a fox that has crept into a house and plundered the pantry. Every surface of Ivy's neatly ordered kitchen is covered in dirty plates, half-empty jars of peanut butter and crumbs of various origin. A stale loaf of bread sits in the middle of a beautiful glass cake stand, like a brick.

'What happened in here?' I ask Alfie, trying not to sound like the long-suffering parent of teenage boys. 'Did you have a party over the weekend?'

Alfie frowns and scans the kitchen like there's nothing wrong with leaving a trail of discarded teabags strewn across the countertops. They look like a network of tiny mole hills.

'Could you clean it up, please?' I ask. 'I've got to pack up the kitchen tomorrow, and it will take me twice as long if I have to deal with this first.'

'You're taking all the plates and cups?' Alfie looks aghast, like this is news to him.

'I have until Wednesday to clear everything out, we talked about this last week, remember?'

'Of course I remember, I haven't lost my marbles yet,' Alfie says, sounding irritated at the insinuation. 'I just didn't realise you'd be taking every last spoon and fork. How am I supposed to eat my dinner?'

'I can leave enough for your own personal use, Alfie.'

'It's Mr Evans to you,' he scowls.

'But as of tomorrow, I'm afraid you won't be able to cook in Ivy's kitchen.'

Now I feel like the chief villain in a pantomime, the kind that would have been pelted with ripe tomatoes in days gone by. But Alfie turns up his shirt sleeves and fills the sink with soapy water, grumbling about people who throw old age pensioners out of their homes, with about as much care as a sack of potatoes.

I head to the quiet of the hallway with my phone. There's a voice mail from Loretta reminding me (unnecessarily) that I have until the end of the day to complete the job at Starcross Crescent. Thanks to Alfie, I won't be finished until late Wednesday afternoon, at the earliest, but I'll break that piece of calendar-altering news to Loretta later. Loretta also informs me that Mr Thurston already has new tenants lined up, and he needs to give the place a fresh coat of paint before they move in, a week from today. It does seem indecently fast. And I need to make sure Alfie's got somewhere to go before I hand the keys back to Thurston. Luckily, he never enters any of the vacant properties until Hobson's have cleared the contents; he knows there's nothing he can do until the rooms are completely empty. And even though I am running way behind schedule, Alfie's days at Starcross Crescent are numbered.

I put a call into Jaya at the council Housing Department, to see if she's managed to arrange some temporary accommodation for Alfie. He might feel a little happier if he knows where he's going on Wednesday.

'I'm still working on it, I'm afraid,' she tells me, when I manage to track her down. 'I'm hoping for a place at the Abbey View Bed and Breakfast, but the manager hasn't come back to me with a confirmation yet, so I'll chase that today. And we're still looking at a wait of several months for the sheltered housing, unless circumstances change.'

'But you'll definitely have somewhere for him to go on Wednesday?' I have visions of Alfie cowering under a railway bridge, in a cardboard box, rootling through the bins outside the nearest takeaway for a few stray burger scraps.

'Don't worry. Alfie will have somewhere to lay his head for the night. After that, I may have to move him again once or twice, three or four times at the most, depending on the situation,' she says, sounding apologetic. 'I'll do the best I can for him.'

I hang up feeling worse than I did before I phoned her. But Jaya knows her job. I have to tell myself that Alfie will be in good hands, and that rehousing homeless pensioners is definitely not a part of my job. I just wish I hadn't seen lots of photos of Alfie as a toddler, being smothered in love by Ivy. This house clearance is already becoming far more personal than I'm comfortable with.

The rest of the morning has a tetchy feel to it. Alfie spends several hours cleaning up in the kitchen, complaining about having prune fingers. He also makes more noise than necessary when he collects up all the empty bottles, tins and cartons, and flings them into the recycling bin outside the kitchen door.

I concentrate on clearing out the rest of the sitting room, sorting table lamps, old televisions and pictures into donate and dump piles. Ivy's plants, a cactus and several healthy-looking maidenhair ferns, will be taken to the communal areas in the housing complex. The 1980s sofa and armchairs will be picked up by Otis, another Hobson's veteran, on Wednesday afternoon. Otis has a long history of turning up on the wrong side of town – at Clement Gardens instead of Clement Close, or on Thursday instead of Tuesday – so it's anyone's guess if he'll actually make an appearance on the day and time arranged. He also doesn't believe in mobile phones, even though Hobson's has provided him with one, and he hardly ever turns it on. So it's impossible to track him down when he's late or totally absent. Hobson's has become the most successful house clearance company in Sholtsbury *despite* Otis and his shortcomings.

By 11.30 a.m., everything in the sitting room has been dealt with. Alfie emerges from the kitchen, a few minutes later, wearing a pair of rubber gloves, Ivy's apron tied around his waist. His face drops as he spots the orderly piles I've made under the window at the far end of the room, the reality of his situation hitting home again.

'Ivy's stuff,' he says. 'What's happening to her pictures?' He peels off his gloves and strides straight over to the largest of the paintings – a herd of deer in a pine forest – that I've placed carefully against the wall. 'She loved the one with the deer. It was a present from Mum. You can't just toss that into a skip.'

'I'll sell all of Ivy's pictures to a second-hand shop I use all the time. The owner's very good, he'll make sure Ivy's pictures go to a worthy home,' I say, hoping it's true.

Normally, I don't have time to think about the fate of any of the stuff I sell or donate. But if Norman, the owner of Sholtsbury Bargain Hut, decides the pine forest picture is too old-fashioned and won't sell, he'll donate it to one of the charity shops on the High Street. And there's a good chance Alfie might stumble across it.

'Do you want to keep the picture?' I ask.

'What would I do with a picture of a pine forest when I've got nowhere to live?' The anguish in his voice is hard to hear.

Alfie retreats back to the kitchen to make some lunch. It's a cheese sandwich today, no soup, thankfully. I take my own lunch — a pasta salad from Boots again — and join him at the table with the box of photos I set aside at the weekend.

'I thought you might want to keep these,' I say, pushing the box over to his half of the table. 'Ivy had some lovely photos of your family.'

Alfie opens the box and pulls out a handful of snaps, his face still stony from our difficult morning. He stops at the image of his whole family together in the back garden, and throws it down on the table with a contemptuous grunt.

'You can get rid of this one, for a start. I don't want it.'

This is why I work alone. There are no family feuds or deeply held wounds to deal with when you're the only person making decisions. I take the photo and place it in my bag.

'And if you've got any more pictures of my dad in that box, you can fling them on the rubbish heap with Ivy's old girdles. I don't want to see his sour face staring back at me from any photos.'

I take the box and find the photo of Alfie's parents on their wedding day. Then I grab a pair of scissors from the kitchen drawer and cut the offending party out of the picture, slipping Alfie's dad into my bag, next to the other photo. Alfie almost smiles.

'That's the only other photo of your dad. Everything else is of you and Ivy, and of Ivy's life.'

Alfie nods and tucks into his sandwich again, and we eat the rest of our lunch in silence. It's not exactly companionable but at least it's lost some of its hostile edge.

'I expect you're wondering why I don't want any photos of my dad,' Alfie eventually says.

He pours himself a fresh cup of tea from the pot and begins to work his way through a packet of chocolate digestives.

'It's really none of my business, Mr Evans. I'm not here to pry into anyone's personal life.'

'You can call me Alfie again,' he says, softening. 'You just took me by surprise this morning, that's all. I like Ivy's place, it's comfortable. I've been coming here every Thursday afternoon for years now, regular as clockwork, for a cuppa and a chat about old times. Ivy always made a fuss on my birthday as well, baking a cake and cooking a fancy dinner. And I suppose I got it into my head that I might be able to stay here, after all. If you explained the situation, Juliette, and put in a good word for me with that weasel, Thurston...'

I lay the remains of my pasta salad on the table, losing my ability to swallow.

'The tenancy was in Ivy's name, Alfie,' I explain carefully, 'and Mr Thurston already has some new people lined up. They'll be moving in next Monday.'

It was his last sliver of hope. I watch it vanish from Alfie's eyes, like the bars on an old electric fire fading after the plug has been pulled.

'Well, that's that then, I'm officially homeless.'

His words cause me a sudden stab of indigestion, or maybe it's just guilt, they feel remarkably similar.

'I've had another word with Jaya from the Housing Department at the council,' I tell him quickly, 'and she assures me she'll have somewhere for you to go on Wednesday.'

'But it won't be Ivy's flat,' Alfie says. 'This has been my home-from-home for years. First Ivy and now this place, it's been a tough week, Juliette, and that's the truth. But I appreciate everything you've done for me. I wouldn't have known where to start myself.'

I resist an uncomfortable urge to take his hand and give it a tight squeeze of support. Alfie will be fine, I remind myself, clearing away my lunch things instead. Yes, he's just lost his only sister and his home, but hope is on the horizon in the shape of the Orton Lodge Sheltered Housing Scheme. And I cling to that thought as I head to the bathroom to clear out the tall cupboards.

Normally, I'd tackle the kitchen next, but Alfie needs some space and time to come to terms with his changing circumstances. The best thing I can do is leave him in peace. I've barely made a start on the first of the cupboards – which is filled with neatly folded towels and bed sheets – when Alfie appears in the doorway and hovers.

'My dad ran out on us when I was two years old,' he says, without any preamble.

I wobble dangerously on the chair that I'm standing on and turn to stare at him.

'He left you, your mum and your sister?'

'Ivy says we came home from the shops with Mum, one day, and he'd left a couple of pounds on the kitchen table, and a note saying he wasn't coming back. And that was that, none of us ever saw him again. There were no cards at Christmas, no birthday presents, letters or phone calls. He never sent any money to help Mum with the bills, or to buy us clothes and shoes. She had to get an extra job at the local biscuit factory just to make ends meet. Grandma Reed looked after us until we were old enough to go to school. Ivy did most of the cooking and cleaning when she got a bit older. Mum was too tired by the time she got home from work. The blisters on her feet were so big, sometimes, we had to stand well back when she popped them with a sterile needle.'

I stare at Alfie until my arms begin to shake under the weight of towels and sheets that I'm still holding, and I have to climb off the chair and dump them on the floor.

'Where did he go, what happened to him?' I ask, shocked that anyone could desert their own family so thoroughly.

'Nobody knows,' Alfie says, with a shrug. He leans against the doorframe with his arms folded. 'Mum tried to track him down, according to Ivy, but none of his family had the faintest idea where he'd gone. The police weren't interested because he'd left of his own accord. And after a few months, Mum just stopped looking. I was too young to remember any of this, but Ivy liked to talk about the old days, in her last few years, and that was one of the regular tales she told. It's not a story I've ever enjoyed sitting through much.'

'Do you know *why* he left?' I ask.

'Apart from the fact that he was a selfish, lazy bastard, you mean? Ivy found out later, from one of Mum's closest friends, that dad might have been involved with another woman. There were rumours, apparently, right before their wedding. Maybe he ran off with her.'

That would explain the solemn expressions in the wedding photo.

If Alfie's mum had a sense, even then, that Joseph Evans wasn't fully committed and that there might be someone else...

'Ivy's always been soft-hearted,' Alfie says, shaking his head. 'She would have forgiven him, even if he'd walked back through her door last week, with his tail between his legs. She would have baked him one of her special chocolate cakes, done his washing and mended his socks, if he'd asked her to. But as far as I'm concerned it was good riddance to bad rubbish.' His face hardens, the muscles around his mouth pulling inwards. 'He did nothing for his family, turned his back on us and his responsibilities as a father. He sent my mother to an early grave, with her constant worrying about money. She was only fifty-two when she died. He may not have been the love of her life, but she felt abandoned and ashamed when he walked out on us. She never mentioned his name again. When she died, and Ivy went through her stuff, just like you're going through Ivy's now, she found some letters.'

Letters can be powerful conduits to the past; they are among the most difficult items to deal with on any house clearance job.

'Ivy said that Dad had written to Mum before they got married,' Alfie says. 'She wanted me to read the letters, but I told her to burn the lot of them. I didn't want to know how he'd charmed Mum into marrying him. Ivy said they were proof that he had noble intentions, once. All I know is Mum deserved better than him.'

'I'm sorry,' I say, seeing how much pain it must have caused Alfie in his life.

'Yeah, so am I. But it's all ancient history now,' he says, looking like it's anything but. Clearly his dad still has the power to make him angry, even though Alfie hasn't seen him for seventy-five years. And he turns back to the sitting room and closes the door behind him.

I spend two hours in the bathroom sorting sheets, towels, pillowcases and duvet covers into donation and dumping piles. I'm well behind schedule. The kitchen is going to be tricky. I haven't even started on the bedrooms or the hallway. And if Alfie keeps telling me his family history, I'll be even more behind.

I throw out a collection of half-used shampoos, bottles of perfume and cotton wool buds. And leave Alfie's razor, soap and English Crab Apple sitting on a lonely shelf in the middle cupboard. The more of Ivy's stuff I sort through, the more obvious it becomes that Alfie owns practically nothing of his own.

It's in the final cupboard that I find something more personal. Pushed right to the back of the darkest corner is a shoe box, held together with a length of frayed pink ribbon. I open it slowly and find a pink baby dress tucked neatly inside, there's also a pair of matching slippers and socks that are so tiny they look like they could have been made for a doll. Everything smells of baby powder. I also find a wristband from the Royal Victoria General Hospital, with the name *Sarah* scrawled across it in pen. Several locks of soft, fine brown hair sit curled inside a small cloth bag. Ivy and her husband clearly had a baby girl, Sarah, who never made it home from the hospital with them. Sarah must have died soon after birth. I pack everything back into the box exactly as I found it, taking extra care with the hair and the wristband. How many times did Ivy come to this box and treasure the memories it held? Judging by how frayed the ends of the pink ribbon are, I'm guessing a lot.

This is not the first baby box I've ever found and I know what to do with it. When I first started my job with Hobson's, Nigel sent me on a course which covered the basics of house clearance, and how to deal with anything I might find. The number one rule is to treat everyone's belongings with care and respect. Imagine what it would feel like if someone was going through your possessions. What would they discover hidden at the back of your drawers and cupboards? Would you want them to judge you solely on some of your less fabulous moments as a human being? Would that judgement be a fair and rounded picture of who you really were?

I was also taught to inform the police if there was any evidence of a crime, which I've only had to do a handful of times. Once, when it was clear that a little old man had been embezzling the funds he'd collected for a charity, over the course of several decades. And another time when some highly descriptive diary entries – and some gleeful holiday snaps following an insurance payout – made it clear that a woman had murdered her husband. Lastly, I was taught that there's only one way to deal with highly emotive personal belongings, like Ivy's baby box; don't get involved. Respect the tragic circumstances of someone's loss with a prayer, or some words privately spoken, and keep going. It may sound heartless, but it's the only way to do this job without being in a constant state of distress.

Tragedy happens.

I've found that the easiest way to deal with baby boxes, spousal boxes or even pet boxes, is to take comfort in the idea of longed-for reunions, on the other side. I'm not sure whether I even believe that's possible. Coming from a family of firm nonbelievers, we weren't exactly big on discussions about the afterlife. But I'd be a fool to rule it out, especially as I have my own tragedy to come to terms with. If I think about being reunited with Jamie in the afterlife, it generally involves visions of us gambolling happily through fields full of meadow flowers, or enjoying lazy summer picnics with scones and jam. It's strangely comforting. But this is still hard. Ivy's loss seems more personal than most. Thankfully, I know exactly what to do with the treasured memories of her daughter. I take the box out to my car so I can deal with it on my way home. And then I pull myself back together again with a handful of tissues and some water. I haven't shed any tears at a house clearance for several years. Alfie, I decide, is throwing me off my rhythm in more ways than one.

With the bathroom and the sitting room now sorted, I decide to concentrate on the hallway. It's far more cluttered than I'd realised, with things squirreled away in every corner: boxes filled with envelopes, pens, old address books, Argos catalogues going back at least a decade. Much of it can be dealt with swiftly. The collection of telephone directories stacked against the wall goes to the recycling bin outside. The coats and scarves on the hall stand are too worn to be of use to anyone but a material recycling company – who will break the fibres down and form them into new materials for someone else to use. But what should I do with the bowler hats? I take them off the wall and lay them out on the carpet. The reasons why Ivy ended up with such a collection will remain a mystery forever. The labels are different inside each of the bowlers and offer no real clues. No charity shop will take such a large number of hats. I do a quick search on the internet and find a local community theatre group, who may be able to use them as stage props and costumes. I send an email explaining my dilemma and stack the hats up in the corner. The hallway is now cleared. Ivy's flat is starting to reveal its bones and the echo is beginning to set in, the one that always sounds like the ghost of a last goodbye.

Alfie has retreated to his own room by the time I'm ready to leave, so I close the front door quietly behind me and try not to disturb him more than I already have. It's been a rough week for the brother of Ivy Edwards. I take the bowler hats to the community theatre on the edge of town. They seem delighted with the donation and instantly start discussing how they could be used in a new musical production. And then I make one last stop at Flint's, the funeral directors on the edge of town. I hand over Ivy's baby box giving instructions for it to be placed in Ivy's coffin, tucked in right next to her body. I can think of no better way to acknowledge Ivy's loss.

When I finally get home, I make a cup of strong tea and sit on the sofa thinking over everything Alfie told me about his dad. How, without a dad, Alfie grew up with no male role model. Maybe that's part of the reason he never got married. He didn't want to turn out like his dad. But in choosing to never move beyond the status of a fiancé, did he deny himself the love and comfort of a married life and a family of his own? I know marriage isn't for everybody. Sometimes it isn't even an option, and it doesn't always work out well when it is. But is it the real reason that, at the age of seventy-seven, Alfie Evans is all alone?

I heat up a frozen macaroni cheese for dinner, wondering how it is that I'm still spending more time thinking about Alfie, when my duty of care is towards his sister, Ivy.

Seven

ON TUESDAY MORNING, I take a slight detour before driving to Starcross Crescent. I want to give Alfie enough time to have his breakfast in peace, before I clean out the kitchen. It already has the potential to become a battleground, Alfie's last stand. I drive through the centre of Sholtsbury and park outside The New Finds Bookshop, which is only just opening as I arrive. It was in this shop, almost seven years ago, that I met Jamie. Back when it was still called The Wise Old Whale Bookshop.

I can't help wishing the new owner had kept Jamie's window display. But the armchair and the flying books are long gone, and have been replaced by a more conventional show of the latest releases in the book world. Today, it's filled with copies of a best-selling thriller with a gaudy cover in serial-killer red. I push my way slowly through the door as soon as the new owner – a tall, elegant-looking woman with an antique watch on a chain around her neck – has unfastened the bolts and turned off the alarm. She gives me a friendly nod but doesn't press for any conversation.

It's not Jamie's shop anymore. A small cafe was recently added at the back of the building, which means a strong smell of coffee now overpowers any subtle hint of freshly minted books that used to drift gently through the premises. The cafe sells chocolate brownies, pecan slices and soy macchiatos and draws a different kind of crowd to the shop. I move slowly through the shelves, now devoid of plants, they too were removed long ago. The maze of shelves was also dismantled and rearranged, so that I can now see all the way through to the cafe. It's impossible not to notice the changes that have occurred since the last time I was here, only weeks ago. There's a collection of rainbow mobiles in the children's section, and a large unicorn beanbag. Several of the comfy chairs – that used to be positioned in private nooks for undisturbed reading – have now gone. I take a moment to mourn their hairy-seated loss. With each visit, the whole shop moves further away from Jamie. But I can still feel his presence everywhere.

I do my own special tour of the shop, hitting all my favourite landmarks in an order that I've worked out carefully over the last eighteen months. I head down a mythology aisle to a set of shelves that Jamie made himself. I have to remove a handful of books and then weave my arm all the way through to the back before I can feel them. Jamie's initials, JM, carved into the wood, his maker's mark. I feel a familiar thrill of recognition, relieved that they still exist. Every time I visit, I'm convinced they'll have been erased. The next stop is right at the back of the building, where Jamie left a perfect boot mark on the wall once. He was carrying some boxes and tried to close the door behind him with his foot, and missed. I've still got the very boots he was wearing at the time. I touch the handle of the door that leads up to the tiny flat above the shop.

Jamie was living there when I first met him, but I never once stayed the night. It was more of a warehouse than any kind of home, with towers of new stock waiting to find their way down to the shelves in the shop. And I refused to hunker down among the scratching mice that ran freely through the walls after dark. Jamie continued to stay in his flat for a few nights every week, after we met. When he stayed at my flat, on the very outskirts of town, he was faced with a long drive right through the middle of every rush hour just to get to work. It was only after we bought our house on Raglan Road that he finally started moving out of the flat, but he never completed the process.

I finish my tour of the bookshop at the counter, where the new owner is opening the morning mail. It's always better when she's in another part of the shop, giving me a few precious seconds alone with the large expanse of polished walnut. The counter is like a map of Jamie's time here, and I am a part of that landscape.

I want to run my fingers over the carving of the books, the one that wraps itself around the entire base of the chunky, solid counter. Bookworms, reading glasses and starbursts are all woven into the magical design, created by Jamie. He put his own love of books into every carving. There's a split in the top of the counter where he accidentally dropped the till once, and a stool that tucks perfectly underneath it. He called it The Perch, and if he wasn't sitting on it quietly strumming his guitar, he was using it as a platform to talk to anyone who came through the door about books. Jamie's book recommendations were legendary for their far-reaching ability to change your life, or your point of view, should either need altering.

I'd love to stop and let the memories come tumbling out, to think about all the times we sat here and talked together: making plans to visit the Design Museum in London, or sharing our dreams about having a house filled with dogs and cats, or just deciding what sandwiches to order for lunch. Once, when the bookshop was closed for the day, we spent three hours arguing about which book was the best ever written, based on title, character names, use of language and the number of times we'd fallen asleep reading it into the early hours of the morning. But none of that is going to happen today.

I take a book from a display next to the till and try to look as if this is the very item that I came in here to buy.

'I hear this is a good one,' the new shop owner says, ringing up the price on Jamie's till. 'Did you enjoy the others?'

'Oh, no, I mean, I haven't read any of the other books.'

She gives me a mildly puzzled look. But before she can follow it up with any kind of question, I take the book and hurry out of the shop, savouring the familiar ring of the antique door bell, as I go. If the woman knew who I was, and in a moment of kindness, let me take anything I wanted from the shop, it would be that bell. Jamie loved it. He found it at an antique's fair in Cornwall. It came from a large private residence overlooking the sea, and was one of the bells used to call the servants up from the kitchens. Jamie got a real thrill out of owning such a piece of history, and from imagining all the tasks – the everyday and the not so everyday – that it had summoned the butler, the housekeeper or the housemaid to perform.

I sit in my car outside the shop, fretting over the diminishing evidence of Jamie's life. One day, none of it will be here. Someone will paint over the boot mark on the wall, or they'll turn the shop into a hairdresser's and replace the counter. But I don't want to think about when that day will come. When someone noteworthy dies, bronze statues are erected, books are written and portraits are painted and hung in galleries, open to all visitors. When someone like Jamie dies — a good, warm-hearted normal person, who never did anything of note other than exist — where are you supposed to go to see the proof of that life? This bookshop is his bronze statue and gallery painting. Sometimes, I just need to pay a visit.

I look at the book I've just bought and will probably never read — *The Tamsin Prophecy*, which is book three of *The Star Tamer's Series*. That explains the questioning look from the new owner. I'll have to make a more careful selection on my next visit, something to show her that I'm not a crazy, random book-buying woman, even if the shoe fits.

It's 10.10 a.m. by the time I reach Starcross Crescent, and I'm still struggling to get my head out of the bookshop. Alfie has cleared away his breakfast things and is waiting for me in the sitting room, in an obvious state of agitation.

'Have you heard from your friend at the council yet about where I'm supposed to go tomorrow?' he asks, as soon as I walk through the door.

'I'll give her a ring right now,' I say, putting my bag down and dialling Jaya's number, trying to focus. This is important. I need to ask the right questions on Alfie's behalf, there's nobody else to do it for him now that Ivy's gone.

'You were fourth on my list of people to call this morning,' she says when she answers, sounding disappointed that I've beaten her to it. 'I've got confirmation from the manager at the Abbey View Bed and Breakfast on Curzon Street, Alfie's going there tomorrow. Shall I give you the address?'

I write down all the relevant details, how to get to Curzon Street, who to ring if Alfie needs to arrange transport.

'Now that I can contact Alfie directly at the B&B, or wherever I have to move him to next, I can keep him posted about the sheltered housing situation. Orton Lodge is a nice place, he should be happy there. It's got a good community feel.'

'What about the B&B?' I ask. 'Is it a decent place too?'

'We've been using it for some years, but it's been a good while since it had an official inspection.' There's a pause as she reads the notes on her computer screen and considers what they mean. 'But it should be fine.'

I don't know if she's trying to convince me, or herself.

I recognise the address of the B&B. It's on a busy main road heading out of town, near a rundown industrial estate. It's miles away from any of the amenities Alfie's likely to want. If I had to stay there for a single night – and I'd probably rather spend it sitting on a bench in the park – I'd take an extra padlock for the door, some noise-cancelling headphones and plenty of flea spray.

'So?' Alfie asks when I put my phone away. 'Where are they sending me? I hope I'm not going to some grotty caravan park, opposite the council tip.'

'It's a B&B on Curzon Street, and I can ring someone to arrange transport, if you need me to.'

'Curzon Street, the one down by the old industrial estate?' He looks less than impressed. 'That's where all the old soaks used to hang out, once upon a time. It's not exactly The Ritz, but I suppose I should be grateful, nonetheless.'

'Jaya says she might move you again quite soon,' I say, trying to ignore Alfie's comment about the "old soaks", and hoping there isn't anywhere worse than Curzon Street.

Alfie folds his arms. 'And I suppose you'll be wanting to clear my room out today?'

'I thought I'd leave that until last. I'll do it tomorrow, give you a chance to get your things together first.'

Alfie frowns but says nothing more and he disappears into the hallway. I head straight for the kitchen to make a start on the cupboards. I've got to get through everything in this room this morning so that I can tackle Ivy's bedroom later. But all I can think about is Alfie's room at the B&B. In my imagination, there are whole continents of mould growing across the cracked ceiling. Wolves howl outside the building, planning how to pick Alfie off as soon as he leaves his room. I can picture a secret door that opens, in the dead of night, revealing a gang of ruthless thieves who are intent on stealing Alfie's last possessions. Even without the wolves and the thieves, it's no place for a man of his age to spend any amount of time. But where else is he supposed to go? He's got no family or friends he can stay with, every single one of them is probably in a housing scheme of their own. And he's too old to sofa-surf anyway.

I power through the kitchen cupboards, getting rid of bags of flour and different kinds of sugars for sweetening and icing – Ivy was clearly a baker. I find a collection of cake recipes piled neatly inside one of the drawers. And I see a sudden image of Ivy standing at the kitchen counter, looking exactly as she did in her middle years, with curly hair and the beginnings of an extra chin. She's weighing out the ingredients for a cake, a smudge of flour making her nose twitch. And then, I can't help it (it's already been a difficult morning), my imagination really kicks in and the cupboard doors are flying open in time to a lively piece of kitchen music. Ivy begins to twirl around the room wearing a sunshine-yellow apron, a whisk in her hand as she grabs a bowl of eggs and begins to beat in time with the music. The rest of her mixing bowls slip and slide gracefully across the countertops, like they're skating over a frozen lake. One of the bowls collides with the scales, and suddenly, the flour it contains cascades around Ivy, covering her hair like a winter's snowfall. She laughs, joyful in her kitchen, loving her baking routines. She hops up onto the table and does an impressive tap dance routine in her slippers, really working the room and the sudden spotlight she appears under. The cutlery shoots out of the drawers and mimics her movements. Ivy Edwards, queen of her kitchen. Just thinking about her in her apron makes me smile for the first time all day.

In the flats and houses where I've worked, I've often been aware of something in the very make-up of the furniture and the kitchen utensils that gives a sense of the person who used them. In Ivy's home, everything feels like it was loved. I'm certain that this was a happy home.

The image of Ivy fades and I hold onto the feeling for as long as possible, before dealing with the rest of the pots and pans. I'll have nothing new and spontaneous to share with Jamie if I keep having these visions of Ivy Edward's life, the musical. But I need the distraction, I realise. Alfie is disrupting my usual house-clearing equilibrium. And these visions are helping me to focus on Ivy.

I manage to set aside a lovely cake stand and some useful storage boxes for donation. But Ivy's cooking pots aren't worth saving; they've already had a long life of service and are fit for nothing but the scrap-metal merchant. I quickly clear out the other drawers, filled with plastic bags and sachets of sugar from a local cafe. And empty the fridge of everything but a pint of milk and a tub of butter for Alfie, who only reappears at lunchtime. He takes a long look at the empty cupboards, standing open and pillaged of everything good and comforting, the heart of Ivy's home no longer beating.

'I'm going down the pub for some lunch,' he says, and he's out of the door before I can offer to share my sandwich.

After I've eaten, I head towards Ivy's room. Alfie's bedroom door is open and I slide inside for a sneaky look. It's the only room in the house I haven't fully investigated yet, I have no idea what's waiting for me inside the wardrobes. If they're packed from floor to ceiling with old documents, photos, or a lifetime collection of holiday souvenirs, I'll have to work into the night to clear them. But it feels wrong to do any kind of exploration now. I'd have to move Alfie's belongings to clear a path to the wardrobes, and they are not mine to touch.

As I suspected, he doesn't have many possessions. A single suitcase sits open on the floor, with a neatly folded layer of clothes on the top, there are two duffle bags and a box marked *personal*. As far as I can tell, Alfie owns nothing else. His whole life reduced down to a small, sad-looking pile of socks, shoes and shirts that wouldn't even fill a car. At least it won't take much to move him to his new home. I shake my head, annoyed with myself for being so heartless.

In Ivy's room, I have to yank hard on the wardrobe doors before they'll slide open, but then I dive straight in. Most of her clothes, in various bold and garish patterns, can be donated. I find several smart suits right at the back of the wardrobe, clothes Ivy obviously made for herself in her younger days. They are beautiful pieces of sewing, fitted at the waist, flawless seams, nips and tucks everywhere. Ivy would have looked like a film star every time she wore any one of them. I set them aside for a vintage shop, along with two pairs of 1960s shoes with cute little bows that are still in good condition. I can't help wondering if Ivy wore them as she danced the night away at the Sholtsbury Dance Hall, every Saturday.

There are three shoe boxes filled with letters, but I don't have time to go through them now. Normally, I scan any personal correspondence relatively quickly, trying not to get lost in the contents, looking for any living friends or relatives who can be informed of the person's death. But this time, I need to pay a little more attention, for Alfie's sake. I take them out to the boot of my car so I can read them at home later.

Alfie returns midway through the afternoon, smelling strongly of beer and looking a lot happier. He flings his coat onto Ivy's bed and sits in a chair by the window, insisting that I need some company as I go through Ivy's jewellery box. I try to tell him it's not necessary, that I'm used to working alone, and that most of the time, I prefer it. But Alfie swats my protests away.

'I remember Ivy used to wear those to work,' he says, as I inspect a pair of silver earrings. 'Did I ever tell you she worked in the Haberdashery Department, at Shimming's?'

I think of the photo I found of Ivy, with her lunchbox tucked under her arm.

'She loved her job, said no two days were ever the same. She liked helping people pick out patterns and materials, and all the zips, buttons and trims that went along with it. And her favourite days were when they had a big new delivery of stock for the autumn or spring. She'd come home, to our old house on Grange Road, twittering away like a budgie about floral this or tweed that. And it only got worse when she bought her first sewing machine.' There's a real brotherly affection in Alfie's voice, his memories and fond feelings freed up by the beer and the sight of Ivy's old jewellery. 'She made Mum a lovely dress once, for her birthday, used two weeks of her wages to buy the fancy material.'

'Did she stay in the haberdashery for long?' I ask, boxing up two gold chain necklaces.

'She was there for twenty-three years, and then they moved her up to the offices on the fifth floor. Mind you, Ivy was ready for the fifth floor by then. Her feet were killing her at the end of the day and she wasn't getting any younger. She moved to Pomphrey's a few years after that.'

Pomphrey's, the only other big store in town, lacks the grace and style of Shimming's, but tries to make up for it with heavily discounted stock.

'She worked in the office. Said she liked the people but the paperwork was a bit dull. She stayed there until she retired.'

'What about her husband?' I ask.

'Stan? He was a carpenter.'

'He made the cupboards in the sitting room?'

Alfie nods. 'Ivy was over the moon. He built them at work using offcuts and any scraps he could scavenge. And then she came home from work on her birthday – it was the same year they moved into the bigger house, on Quince Road – and the cupboards were sitting in the front room, all tied up with a bow. Ivy squealed when she saw them.' Alfie smiles at the memory. 'He was a good man, Stan, I knew him all my life. He lived at the end of our street and was born three days before Ivy. She was lost when the stupid bugger died at the age of sixty-three. Didn't know what to do with herself for a few years after that.'

I don't have to reach far to imagine how heartbroken Ivy must have been to lose the love of her life. It was hard enough losing Jamie after only five years. I concentrate on Ivy's collection of rings, making no eye contact with Alfie. He's now sitting quietly, thoughtfully, possibly losing consciousness after his liquid lunch at the pub. I let him snooze as I clear out the last of Ivy's boxes from the wardrobe, containing more old patterns and some Christmas decorations, which look like family heirlooms. I take a beautiful red and green bauble with a hand-painted Christmas tree on the front, and creep silently into Alfie's room, tucking the bauble inside a pair of his socks. He should have something to remember that time too.

When Alfie finally wakes up, he's bleary-eyed and desperate for a cup of tea. He takes himself off to the kitchen and returns with the only two remaining cups, on a tray, and sits down again. He can't have had much company since Ivy died, I realise.

'Do you have any hobbies, Alfie?' I ask, as I drag a heavy sewing machine out from the bottom of the wardrobe. It has a post-war industrial appearance, with a bobbin of red cotton still wound and ready to use. But Ivy won't be needing it again.

'I've never had much time for hobbies,' Alfie says. 'Crossword puzzles in the paper, and I used to go to the football on a Saturday afternoon with my mates. I didn't always have a lot of spare time with my job.'

'What did you do before you retired?' I ask.

'You could say it was a job of grave importance, in the dead centre of town.' He grins at the nonplussed look on my face. 'I was a gravedigger.'

I stop struggling with the sewing machine and study Alfie, with his neatly brushed hair and clean fingernails. It's almost impossible to imagine him in a graveyard, wielding a shovel, standing waist deep in a hole in the ground.

'That's the reaction I get from most people when I tell them what I did,' he says, looking pleased that he's managed to shock me.

'Did you enjoy it?'

'It was good solid work, kept me fit and healthy and out of mischief. I was young when I started out, barely sixteen, and at that age, you think you're immortal. It never crosses your mind that you'll be old and wrinkly one day, that's for other people. But a few years of digging graves teaches you a thing or two about life, and what's really important. I saw plenty of youngsters buried before their time and it makes you think.' He nods to himself as he says it and then his head slowly droops. He's in danger of falling asleep again but he manages to rally. 'My old boss made me attend every funeral that we ever dug a grave for, at a distance, of course, to pay our respects. And that's when you learn what really makes people tick. Their guards are down, you see, when they're at a funeral. They tend to say what they mean, pass on pearls of wisdom. Grave digging isn't so much a job, Juliette, as a philosophy on life.'

I stare at Alfie, stunned into silence again. We have so much in common and I didn't even realise. We both deal with the dead – sometimes because there's no one else left to do it – trying to give them the respect they deserve. I sit on the carpet wondering why it's taken me this long to ask Alfie more about himself, but I already know the answer to that question. I don't want anything or anyone to distract me from Jamie. It's far better to keep the living at arm's-length. Dead people don't ask any awkward questions. House clearance is usually the perfect job for me.

'I was a gravedigger until about the age of forty-five, when my knees gave up on me. And then I moved into parks and gardens with the council instead, and by that time it was a welcome change,' Alfie says, happy to continue with his story. 'I got the youngsters to dig all the holes and I stuck to cutting the grass, pruning the shrubs and planting up the flower beds. It's satisfying work when you see everything in bloom, and people stopping to admire the colours and the arrangements. Although it feels like I spent my entire working life mucking about with spades.'

Alfie is a man of many surprises.

'I still take a weekly walk through all the parks and gardens where I used to work, just to see how things are coming along. I prune the odd shrub too, if it needs it. All the gardeners know me and they don't mind. Half of them still ask me about the right time to cut back the azaleas and the camellias. And some of the trees in the town parks are like old friends. There's this one ancient oak that's my favourite. I like to sit beneath it in the summer months, and listen to its leaves rustling in the breeze. That's how trees talk to you, you know, through their leaves.'

I definitely didn't have Alfie down as a tree-hugger, but I like that about him. It shows true strength of character – the ability to appreciate the wonders of the natural world, and to listen when the trees talk.

'What about you, Juliette, have you always been in the house clearance business?'

This is the first personal question Alfie has ever asked me. I shift positions on the carpet. 'I left school and went to study English at university, but that didn't really help me get a job. So I went to work in administration at a big telecommunications company, and hated every minute of it. I also worked at a garden centre for a while, just keeping things tidy, watering trays of plants.' Again, the similarities between Alfie's life and mine are so striking they're unsettling. And this suddenly feels way too personal. He'll be asking me about husbands or partners next, and that is a place I do not want to go.

'I'd better go and do something with this,' I tell Alfie, gathering up Ivy's jewellery.

I scuttle out of the door and retreat to the sanctuary of my car, hoping Alfie will have wandered back into the sitting room to watch some TV, by the time I return. I know I'm being a coward, possibly even rude, but I don't want to share anything about Jamie with Alfie Evans. And I have no imaginary friends I can call on to get me out of this encounter. I have to finish my work here.

I spend the rest of the afternoon finishing up in Ivy's bedroom. Stripping the bed of its covers is the last job, and then Ivy's presence has been thoroughly removed. The room looks dark without Ivy's pink possessions to lend it a softer glow. This house clearance already feels like it has taken months, I realise, as I pop my head into the sitting room to tell Alfie I'm leaving. But he's asleep in the chair, and

I go without waking him. Tomorrow is my final day at Starcross Crescent, my final day with Alfie. By the end of the afternoon, every last trace of Ivy will be gone, including her brother. For some reason, the thought makes me anxious.

I pick up a Chinese takeaway for dinner on the way home. Then I park outside the house and wait, hoping that Jamie will make an appearance today. I'm just about to give up and take my dinner inside, before it's completely cold, when he's suddenly sitting beside me, smelling the spring rolls and the chicken chow mein like it's the food of the gods.

Eight

JAMIE DOESN'T USUALLY SURPRISE me just as I'm about to climb out of the car, and it takes me a few moments to steady the erratic rhythm of my heart.

'Did you get this from the Golden Wok on Ashfield Road?' he asks, taking another long sniff of the food.

'Of course, where else would I go?'

The Golden Wok was always our favourite place because of the fresh ingredients, and the uncannily accurate wisdom contained within the fortune cookies – which once told me that the dark-haired man in my life would bring me nothing but joy. On another occasion, the cookies told Jamie that his feet were the foundations of his happiness and that was enough to send him to the podiatrist, the very next week, to get his bunions looked at.

'Can you actually smell the egg fried rice?'

'I'm not sure if I can smell it for real or if it's just the memory of the smell. But either way, it's making me hungrier than a cat locked out of a creamery. What I wouldn't give for just one tiny bite of a spring roll,' he says, wafting the aroma towards his nose with both hands, inhaling deeply.

'It's good to see you,' I say, taking a proper look at him.

He's wearing a coat that he lost years ago at a concert, and he also has a goatee beard, which he never even considered growing when he was alive. It doesn't suit him. It makes him look like a villain from an old black and white movie, the kind who were always wringing their hands with evil glee as they tied a helpless waif to the railway tracks. I wish I could close my eyes, wiggle my nose and restore his face to its normal state, but it won't work. I've tried many times before, like when he appeared in the car with strange black-tinted eyes. Or with glittery eyebrows that were so distracting I couldn't think of anything but an old disco tune, for his entire visit, and I was almost glad when he left. There was also the occasion that he turned up in the seat beside me completely bald, with a tattoo of a grand piano on the top of his head. And once when he spoke nothing but French, and the only word I understood was *baguette*. I try not to focus on his evil-villain beard (it could have been a lot worse) and concentrate instead on his eyes.

'I went to your bookshop today,' I tell him.

He loves to hear about the shop, but for some inexplicable reason he's unaware of the changes that have taken place there, since he died. I haven't had the heart to tell him that the armchair and flying books disappeared from the window just months after his death, or that it's no longer called The Wise Old Whale Bookshop. It was a name Jamie loved because of its reference to his childhood, and the fact that when he was learning how to read, he kept getting owls and whales mixed up with each other. I don't understand how he can know every detail about Robert Butler's funeral, as if he was sitting beside me in the crematorium, but he's clueless (the opposite of omnipotent) when it comes to his beloved shop. There aren't exactly any rules out there telling me how to handle these visitations either. So, for now, I've got no reason to tell him the truth, it would break his heart.

'How's the old place looking?' Jamie asks, with an affectionate tone in his voice, like we're discussing a faithful Irish terrier. 'Has Alonzo got that broken windowpane fixed in the flat yet?'

I've also told him that the shop has been taken over by his old friend, Alonzo Rodriguez, another lie. I haven't actually seen Alonzo since the funeral, eighteen months ago, but it makes Jamie happy. He knows that if Alonzo has taken over the lease, then it's in the hands of a kindred spirit, a fellow book-loving, guitar-playing soul who will water the plants, and encourage people to purchase better books than the ones they went into the shop with every intention of buying.

'I've already reminded him that the window needs replacing, but you know Alonzo, he'll get around to it in his own good time,' I say. 'He's more interested in rearranging the books in the architecture section, and practising his favourite 1980s songs for the open mic night at The Rabid Dog.'

Jamie smiles, enjoying the images I am creating for him. I'm so used to weaving a tangled vine of details around the lives of my imaginary friends – Vanessa, Angelique and Lauren – that I've now got the skills of a Hollywood scriptwriter when it comes to spontaneous lying.

'So, you're still making your way through Ivy Edward's flat,' he says, turning towards me in his chair, rubbing his eyebrow with his knuckle like he always used to. 'This one seems to be taking much longer than usual.'

'It's Alfie's fault,' I tell him. 'It's difficult to sort through Ivy's stuff when he wants to make some lunch, or tell me about his grave-digging days.'

'I liked hearing about that, he's a natural storyteller,' Jamie says. 'Alfie's a real character. Will you be visiting him at the B&B on Curzon Street, to make sure he settles in okay?'

'What? Why would I do that?' I say, suddenly feeling irritated. 'Alfie's not my responsibility. I've done everything I can to help him. He'll be fine once he moves into the sheltered housing scheme.'

'He's an old man and he needs someone to care about what happens to him, Juliette. And for reasons that none of us quite understand, that someone seems to be you.'

'Why is it my responsibility? Just because you'd rescue a snail if it fell into a bucket, or help a lost-looking ant find its way back to its nest.'

I've watched him do both of those things, and at the time, thought it was adorable; a real testament to the depth of his respect for all life, no matter how microscopic. But I do not feel that way about Alfie Evans.

'You do feel that way about Alfie Evans, you just don't want to admit it to yourself,' Jamie reasons. But he's not getting me on his side that easily.

I fold my arms and turn to face the windscreen, so he can see nothing but the side of my face. 'Just because you can apparently read my thoughts, it doesn't mean you should. And anyway, you're wrong. I don't feel responsible.'

'Then why are you getting all hot under the collar about it?'

I can't tell him the reason because he'll just give me another lecture about moving on with my life, letting other people in, letting him go – blah, blah, blah, blah. And I don't want to hear it. So I continue to glare through the windscreen instead, until he's prepared to change the subject and stop giving me a hard time. This is the first real disagreement we've had since he died. Up until now, I've been so grateful to see him every time he's appeared that I've felt nothing but love, longing and joy in his presence. But this is none of those things. This is a timely reminder, in fact, that when he was alive Jamie was far from perfect, not even close to walking the road to sainthood. He had an uncanny ability to tell what I was thinking; books weren't the only things he could read and understand with the skill of an Oxford professor. But there were other times when he misread the cues, failed to see that my escalating anger did not want to be appeased by a quote from an Eastern mystic. It wanted him to stop talking, back out of the room immediately and let me work it out for myself.

I sneak a sideways glance at him, and he gives me a familiar smile, his *I'm sorry for being such a jerk* smile. It's the one he always used to give me when he'd left his clothes all over the bedroom floor, and I'd just tripped over his shoes. Or after he'd had a late-night takeaway from the Golden Wok, and I'd gone downstairs, the following morning, to find congealed grains of rice stuck to spoons, plates and the bottom of the kitchen sink, like tiny slabs of concrete. It took a hammer and chisel to dislodge the starchy little buggers. This is the first time I've really remembered any of the things that used to annoy me about him, I realise. There's so much good stuff to feed my ever-hungry grief that I've never needed to think about any of Jamie's imperfections before. And I don't want to think about them now, not when he's sitting right beside me. I have no idea how long it will be before I see him again.

I take a deep breath, ready to apologise for my defensiveness, but in the blink of an eye he's gone. The only thing sitting beside me now is my dinner.

'Jamie?' I say, resting my head back against the seat. 'Please come back, I'm not done with you yet. I promise I won't sulk.'

I wait, hoping, but this never works either. I've tried it before, along with crying, begging and cajoling, but it seems that when he's gone, he's gone. I take my egg fried rice and lock the car, wishing we'd ended our conversation on a happier note.

I don't feel much like going through Ivy's letters after I've finished my takeaway, my thoughts still revolving around Jamie and the less than perfect conversation we've just had. But everything at Starcross Crescent has to be finished by the end of tomorrow afternoon, when I hand the keys back to Thurston, so it's now or never. I take the letters into the sitting room. It's been a long day and I need to put my feet up, but I can't get comfortable. I'm so restless I have to sit on the floor instead, with the letters spread out on the carpet before me.

Ivy's letters span at least six decades of her life. Most of them from close friends who moved away to Nottingham, Glasgow or Whitby, after getting married or finding a new job. There are several from Alfie, written when he was thirteen, fourteen and fifteen years old, and went to stay with an ancient aunt in Lancashire for a few weeks in the summer. They're cheeky missives, filled with jokes and vivid descriptions of his aunt, who apparently smelt like fried liver. And who chased Alfie around the kitchen with a broom, when he accidentally dropped a pork chop onto the floor. It got eaten by the dog before anyone could rescue it. I can't help laughing as I picture the chaotic scene, Alfie's gift for storytelling revealing itself at a young age. Most of Ivy's correspondents stop writing as the years go by, and by the end of her life, the letters have dried-up completely.

I put aside the letters that Alfie sent to his sister from Lancashire, along with a few photos that I find tucked inside letters from some of Ivy's old friends. There is no trace of the letters that Ivy discovered when her mum died, the ones written to her by Joseph Evans. And I wonder if Ivy destroyed them after all.

At the bottom of the final box, I find a small bundle of letters with Australian postmarks, the only foreign mail in Ivy's hoard. The name and return address are the same on each of the envelopes – Mr Wilson, Lost and Found Agency, Barkers Road, Perth, Western Australia. A quick read of the first letter reveals that Ivy had tried, on several occasions, in the 1980s, to find her dad. And that she clearly had some reason to believe he had emigrated to Australia. Mr Wilson confirmed that Joseph Evans had arrived in Freemantle on the 7th February 1949, after disembarking from a ship called the Georgic. After that, however, the trail appeared to go cold very quickly. There was no mention of him on any electoral rolls, criminal records, or on any official records relating to births, deaths or marriages. Mr Wilson told Ivy that he'd made all the other usual enquiries – he didn't bother explaining what those were – but that Joseph Evans had simply disappeared. His best guess was that he had probably got a job with one of the big mining companies in Western Australia, and wouldn't surface again until a death certificate was signed.

I decide I don't like Mr Wilson or his pompous tone.

The final letter from the Lost and Found Agency is dated several years later. The same Mr Wilson wrote to inform Ivy that her dad had emerged somewhere called Karratha, in the Pilbara region of Western Australia. He'd been working in the iron ore extraction industry, and now had a wife (Elizabeth) and a daughter (Abigail). A copy of a rental agreement that Joseph Evans had signed on a property in Karratha had been included in the letter as proof. But by the time the Lost and Found Agency went to investigate, Joseph Evans had already moved on again.

I stare at the rental agreement trying to process this new information. Alfie's dad had another family. He abandoned his wife and children and moved to the other side of the world for a new beginning, which he apparently found with a woman called Elizabeth – who he only married after Frances Mary had died. There was nothing in the rest of Ivy's belongings to indicate she ever had any contact with her dad, or his daughter. And I realise that Alfie has no idea he has a half-sister. Ivy never shared any of this with her brother. I would have heard about it by now if she had.

I gather up the letters, stretch out my stiff legs and retreat to the dining room, so I can do some investigations of my own. As soon as my laptop is plugged into the power, I key in the *Lost and Found Agency, Perth*, but there are no results. The last letter they sent to Ivy was dated 1986, so I know the chances of the agency still existing are slim. I find Barkers Road in Perth, the last known address for the agency. It looks typically Australian, to my untrained eyes, houses and buildings half hidden behind sumptuous greenery that I can't identify. Number seventy-eight sits between Alfredo's Perfect Pizzeria and The Aussie Shoe Emporium, but it's now a dry-cleaner's.

I type in the address on the rental agreement instead, Wycliffe Way, Karratha. Karratha was established in 1968, according to my search engine, to accommodate the workforce for one of the iron mining companies. It looks arid and isolated. And in the pre-internet days of the 1980s, it would have been the perfect place for someone to settle for a while, if they didn't want to be found. I click on the street view for Wycliffe Way, but it's hard to see anything of the actual house, except a driveway and a red corrugated-iron roof. There's a front garden filled with green shrubs and a swing seat. Did Joseph Evans stand in that garden watching an Australian sunset? Did he ever think about the life he'd left behind, the wife and kids he'd abandoned, the trouble and heartbreak his absence had caused?

I keep the tab open and do my own research on Joseph Evans, linking his name with Karratha and all the names of the mining companies I can find, but there are no results. It seems he was very careful not to leave a trail behind him. When I type Abigail Evans into the same search engine, it brings up so many possibilities that I don't know where to start. I close the laptop, thinking.

I'll need to narrow my search down somehow, but is any of this a good idea anyway? Wasn't I just arguing with Jamie about this very thing, the fact that Alfie is not my responsibility? I'm supposed to do my job, clean out Ivy's flat so somebody else can move in. And I have done that to the best of my ability. The things my job doesn't include are finding emergency housing for unexpected tenants, or tracking down relatives they know nothing about. But if I destroy Ivy's letters, Alfie will never know his dad moved to Australia and started another family. He'll never know he may have a half-sister, a blood relative, who might be very happy to discover Alfie's existence, if she doesn't already know. But would Alfie be happy to discover anything about Abigail Evans? Doesn't she just prove that his dad was a quitter, who moved halfway around the world and started a new life without ever bothering to find out what happened to the family he already had? Hasn't Alfie already made his feelings about his dad clear?

Nobody else at Hobson's House Clearance would have taken the time to read any of these letters. All evidence of Alfie's half-sister would have gone straight into the bin and been lost forever. It is by chance alone that I was sent to Starcross Crescent, instead of Alan or Carmel. I take the letters from the Lost and Found Agency and place them on the mantelpiece. The rest of Ivy's letters, apart from the ones I've saved for Alfie, can be incinerated in my backyard. But what am I supposed to do about Abigail Evans? Should I tell Alfie? Or should I let some very mangy sleeping dogs lie in the hot Australian sun?

Juliette and Jamie
II
Wedding Bait

THE HOUSE ON RAGLAN Road was the fifth property we'd looked at together. The first was too far out of town. The second had a tiny second bedroom that was good for nothing but storing Jamie's large book collection, which was like an overflow from his shop. The third house, a fantasy viewing, was way over the top end of our budget. Jamie fell in love with the long, meadow-like garden at the back and the sun-soaked kitchen. I had my head turned by house number four, a semi-detached 1970s classic in a rural location, filled with internal dimpled-glass partitions. It had an airing cupboard big enough to dry a tent, but it was too isolated to be a practical possibility. As we pulled up outside house number five, I was starting to feel nervous about our chances of finding anything that would suit us both, or our budget. So far, we couldn't afford anything we truly wanted, and we didn't want anything we could realistically afford.

'I like the look of this place,' Jamie said, peering up at the frontage through the windscreen of my car.

This had quickly become a house-hunting tradition, we'd sit and take a good look at the bones of the house first, trying to get a feel for the place. Jamie always saw faces. I saw renovation costs spiralling out of control, before we'd even walked through the front door.

'This place has got a happy expression,' he said, 'it looks like it's winking at us.'

This time, I could sort of see what he meant. One of the blinds upstairs had been half drawn, like a winking eyelid.

'Don't you think it looks a bit small?' I said, noticing how close the neighbours were on both sides of the property. I'd already seen several net curtains twitching.

'These old Victorian terraces are always bigger on the inside.'

Jamie was already clambering out of the car, unfolding his legs from the cramped footwell, like a young colt eager to gallop across a field just for the fun of it. I'd decided, long ago, that if Jamie was an animal, he'd be a wild fell pony, his mane speckled with teazels and caught in a constant gale. Jamie had once compared me to a unicorn, for my love of rainbows and things that glittered. I was still trying to decide if it was a compliment or not. But the idea always made me smile. A lot of things about Jamie made me smile, and in a way that I'd never smiled with anyone else before. It was like Jamie had excavated a part of me that I hadn't been fully aware of, until I'd spent some time in his company. Even after almost five years together, I was still discovering previously unused facial muscles. Nothing about my earlier partners had prepared me for how much fun it was possible to have with a person who was a true and proper fit. The closest I'd come to it, long before Jamie, was with Pete Bowman, a chemistry teacher. He was thoughtful and caring, and on paper, a really good bet for long-term happiness in a romantic partnership. But ten months into our relationship, when I started trying to remember the lyrics to old Christmas carols almost every time he spoke, I knew it was time to call it quits. I broke it off as kindly as I could.

With Jamie, no distractions were necessary. He was fun, inventive, and eternally curious about the world, and what other people thought of it. We could spend whole weekends together without the slightest hint of tedium setting in. On our first date, when he came round to my flat to cook dinner, I laughed so hard I pulled a muscle in my stomach and couldn't walk fully upright for three days afterwards. As soon as I could move again without wincing, we met up for a long stroll through the park in the centre of town. The following week, he came round to my place for dinner again and never really left. Our lives slotted so seamlessly together it was like building a future out of Stickle Bricks, every piece was a perfect fit. And not in a sickly way either. We had our disagreements and differences, just like everyone else, but they never had the power to pull us apart. It had taken some time to get used to the ease of our relationship, the lack of drama. And now, we were buying our first house together. No longer content with squeezing ourselves into my small, edge-of-town flat, we had finally taken the plunge.

I caught up with Jamie outside the front door. Due to some kind of mix-up over appointments, the estate agent had been happy to give us the keys so we could look around the house by ourselves. The owners had already moved out, we could take as long as we wanted.

'I've got a good feeling about this one,' Jamie said, kissing the key for luck before turning it in the lock.

'You say that about every house we look at.' I peered impatiently over his shoulder as he pushed the door open. The hallway was dark but the floor was tiled and the ceiling high.

'Nice big sitting room.' Jamie was already opening internal doors. He always wanted to see what was around the next corner. 'It might need a bit of love and attention, though.'

What it needed was a sledgehammer. 'Jamie, this place is a ruin!'

The fireplace was an old Victorian classic, with blackened grate and iron surround, the kind that I already loved. But the peeling wallpaper revealed crumbling plaster beneath, the ceiling was a crazy paving of cracks and holes. The windows had either been hit by the stray fragments of a previously undocumented meteor strike, in the road outside, or had been the victim of a particularly vicious attack from a small boy with a catapult. The tiny holes were clean, round and worn smooth with age.

'The agent said the couple who lived here bought it in 1965.' Jamie took my hand and led me into the centre of the room, so I could see it from all angles. 'It's been their home for almost sixty years. If we live here for that long, we'll be over a hundred years old.'

'It's been at least a hundred years since anyone has decorated this room.'

Jamie laughed but he wanted me to love it, I could tell he was already smitten with the high ceilings and the bay window. It had history, great proportions, potential and size. The sitting room alone was almost as big as my entire flat. I tried to ignore the original cornicing and the ceiling rose, but they drew my gaze upwards, forcing me to swivel my head so I could admire them fully.

The rest of the downstairs was in a similar state of disrepair. The dining room looked like it had been used as a coal cellar, with soot from a boarded-up fireplace creeping all the way up the chimney breast and across the ceiling. The carpet had been ripped up and one in every three floorboards was simply missing. We had to walk around the very edge of the room to reach the kitchen safely. Jamie led the way, and even from behind I could tell he was smiling. The renovation work didn't faze him at all, missing floorboards were a minor inconvenience, not a huge red flag flapping in the breeze. The kitchen was a suntrap, which highlighted the extent of the mould on the ceiling and picked out, in fine detail, the large crevice running down one wall. None of the cupboards had doors. The sink was a porcelain relic; the kind that belonged in a museum where schoolkids were sent to learn about how life was lived when Queen Victoria was still on the throne.

Jamie rested his hands on my shoulders and steered me out into the backyard, before I could comment on the cracked floor tiles. I could see that he'd already lost his heart, it was a hopeless case.

'So, what do you think? Could we make this place our own? I know it could do with a lick of paint in places—'

'Jamie, the place is virtually falling down,' I said, trying to be the sensible one, the practical one. We'd never really discussed doing a total renovation before. It was a daunting prospect. 'The kitchen needs ripping out, the windows need replacing, the walls will have to be replastered and the electrics are probably a fire hazard.'

'But it feels like home, doesn't it?' Jamie squeezed my hand, ignoring every practicality. Caution wasn't in his vocabulary.

And there was a part of me that felt it too, I couldn't deny it. The house was cosy and homely. It had all the best intangibles that made you want to ignore the crumbling plaster and the holes.

'I can see us here, in the winter, cuddled up by the fire. And the dining room could double up as a crafting space.'

'That's not fair, Jamie.' I pulled my hand out of his. 'You promised you wouldn't use the idea of a crafting space to persuade me to buy any house, we had rules.'

Jamie grinned but he was unrepentant. 'I think we should ring the agent and put in an offer.'

'We haven't even seen the upstairs yet. There could be an infestation of cockroaches in the bathroom, or mice scampering through the wardrobes.'

'But can't you just see us having our wedding reception in the backyard, love, with all the windows open and some smooth soulful sounds filling up the warm evening air?'

I folded my arms. 'You also promised you wouldn't use our wedding reception as property bait.'

'But it's perfect, Juliette. I can imagine all of our friends with a glass of champagne, toasting our future together, and the wedding cake could sit on the dining room table.'

'Assuming we put a dining room floor down first.'

'We can fill the yard with candles and ask the photographer—'

'You mean your dodgy mate, Dave.'

'Okay, we can ask Dave to take lots of lovely candid shots of your mum swigging back the sherry, and my sister dancing like a loon. I can almost smell the scented candles wafting through the air.'

He paused, hopeful, waiting for me to crack. The candles (wrapped in fairy lights) were my idea anyway. He'd deliberately planted the vision in my head, so I'd ignore the fact that the house was a whisker away from a date with a wrecking ball. He wanted me to put aside my very real worries and be as reckless as him.

'I know it's not as grand as the 1970s house, and it doesn't have a meadow out the back, but it suits us.' He paused again searching for any extra inducements he could find to tempt me. 'And if we buy this house, I promise I'll let you book a piano player for the wedding reception who can belt out all the hits that Skara ever had.'

Skara, a Swedish pop group, were my favourite band of all time, a love affair that had begun when I was nine years old and was still going strong. Jamie had once compared them to a virus.

'But you hated the idea when I suggested it,' I reminded him. 'You said, and I quote, "having a wedding reception full of Skara songs would be like celebrating our union at a Swedish meatball festival."'

'Juliette, love, I'm more than happy to embrace the idea of Skara for one day. I would have come around to it anyway, I know how happy their music makes you. But this house, I want it to be for the rest of our lives together.'

He had me and he knew it. He'd seen some micro-movement in my face, seen it and understood what it meant before I was even aware. I could hide nothing from him. I wanted the house too. It felt like it was already ours.

'Only if you swear on your precious Triumph motorbike that we won't still be renovating this house in five years' time. I want a home not a building project.'

'Cross my heart and hope to die,' Jamie said, suddenly solemn, knowing that I'd hold him to it. 'I'll even put it in writing if it makes you feel any happier.'

'I haven't ruled it out.'

Jamie enveloped me in a bear hug, lifting me off the ground and swinging me around, until we were both dizzy and giddy with the idea of owning our own house on Raglan Road.

'We'll make a proper plan,' Jamie said, when he finally put me down, holding me by my elbows until I'd got my balance back. 'We'll deal with the basics first, plumbing, electrics, heating, floors, this place will be toasty and warm in no time.'

'We could have a proper housewarming party, or a wallpaper stripping party, and get everyone to bring a scraper.'

Once I'd made up my mind about the house, I couldn't stop my own imagination from running wild. There was nothing we could do to make my boxy, 1980s flat more interesting, no matter how many coats of paint we covered it in. But this place was a broken-down blank of a canvas. We could transform it into something beautiful and unique, although I'd already had to veto Jamie's suggestion to install a fireman's pole next to the staircase. Sometimes, his imagination got a little too out of control. We were still negotiating on the idea of an old submarine periscope placed high up in the attic, so he could study the clouds. Although the more he talked about that particular idea, the more I liked it anyway. Being with Jamie meant accepting the unconventional. It had been a liberating experience. I had taught him how to bake chocolate brownies and Madeira cakes, how to appreciate the beauty of Victorian architecture and the joys of spreadsheets. We were a good match; we brought the best out of each other. I couldn't wait to find out what that partnership looked like when we papered it over the walls and ran it under the edges of the skirting boards. The thought of white gloss paint had never been so exciting.

By the end of the day, our offer on the house had been accepted. At two o'clock in the morning, we were still making plans.

Nine

WEDNESDAY FEELS LIKE IT'S going to be a difficult day as soon as I wake up. The first person who drifts through my thoughts is Alfie, followed by his half-sister, Abigail Evans, and it's only then that I think about Jamie. I try not to replay the conversation we had in my car yesterday, or brood over the fact that he left before we could patch things up properly.

I let myself into Starcross Crescent with a knock on the door. It feels strange. I'm not used to announcing myself. The dead don't need any warning so they can put their teeth in or tighten the belts on their dressing gowns. Alfie is in the kitchen, already dressed and neatly groomed.

'Well, this is going to be a strange day, Juliette.'

He greets me with a cup of tea. There's no teapot, so it's just a bag, a spoon and a dash of milk.

'There's never been a day in my life when I couldn't turn to Ivy for help, or company, or just for the pleasure of talking about old times at Grange Road. Today is the last day I'll ever spend in Ivy's flat. I'll never be able to visit her again.'

'I'm so sorry for your loss, Alfie,' I say, wondering if this is the first time I've actually offered him my condolences.

On top of everything else that's happening to him, he's dealing with the loss of his sister. Alfie just nods. This is definitely not the right moment to mention the fact that he could have more family than he thinks. But I hand over an envelope filled with the letters he sent to Ivy from Lancashire. It barely raises a smile.

'I'll move all of my stuff into the sitting room, so you can go through my bedroom,' he says, matter-of-factly. He's clearly given in, accepted that his fate is not to stay at Starcross Crescent.

Alfie's room is the last area of the flat to deal with before Otis comes to take all the furniture, before the cupboards in the sitting room disappear. I close the door, so Alfie doesn't have to listen to the sound of his room being cleared, and work as quickly as I can.

The wardrobes contain lengths of unused material, more sewing patterns and a large number of zips, reels of cotton and trims. There's also a short rail filled with men's clothes, which must have belonged to Ivy's late husband, Stan. The clothes are ordinary and workaday in cheap cottons and synthetic blends, with none of the style and flair that Ivy's clothes possessed. A box of old lamps and ornaments is easy to set aside for donation. I find a neat stack of jigsaw puzzles, an unused wine-making kit that looks like a Christmas present, a box of curtain rings and header tape. A bedside cabinet contains a couple of well-read paperback novels and an ancient camera. But there's no film inside it, no undeveloped snippets of Ivy's life left to discover. And that's the last of it. I've now seen and dealt with everything Ivy still owned at the time of her death. All that was precious to her has passed through my hands, all the things she'd forgotten about at the back of the wardrobe, and all the things she used every day without giving them a second thought.

I sit on the floor with my back pressed against the wall, and take a few moments to picture Ivy in her house and the life she must have lived, her daily rhythms and routines, baking cakes in the kitchen, laughing with Alfie at the table. The musical number of her life, the one that I could so easily lose myself in at this moment, tries to take over my thoughts. But I resist, deciding to save it for after the funeral service when I can share it properly with Jamie. At least Alfie will be at the funeral too, and we can remember Ivy together. I'm glad I won't be the only mourner. I know so much more about Ivy because her life was entwined with Alfie's, his memories overlapping with hers. I almost feel like I've lost an old friend.

I sit with Alfie at lunchtime, as he nibbles on a cheese sandwich. The last of the food from the cupboards sits in a cardboard box on the countertop, ready to go with him to the Abbey View Bed and Breakfast.

'How are you going to get all your stuff to the B&B?' I ask. 'Do you need me to ring someone for transport?'

'I've got a mate who owns a taxi and he's picking me up at the end of his shift. I saw him down the pub the other day. Don't you worry about me, Juliette. I can take care of myself.'

I want to tell him I'm not worried, but it isn't true. Alfie Evans and his stories about his grave-digging days, his sister and his dad have made an impression on me that won't be easy to shift.

Otis turns up an hour later than arranged, at 2.46 p.m. He tugs on his grizzled beard and grumbles about confusing work orders, mistakes being made at the office, blaming everyone but himself for his poor time keeping. Then he helps Owen, his trainee, wrangle the sofa out into the hallway. It's followed by Ivy's armchairs, mattresses, chests of drawers, kitchen table and chairs. All the white goods are staying with the flat for the next tenants. The bedside tables are the last items to leave Starcross Crescent. I check all the rooms to make sure nothing has been left behind. But all I find is Alfie, sitting on his suitcase in the empty kitchen, looking forlorn. It's one thing to lose your only sister, but then to watch as her home is swiftly dismantled around you by strangers...

By 4.57 p.m., the tall cupboards in the sitting room, the last of Stan's craftsmanship, have been collected. There's nothing left for me to do but close the front door and hand the keys back to Thurston. But Alfie is still waiting in the kitchen, like the lone survivor of a shipwreck, bobbing about in the ocean on his luggage.

'What time is your friend picking you up?'

He looks at his watch. 'He should have been here over an hour ago, the daft old codger must have forgotten.'

If he even exists at all.

'I've got to give the keys back to Mr Thurston,' I tell him. 'Alfie, you can't stay here.'

'So, you're chucking me out onto the street?'

Ivy's flat opens out onto a lovely communal garden and tree-lined car park, but it seems churlish to point that out. 'I'm not throwing you out. I'm giving you a lift to Curzon Street.'

I know I'll be happier if I see him settled into his new temporary home for myself. I pick up the box of food and carry it out to my car before he can protest. Alfie follows slowly behind with his suitcase, and it takes one more trip to grab the rest of his stuff. Then I wait in the car while he says his last goodbyes. Ten minutes later, he lowers himself into the passenger seat with swollen eyes, and stares out the window with his head turned away from me.

I leave him in the car as I take the keys into the office. Luckily, Thurston's on the phone and I escape without having to talk to him. Then we hit the rush-hour traffic as we head slowly for the edge of town. Alfie says nothing, and I don't even try to make small talk. What could I possibly say that would make him feel any better at this moment?

The streets become progressively more down-at-heel the closer we get to the B&B. It's hard to ignore the sullen, oppressive feel of the abandoned industrial units, the endless off-licenses and takeaways. Empty burger wrappers and polystyrene food containers clog up the gutters and drains. There's nothing at this end of town that I want to see more of. It's such a contrast to the welcoming feel of Starcross Crescent, that even if Alfie was up to making eye contact, I couldn't return it.

By the time we reach the Abbey View Bed and Breakfast it's already dark. We both stand beside the car and study the tall, grim, Victorian exterior of the building, which resembles a final resting place for homeless gargoyles. Mr Fenchurch, the owner, meets us as we enter the hallway. He doesn't make a good first impression. He offers no words of welcome, and it's obvious he has no interest in Alfie. I get the feeling we've dragged him away from his phone or his TV. He keeps glancing back towards his office, where, I decide, he probably spends most of his days rolling around in the heaps of money he makes from the council.

He leads the way to Alfie's room, passing through several fire doors. I recoil at the pungent smell of stale smoke, which must have been working its way into all the walls, ceilings and carpets long before smoking was banned on the premises. The ceiling has almost caramelized with nicotine, I notice, as we begin to climb the stairs. It's the same sickly shade of brown as the long, witch-like fingernails of Mr Fenchurch. I can hear deep, phlegm-filled coughs coming from some of the rooms, there's the sound of a football match on a loud TV and someone is shouting into a phone. Alfie's room is on the top floor, even though I told Jaya that he couldn't manage any stairs, it's the very reason he was forced to leave his own flat in the centre of town. But it's when old Witchy Fenchurch unlocks and opens the door that I finally lose my cool. The room is the size of a shoe box, with sloping ceilings and one tiny window. The curtains are swaying in a fresh breeze, even though the window is closed, and the carpet is so threadbare in places I can see the floorboards beneath.

'No,' I say turning angrily towards Mr Fenchurch. 'Alfie can't stay here. Don't you have a better room?'

'This is the only vacant one I've got. The lady at the council seemed to think it was okay.'

'The lady at the council obviously hasn't seen this in person, or she'd have closed you down for breaching at least a dozen health and safety laws.'

Mr Fenchurch folds his arms over his capacious belly, and is clearly about to give me a piece of his mind, but I turn my back on him before he can speak and swiftly take a photo of the room. I need to let Jaya know it isn't fit for mice to sleep in. As soon as Alfie reaches the top of the stairs, I grab his arm and turn him around.

'What's going on?' He's winded and wincing with knee pain.

'You can't stay here,' I tell him, helping him back down the stairs before he can object. 'It's way too Dickensian. Even a poor, undernourished Victorian pickpocket would have had trouble folding himself into that bed, without banging his head on the ceiling.'

'So, where are you taking me?' he asks, looking worried.

'I'm taking you home with me.' I say the words before I can truly consider what they mean.

'But I don't want to be an imposition.'

'If you're imposing, I'll let you know. It's only until you get your place at the sheltered housing scheme, I'm not adopting you or anything.'

Alfie smiles with obvious relief and lets me lead him back out to the car. Mr Fenchurch slams the front door behind us. The feeling is mutual. I have a suspicion that the last time this place was inspected by anyone in person, it didn't look like the fleapit it now resembles. And that Mr Fenchurch clearly has some extra rooms he's decided to let out, without anyone's approval, just to make more money.

'Are you sure about this, Juliette?' Alfie asks, buckling himself in with his seatbelt. 'I don't want to be any trouble.'

Alfie has already been more trouble than he'll ever know, but what choice do I have? Jamie knew I could never leave Alfie at the House of Horrors B&B, so he cleverly planted the seed that has led to this rash but inevitable moment. He was right. Someone needs to take care of Alfie Evans. And for reasons only the universe will ever fully understand that someone is me. But that doesn't mean I'm jumping over the moon with joy about the situation, like a cat or a cow with a stupid fiddle.

'It's no trouble, Alfie,' I say, keeping a neutral expression on my face. 'I've got plenty of space and a spare room you can sleep in.'

'I seem to be spending a lot of time in spare rooms just lately,' he says, sounding amused. But I can tell he's genuinely grateful that I didn't leave him at the mercy of the nauseating Mr Fenchurch. 'Thank you, Juliette.'

I grip the steering wheel with both hands and concentrate on driving to avoid any more conversation with Alfie. This is definitely not part of my job description, housing homeless pensioners. In fact, no one has stayed at my house since Jamie died. I've had a few visitors, the gas man, and Mrs Lafleur, my neighbour, who came to borrow a cheese grater once. But I think she was just checking that I was still alive. The walls between us could be thicker and she may have heard some wailing. Poppy has been round a handful of times for coffee, and to deliver some lectures about me spending too much time on my own. But I've managed to keep everyone else out. And that's the way I like it, with just me, living in the soup of my sorrow and my memories of Jamie. I'm not sure I'm ready for that to change.

By the time we reach home, Alfie looks exhausted. This day has taken its toll on both of us. I make some tea and install Alfie in the sitting room, with a plate of biscuits.

'And you're absolutely sure you don't mind me being here?' he asks for the tenth time, as he eases off his shoes and rests his feet on my favourite vintage velvet footstool. 'Your feller won't mind another man staying in your house?'

'That isn't a problem. I mean, there is no... I haven't got a husband or partner,' I say, not willing to explain anything more to him. Or to point out that I don't need permission from any husband or boyfriend before I invite someone to stay in my own home. I'm too tired to enlighten Alfie on the finer details of such a modern concept. 'I just need to go and make some space in the spare room.'

But I stand by the door for a few seconds first and watch as he selects a biscuit, dunks it in his tea, and makes himself at home with remarkable speed. I've spent so much time with him in Ivy's flat, over the last week, that having him here doesn't even seem strange – which is possibly the most bizarre aspect of the whole situation.

I leave him to his tea and biscuits and head upstairs to the spare room. It's so long since I've been in here that I've forgotten how jaded it looks. It needs a new carpet, new windows and a fresh coat of paint, but it's a good size and a vast improvement on the room at the Abbey View Bed and Breakfast. Alfie will be comfortable here. It hasn't been used for guests since before Jamie died, and most of the floor space is covered in boxes. This is where I dumped everything after me and Poppy cleared out Jamie's flat above the bookshop.

It was two months after his death. Poppy had contacted the owner of the building and Jamie's lease had been terminated, but we now had a small window of time to clear out his flat before the new owner took possession. Poppy came to help, and I was grateful for her presence. Jamie's flat was a tiny bedsit with yellowing walls and grey carpets, and just enough room for a two-seater sofa, a small double bed and a wardrobe. There was a kitchenette on one side of the room, with a single ring for cooking, a minuscule fridge and one cupboard. The bathroom was only just big enough for a shower, basin and toilet, which all seemed to overlap each other in a way that reminded me of the paper folds in origami. But Jamie's presence saved it from being a soulless box. He'd made it feel lived in.

Clearing out the space of someone you love is entirely different to the professional art of house clearance. I should have been good at it, but Jamie's flat almost killed me. To suddenly be standing in such a Jamie-filled space again – where everything had been chosen by him, used by him, or chucked on the floor by him – was overwhelming. It was a time capsule of his last few days on this earth, and one that I hadn't seen until that moment. But the details started leaping out and showing themselves to me almost instantly, and I could piece them together into a storybook. He'd worn his favourite T-shirt and then thrown it onto the sofa to be washed, someday. He'd bought some oranges from the market and left the peel in the sink; it made the whole flat smell like Christmas. He'd been reading a book about South America and had used an empty crisp packet as a bookmark.

I picked up his T-shirt and inhaled the scents still clinging to the fibres, like they'd been waiting for me to come and liberate them. And it smelled exactly like him. Jamie always smelled as fresh as a laundry cupboard in an expensive London hotel. Even when he'd been mopping the floors in the shop, or building shelves on a hot summer's day, somehow his skin still smelled like fabric softener, with hints of calendula or rosemary. I stepped carefully over his second favourite pair of boots, the ones he'd bought from a genuine cowboy on a road trip to California. The bed was crumpled, sheets unruly, rippled and cold.

'Jamie never could make a bed to save his life, even when he was a kid,' Poppy said, half-smiling, until she realised what she'd said.

She hugged me tightly and we stood in the middle of the flat, clinging to each other for comfort, trying to hold onto the last strands of Jamie. A pile of his silver rings sat by the bed, like they were waiting for him to come back to the flat and put them on his fingers one last time. I slipped them into my pocket, sliding them on and off my own fingers instead. Then I surveyed the heap of unwashed socks, jeans and sweatshirts that Jamie liked to call his laundry mountain. Poppy picked the first few items off the top and folded them neatly into a bag, before losing heart and sinking onto his bed.

I wanted to keep every discarded chocolate bar wrapper and mouldy piece of fruit. Poppy, thankfully, took control and saw to it that all food and perishables were thrown out. And then we set about the grim task of sorting through his belongings. Poppy took a few things that had special meaning for her, and for her parents. But I took everything else. We'd spent virtually no time in the flat together, due to its store cupboard dimensions, but it was still Jamie's. Saying goodbye to it for the last time almost tipped me over the edge. It was the end of another chapter, another closed book.

I brought all his stuff home and put it in the spare room, the room that I hardly ever entered. The spirit of Jamie may have roamed freely around the inside of my head – and sat with me in my car – but one glimpse of his favourite jumper or a bookmark that he'd once used, and I was instantly unstuck. I'd already packed up most of the things that Jamie had left scattered around our house in Raglan Road, for that very reason. Only a few rare items had escaped the roundup, and then only because for some peculiarity, I could look at those objects without feeling crushed by the weight of my loss. Everything else had been entombed in the spare room, the room that I now have to tackle because of Alfie Evans.

I survey the boxes stacked on the floor, thinking about where to relocate them. Now that Alfie is moving in – temporarily – it will all have to go somewhere else. There's no room in the wardrobe, Alfie needs that for his own clothes. The dining room is too small, and I'd see the boxes every time I went to make a cup of tea or a sandwich. The only place the boxes can sit is in my bedroom. They will be an unavoidable presence. I'll be forced to encounter them every night when I go to bed, and every morning when I wake up. But what other choice do I have?

I carry some of the smaller boxes into my room and place them under the window, being extra careful not to open anything, or even look at the labels. The bigger boxes are cumbersome to carry, and I have to pile them up on the far side of my bed. It's the only place they'll fit. After thirty minutes of hauling, dragging and shuffling, I've created a wall of Jamie's old stuff. These are the very possessions he wants me to get rid of, but I feel like I'm a custodian. The last remnants of the life he lived on this planet are in those boxes, and it's my job to keep them safe. That does not, however, make for a good night's sleep.

Alfie is watching the news when I return to the sitting room, already looking like a part of the furniture. I take his meagre possessions up to the spare room, and make up the bed with fresh covers and sheets. We are, at least, separated by a bathroom. If he snores, only the basin and the shower will hear it. I'm suddenly grateful for Victorian house design.

I say a quick "hello" to Jamie as I grab a clean towel for Alfie from the airing cupboard. Jamie's ashes are sitting in a jar at the back, wrapped in a blanket. I've never gained much solace from having his ashes in the house. The jar might as well contain the remains of an old kitchen chair for all the comfort it brings me. It just doesn't feel like Jamie is in that jar.

I make a basic dinner of pasta and sauce, with added mushrooms and peppers.

'I could have helped with that,' Alfie says, when I carry it into the sitting room. He grabs a cream, bee-print cushion to protect his knees from the heat of the food. 'One thing about living on your own, it teaches you how to cook.'

'I'll bear that in mind,' I say, trying not to wince at the little flecks of red sauce that are already making their presence felt. The dining room table needs to be cleared, and quickly, I decide, before Alfie can ruin all of my soft furnishings.

We watch TV as we eat. I'm grateful for the background noise because when Alfie chews, something strange happens with his teeth, and it's all I can do not to leap up and finish my dinner in the kitchen, alone. He insists on washing-up afterwards, and I let him, making the most of the solitude for a few precious minutes. Alfie takes up a lot of space. But I know I made the right decision. I send the photo I took of the room at the B&B to Jaya, so it will be in her inbox when she checks it tomorrow morning. If Mr Fenchurch is running some kind of rental scam, I'm certain that it won't survive the scrutiny of Jaya.

Alfie's bedtime routines are an eye-opener. He likes to soak in a bath for about an hour and a half, leaving a visible rim of dead skin around the high-water mark. I have to scrub it clean before I can even contemplate stepping into the shower. His toiletries have somehow multiplied now that they're out of his suitcase, and my lotions and creams have been squashed to the very edge of the only shelf in the room. His towel is hanging from the shower curtain-rail, steeped in the scent of English Crab Apple and dripping onto the floor. And he's drawn a smiley face in the steamed-up mirror. The smiley face almost makes me laugh. It's exactly the kind of thing Jamie used to do. But as for the rest of it, I am horribly out of practice. I've been on my own for so long now that these new living arrangements are going to be a big adjustment.

I wonder fleetingly if the B&B was really that bad, after all. Maybe I had a kneejerk reaction to what could have been a perfectly charming room with Alfie's stuff in it. But I know my gut feeling was right. For better or worse, Alfie Evans is now a guest in my home. Up until this moment, I couldn't even contemplate having another man in my bathroom, or clattering his way around the kitchen, or sitting with his feet up on my footstool. This is going to be odd for both of us.

I hurry into bed so I don't have to look at the boxes looming over me, but I can already feel their presence. They change the way everything sounds. I know that if I opened just one flap, I'd catch a glimpse of a photo, a battered guitar strap or one of Jamie's favourite books. Jamie calls it junk, and I'm painfully aware that nothing can ever bring him back. But to me, even the lowliest sock is a piece of treasure, so why should I have to get rid of any of it?

I can't hear anything coming from Alfie's room, even when I listen really hard for any shuffling, bumping or snoring noises. But the house still feels different with another person resting inside it, and sleep takes a long time to find me.

Ten

WHEN I VENTURE OUT of my room in the morning, Alfie has made toast and proper coffee for breakfast – and a proper mess of the bathroom again. I may have to lay down some ground rules. But it seems ungrateful to say anything when he's handing me a steaming mug.

'Are you sure this is *my* coffee?' I ask, taking an experimental sip. It tastes nothing like the insipid, burnt brew that I manage to make on a daily basis. 'Why can't I ever get it to taste this good?'

'It takes time and patience, Juliette, time and patience,' Alfie says, sounding like a cross between my old home economics teacher and a coffee guru. 'And you need to give it a stir before you let it stew.'

'Do you know what you're going to do today?' I ask, slathering a slice of toast with a generous helping of orange curd that I'd forgotten I had in my cupboards.

'Thought I'd go for a wander, get acquainted with the local area.'

'There's a park about ten minutes away, an easy walk, I'll draw you a map.' I grab a piece of paper and also draw in the local shops, the library, two pubs and a bakery.

'Will you be home for dinner? I'd like to cook you something nice to say thank you for taking me into your home,' he says, with such a grateful smile that I have to look away, staring into the depths of my coffee mug.

'That's really not necessary, Alfie. And I'm meeting my friend, Vanessa, after work,' I say.

I feel oddly like part of a married couple as I grab my bag and a jacket and head out the door, leaving Alfie with the washing-up. I haven't thought about Vanessa in days, but I have a feeling that tonight, she may keep me talking until at least 10.30 p.m.

I drive into the office to file my paperwork for Ivy Edwards and Starcross Crescent. Ivy's funeral won't be for another few weeks, according to Flint's, the funeral directors. Ivy paid into a funeral plan for a number of years, deciding on the flowers, coffin and order of service a long time ago. I'm relieved that it won't have the feel of a public health funeral.

I file my report as quickly as possible, with one eye on the door. Loretta is the only other person in the office today, and when she types – with her extra-long fingernails – it sounds like a troupe of rats dancing on her keyboard. We also have nothing to say to each other, and I get the feeling she'll be much happier when I've gone, and she can reclaim her filing-cabinet kingdom.

'There's a job for you at Station Road,' she says, when I've sent her a copy of Ivy Edward's paperwork. I haven't mentioned Alfie or his half-sister anywhere on the forms. I wouldn't know where to begin. 'Nigel was a bit unhappy that the last job took you so long to complete,' Loretta says, enjoying her moment of power. 'He's asked me to tell you he wants this one done in two days.'

She stays in her seat and holds out a sheet of paper containing the details of my next job, forcing me to walk over to her desk to retrieve it, the spider in her web. The date that I'm expected to finish by has been clearly marked and underlined, with unnecessary force.

'I'm not making any promises, and Nigel knows how I work,' I say, folding the sheet of paper into my pocket. 'I'll just talk directly to him if I have any problems, there's no need for you to worry about anything, Loretta. I know you must be busy, filing.'

I turn my back on her before she can respond and head out of the door. I'll pay for my moment of insolence. The next time I have to come into the office, there'll be a very tricky house clearance to attend, or some disappearing paperwork that needs to be rewritten. But it was worth it.

Station Road is on the far side of town, close to the Abbey View Bed and Breakfast. It's nowhere near as nice as Starcross Crescent, but the flat itself is decent enough. There are large windows in the lounge, a comfy sofa and a good quality carpet in the bedroom. It belonged to Ravindra Singh, according to Loretta's notes, no known family or close friends. And a quick tour of the flat tells me Ravindra struggled with cleaning and tidying in the last months of his life. I'll have to double glove and get stuck in, but at least there are no unexpected guests in the spare room. It almost seems strange, having the place to myself.

Ravindra's kitchen is such a contrast to Ivy's that I find it difficult at first. It smells of neglect and boiled eggs, and even with the windows wide open, I can't shift the unpleasant odour. I do the dishes first, some of which have obviously been stacked on the draining board for some time. I've already cleaned out the fridge and most of the food in the cupboards when the first phone call interrupts me at 11.22 a.m.

'Juliette? It's me, Alfie.' I have to hold the phone away from my ear as he yells at me from the phone in my hallway at home. 'I was just ringing to see if you like chicken. I've got a great recipe for a casserole, but I thought I'd better check with you first. You're not a vegetarian, are you, or one of those vegans?'

'Alfie, you really don't have to cook me anything,' I tell him. 'Like I said, I'll be out for most of this evening with my friend, Vanessa.'

'It's no bother, I like cooking. And no offence, but all I can find in your cupboards are jars of pasta sauce and spaghetti hoops. I can leave it in the cooker on low, so you've got something warm to eat when you get home.'

He rings off before I can protest again.

Normally, there's nobody around to notice if I eat jelly babies for breakfast, or a peanut butter and jam sandwich for dinner, five nights in a row. But Alfie has already come face-to-face with my bad habits. What else is he going to find lacking in my life? I do a quick mental inventory of the cupboards in the kitchen, wondering what he'll say when he finds the jumbo pack of instant noodles, and the hideously unhealthy breakfast bars. I also get a sudden vision of Alfie being confounded by the digital settings on my cooker. What if he accidentally leaves a ring on when he goes out to buy some chicken, what if the paper towels that sit next to the cooker catch fire in his absence, and my entire house burns to the ground? I'm just wondering if there's any kind of lock you can buy to keep your appliances safe from houseguests, when my phone rings again.

'Alfie, what's wrong? Is everything okay?'

'Everything's fine, I was just wondering where you keep your casserole dishes. This chicken won't be the same if it doesn't go in the oven. And all I can find in your cupboards are pots and pans.'

'I haven't got a casserole dish,' I say, relived that he's not shouting at me above the wail of sirens in the background, 'and I've already told you, you don't have to—'

'It's okay. I'll just nip next door and borrow one from your neighbour.' And he's gone again. How many times do I have to tell him? I don't want him to make a casserole. I don't want him in my house.

I feel twitchy for the rest of the day, but Alfie doesn't phone again. I manage to resist the urge to speed all the way home and do a slow drive past the house on Raglan Road, searching for signs of smoke, flames escaping from the windows and doors, Alfie sitting on the kerbside, singed. I'm finished for the day by 3.37 p.m., and I'm supposed to be meeting my imaginary friend, Vanessa, for a drink. Normally, when I'm lying to someone else about what I'm doing, I head straight home. But home is not an option today, so I drive over to see Poppy instead.

I love Poppy's house, even though I find it difficult to visit. Every square inch of wall space is covered in art, mirrors and fairy lights. She also has more cushions, rugs, candles and woollen throws than the entire Home Decor Department at Shimming's. The glorious clashing of colours and textures is just what I need right now. Zarina's influence is more obvious in the bathrooms – neatly ordered towels and pristine tiles. She also has dominion over all the drawers and cupboards, which have been organized and categorized so that every garlic crusher, roll of sticky tape and pillowcase has its own home. Most of the time, the garlic crusher ends up sitting in a drawer with the shower gel, if Poppy has anything to do with it. But I admire Zarina's persistence and her faith that, one day, Poppy will be converted to the joys of living an organised life. Long ago, I had similar hopes for Jamie, but I had to bury them along with every other dream I had for the life we should have lived together.

It's been some time since I visited Poppy's house, and I've missed the happy sound my knuckles make as I rap on the door. She knows me so well, however, that she can tell I'm troubled within three seconds of opening the door.

'What's happened?'

She takes my hand and leads me into the kitchen at the back of the house, guiding me down onto the sofa by the patio doors that open out to the garden. This has always been my favourite place to sit in her house. The big, soft sofa cushions are so squashy that they immobilise the lower half of my body, preventing all attempts at escape. She places a glass of wine in my hand, I don't even protest. She's wearing a full-length canvas apron, which is splattered with large blotches of crimson-red paint, making her look like she's been butchering bunnies all day. I also catch a whiff of turpentine as she sits down next to me. I've clearly interrupted her work.

'Juliette, tell me what's wrong?'

'I've accidentally moved someone into my house,' I tell her.

It's not what she was expecting me to say. I watch as she struggles to contain the shock my words have caused; shock that would usually leave every opening on her face flared, gaping and stretched to the limit of its hinges.

'Juliette,' she says, as calmly as she can manage, 'are you seeing someone? I mean, it's been eighteen months since Jamie died and nobody would blame you.'

The idea is so absurd that I burst out laughing. A few undignified snorts also escape me before I have it all under control again. Poppy has the decency not to comment.

'His name is Alfie,' I explain, surrendering myself to the cushions. 'And I've only known him for about a week.'

'For a week? Have you gone completely insane?'

'Are you going to let me finish telling this story?'

'Sorry,' Poppy says, pretending to zip her mouth closed.

But it's unfair to leave her hanging, so I explain myself quickly, before something inside her, with a vascular origin, can no longer take the strain and pops.

'Alfie Evans is seventy-seven years old, and I moved him into my house because he had nowhere else to go.'

Poppy scratches her head. 'I know I've been saying that you spend too much time on your own, but there are easier ways of finding company than picking up a random old man off the streets.'

I tell her everything about Ivy Edwards, Starcross Crescent and the moment I found Alfie in the spare room. I describe the long waiting list for the sheltered housing scheme, the Dickensian B&B on Curzon Street and my moment of reckless generosity. I don't tell her about my conversations with Jamie on this or any other subject. Even Poppy might have trouble accepting that as normal behaviour.

'So, you could be stuck with Alfie for a couple of months?'

I take a big gulp of wine and nod. 'He's in my kitchen right now, cooking a chicken casserole.'

'And you don't like chicken casserole?' There's a hint of a smile on her face.

'It's not just that, I'm not sure I'm ready to have someone else in my house.'

'You mean someone who isn't Jamie.'

'It just feels wrong.'

'Then think of this as a practice run because one day, whether you believe it or not, you might meet someone who you do want to live with.'

That seems like such a ridiculous possibility that I'm tempted to snort again. I take off my shoes instead and curl my feet up underneath me, snuggling into the warm embrace of the sofa.

'You're doing the right thing,' Poppy reassures me. 'Jamie would approve.'

Jamie was the one who put the idea in my head in the first place. But that doesn't mean I'm happy about it. Alfie disturbs the air and the memories. I haven't been able to think straight for a solid twenty-four hours and it's very discomforting.

'There's another problem,' I say. 'When I was going through Ivy's stuff, I found some information that could literally change Alfie's life, and I don't know what to do about it.'

I spend a whole hour recounting the personal history of Alfie Evans. I tell Poppy about Joseph Evans, Ivy's search for him later in life and the appearance of Abigail. I even show her the photos I slipped into my bag, the ones Alfie asked me to destroy, showing Joseph Evans on his wedding day and with his family in the back garden of their home on Grange Road.

'And you think Abigail Evans is still alive?' Poppy is gripped by the tale. Her glass of wine sits forgotten and her whole body is turned towards me, like I'm reading her the best bedtime story ever.

'I think it's a distinct possibility. And Ivy was clearly willing to hear her dad's side of the story,' I say. 'But Alfie...'

'I think you should find her,' Poppy says decisively. 'What's the worst thing that could happen?'

'Alfie could complain to my boss, and I could lose my job for being an interfering old biddy.'

Poppy waves my concerns aside. 'Nigel already knows about your old biddy potential and he still sends you out to clear houses.'

'It's also a betrayal of trust. Alfie told me those things in confidence. He didn't ask me to go snooping into his private life.'

'But you didn't, you went snooping into Ivy's,' Poppy says, like that makes everything okay. 'Look, Alfie's been through too much already, you can't tell him what you've just told me and expect him to be interested in a big, tearful, family reunion. He's much more likely to be open to some kind of communication if you track Abigail down first, and check her out.'

Or he might tell me to mind my own bloody business, and he'd have a fair point. I'm supposed to be respectfully finding a final resting place for Ivy's possessions, not dragging bits of ancient history to the surface, like bad pennies rescued from the gutter.

'Juliette, this is not the time to get all moralistic about things.' Poppy can see the doubtful expression on my face. She heaves herself off the sofa and collects her laptop from the kitchen table before she returns. 'Alfie Evans has no one left in the world, as far as he knows. You can't keep this a secret. If there's even a remote possibility that someone shares most of his DNA—'

'Okay, okay, let's see if we can track Abigail down first,' I say, still not convinced we're doing the right thing. 'Then I'll decide what to do about Alfie.'

Poppy is already typing *Abigail Evans* into her laptop. For the next three hours, we investigate all the likely looking options, ruling out some of the Abigails immediately on the basis of age, location and obvious lack of family resemblance. We use the photo of Joseph Evans for reference on the shape of eyes, faces, hairlines and noses. I try to point out that this is not a foolproof way of searching, that Abigail Evans might not be on any kind of social media, she might have got married and changed her name. But Poppy isn't interested in excuses. She continues to eliminate every Abigail possible, until we are left with a shortlist of six potential half-sisters. Poppy writes their details onto a piece of paper and then tears the sheet in half, giving three of the names to me, and keeping the rest for herself.

'You try and contact those three, and ask them if their dad was an Englishman called Joseph Evans, and I'll do the same with mine.'

'Don't you think that's a bit direct?' I say, staring at my list uncertainly.

'How else are we going to find out if we've got the right Abigail Evans? We literally know nothing else about who she is or what she does. All we know is that she's the daughter of Joseph Evans.'

Poppy makes us both some dinner, filling me in on the latest news about the publication of her picture book, but I'm only half listening. Now that we've finished discussing Alfie and his half-sister, my mind is wandering back to all the times I've visited Poppy's home, over the years, with Jamie. I've sat with him dozens of times on this very sofa, as we watched the squirrels in the garden, or the sun setting behind the rickety old fence. I've listened to him and his sister talking about the crazy apple-eating competition they had in an orchard, when they were young, goading each other on until Jamie had eaten so much fruit that he puked. To this day, Poppy claims she can't even look at an apple pie without heaving. One of my absolute favourite stories is about the time Poppy fell off her bike and into a nettle patch. And before Jamie heroically rescued her, he grabbed a generously-sized bra from the neighbour's washing line and strapped it over his head, to protect his ears from nettle stings. This kitchen is literally simmering with memories.

'Juliette?'

I stare at Poppy, who is clearly midway through telling me a long tale. Wisps of hair have escaped from her ponytail, a sure sign that the story was a good one. She's pointing a chopping knife in my direction, waiting for a reaction I should have given.

'Absolutely, I couldn't agree more,' I say, deciding on a strong response, hoping it's the right one.

Poppy narrows her eyes at me, shakes her head and goes back to her chopping. It's so long since I've been a visitor in someone's home that I've forgotten how warm, comforting and familiar it can feel. Just to sit on a friendly sofa in good, trusted company – with the smell of gently frying onions drifting out of the kitchen – is immensely soothing. But as soon as we've finished dinner, I make an excuse about needing to check on my house, in case Alfie has flooded the kitchen with the washing machine, and leave.

I sit in my car when I get home, patiently waiting for Jamie, but he doesn't show.

'I've just been round to your sister's place and she cooked me a lasagne,' I tell him.

Lasagne was Jamie's favourite. I'm hoping that if he can smell the lingering aroma of garlic and onions on my clothes, he might settle into his usual seat for a chat. But after twenty minutes of sitting with the windows shut, letting the garlicky smell build up all around me into a concentrated crescendo, it's obvious that he's not going to keep me company this evening. And I reluctantly head indoors.

All the lights are off, and I can't hear the TV. Alfie has gone to bed. I breathe a sigh of relief and go quietly into the dining room, closing doors behind me so I won't disturb him. There's a single flower in a vase on the dining room table. A knife and fork have been neatly laid out next to a note: *Dinner's in the oven, Alfie*. So, he made the casserole anyway. I should be annoyed that he ignored everything I said about cooking dinner, but the casserole smells delicious.

I take the dish out of the oven, which has been left on low – no firefighters required. The casserole tastes as good as it smells. And even though I've already had plenty of lasagne, I eat about half the chicken dinner straight from the dish, and then put the rest in a bowl in the fridge. After weeks of living off snacks and microwave dinners, I've had two home cooked meals in one night. I have missed the solace of real food.

The bathroom is in a less than perfect state, with smudges of toothpaste on the floor. The pools of water beside the bath could rival the aftermath of the dolphin show at SeaWorld. And the toilet seat is up. Alfie might be a whizz in the kitchen but he's more of a troll in the bathroom. I remove a soggy towel from the side of the bath, where it's been flung, mop up the water and go to bed. I stare at the bedroom ceiling for some time wondering if I should call Jaya at the council, in the morning, and ask if she can speed up Alfie's removal to the sheltered housing scheme. If there's any committee I can sit in front of, I'll be happy to beg. Because Alfie is quickly colonising my home, and I don't like it.

Eleven

'ISABELLE HART WAS A well-loved member of the community at the Risley Manor Retirement Home, where she spent the last fifteen years of her life. I am very pleased to welcome some of her friends from Risley here today, along with her favourite members of staff.'

Every now and again, I get sent to a place like Risley Manor; a big, sprawling seventeenth-century house that has been converted into a luxurious retirement home. It's a beautiful house that might have been bulldozed, or fallen into a sad state of dereliction, if it hadn't been bought by the new owners and transformed into a home.

If I'm ever faced with the prospect of picking a retirement home to live in, I'd sign my name up for Risley Manor in a heartbeat. The manor is set in thirty acres of grounds, littered with stone fountains and benches. Stately conifers surround the house like ancient guardians, and the manicured flower beds are overflowing with twenty different types of roses. On the inside, dark oak panelling gives every room a traditional Old English feel. The plasterwork and cornicing could rival anything at Hampton Court Palace. The history has been preserved for everyone to enjoy. The old Risley family crest displayed proudly in the entrance hall. Each resident has their own sitting room, bedroom, dressing room, bathroom and a balcony. And the suites are worth every penny, with high ceilings and the space to breathe and feel at peace.

Some of the places I've visited, in the course of my job, have had more in common with a hospital ward than a home; squeaky linoleum floors, generic paintings and decorations picked straight from the same wholesaler that also supplies council offices and leisure centres.

Rooms so small and dull it's an insult to the people who live there. Not everyone can afford to live in a grand place like Risley Manor, but what's so wrong with giving people space? I've had this argument with Alan at work a hundred times over the years. He's firmly on the side of economics, fiscal policy, bang for your buck. He talks for what seems like hours about overcrowded towns and cities, and poor cash-strapped councils. But none of his arguments can ever convince me that people don't deserve to spend the last years of their lives in peaceful, interesting surroundings. If nothing else, surely, they've earned the right to a room that's big enough to house their most treasured possessions, or to receive their private visitors, or to accommodate their hobbies? If the walls are thinner than water crackers, and you can hear the person in the adjoining room as they turn over in bed, something has gone horribly wrong with the whole system.

At least Isabelle Hart had space, dignity and privacy. Her rooms were at the front of Risley Manor, overlooking a magnificent sweep of lawns and gardens. All she could see from her windows were pine trees, flowers and sky. Isabelle Hart invested in her own comfort, but she clearly believed that her favourite animals deserved the same high standards of care. I found stacks of cards in her rooms thanking her for the generous donations she'd made to various animal centres over the years. Her favourite was clearly a local donkey sanctuary. She had dozens of photos of the playful creatures romping across daisy-filled fields in the sun. There were ring-tailed lemurs in Madagascar, spectacled bears in South America, cats and dogs at another centre close to Risley Manor. Her generous contributions, according to one note, had allowed for the total refurbishment of the cat accommodation, with much bigger, comfier rooms, containing snuggle cushions, heat lamps and climbing posts.

It's also nice to have company at the crematorium. There are six residents from Risley Manor and a handful of staff, who must have known Isabelle Hart well. It was obvious, from the way she occupied every inch of her rooms, that she considered it to be her home. But with no family to deal with her possessions, that became my job. I think I would have liked Isabelle Hart. She had expensive taste in silk scarves, some of which came straight from the most luxurious Parisian fashion houses. True to her generous nature, she'd left instructions to gift the scarves to the other residents and staff. She had a huge collection of books on gardening, and so many house plants that her rooms smelt like the Palm House at Kew Gardens, moist and deliciously earthy. There were photos from Peru, Brazil, Alaska, Switzerland and Australia. Well-travelled, well-heeled and well-liked. Not a bad way to live a life.

I close my eyes as the Reverend Adebisi – who is a much more compassionate human being than Amos Stickythorn – continues with the service. And I can't stop the images from coming. The musical of Isabelle Hart's life begins to form, even though I'd prefer to see it for the first time when I'm with Jamie. But the visions are so strong it's impossible to contain them.

I'm in Isabelle's room and night has fallen, cicadas fill the tropical space with such a rich resonance of sound that it makes the air feel dense. Isabelle wafts into the scene wearing a long, flowing dress made from all of her silk scarves, it is worthy of its own spot on any haute couture catwalk. She sashays through the room like a fashion model, enjoying the music of the night creatures. But as she stands in front of me waiting for her next move, in this fantasy that I am creating, the picture stalls. I have no idea what to do with her next. I have plenty of options, animal sanctuary scenes with a complicated mop and bucket dance routine, performed by the staff, donkeys carrying her across a field in a grand carriage inlaid with gold. I have her entire collection of records (spanning the 1950s to the 1970s) to draw on for the soundtrack to her life. But the only thing I suddenly have in my head is Alfie Evans. Alfie Evans and the stripy red and blue dressing gown that he was wearing, when I saw him in the kitchen this morning. The dressing gown that was too short to cover his knobbly knees, that set off the varicose veins in his legs, and failed to shield me from the sight of his bare white feet, planted firmly on my kitchen floor.

I shake the image out of my head, adjust my sitting position and think about Isabelle Hart again. This time, I can see her on her balcony, hosting a tea party for the other residents. A giant pink, sugary cake revolves on an impressive china stand. I can practically taste the marzipan, the soft fondant icing and moist vanilla sponge. My mouth begins to water... and my stomach rumbles loudly. I open both eyes and glance furtively over my shoulders, checking that nobody else heard the loud, complaining grumble. All I've had for lunch is a banana and a yogurt. And I was so keen to get away from Alfie and his feet this morning, that I skipped breakfast altogether. I'd already set my alarm half an hour earlier than usual, hoping to evade any encounters, but apparently Alfie is an early riser.

There was no avoiding him as I tiptoed into the kitchen, carrying my shoes and bag, ready to leave the house stealthily.

'Juliette,' he said, looking pleased to see me. I tried not to stare at his knees, but they were pointing straight towards me like two lumpy daffodil bulbs. 'I didn't hear you coming in last night. Did you have a nice time with your friend?'

'Um, yes, thanks.' I poured myself the last of the coffee from the pot. 'We went to that new Italian restaurant in town. Vanessa had tiramisu, but I felt like pistachio ice cream, and it was lovely. There was a mandolin player, and a sumptuous bougainvillea plant that the owner brought all the way from his mother's garden in Tuscany.'

I was so used to living in the world of my imaginary friends that it was scary how easily the fabricated details presented themselves to me. Even when I didn't want to share my made-up life with Alfie, I couldn't seem to stop myself.

Alfie smiled. 'I see you saved a bit of room for my casserole, though.'

He'd already washed-up the dish and left it to drain.

'It was really tasty, Alfie,' I said, reluctantly. 'Thank you, but you don't need to cook for me. I can take care of myself.'

Alfie nodded like he'd heard the words and understood them, but I got the distinct feeling that another hot dinner was going to make an appearance that evening.

'I borrowed the casserole dish from your neighbour, Marina.'

I put some bread in the toaster and frowned. 'Who?'

'Mrs Lafleur, next door. Lovely woman, she asked after you.'

'She did? I mean, I barely know her.'

Jamie and I had only moved into our new home a few months before he died. And apart from a couple of "how are you settling in?" conversations, we hadn't had enough time to get to know any of the neighbours. Since Jamie's death, I hadn't had a single interaction with any of my fellow Raglan Road residents. In fact, I had perfected my wave, the one which said *I've seen that you're smiling at me, but I'm already late for work/ dinner/ an important social engagement, and I can't possibly stop and talk to you now. Sorry.*

Once, on a particularly lonely Thursday evening, I'd been waiting for Jamie to make an appearance in my car, and I almost didn't notice when Mr Buckley, from number eleven, started walking towards me with a concerned look on his face. I quickly pretended to be on my phone, laughing brightly, until he retreated inside his house with his wiry little dog (who Jamie called Snarly Face) in tow. But it was a close call and I'd had to be more careful since then.

I avoided putting the bins out at peak neighbour-congregating times, and they were the biggest bunch of congregators I'd ever come across. The small square of garden outside the house had taken on the appearance of a scientific experiment, like I was trying to establish the height that weeds could climb to, if left to grow untamed by human hand. It was the only way I could avoid having to talk to anyone who happened to be passing, as I cut a path through the vegetation with a scythe. But now Alfie had borrowed Mrs Lafleur's casserole dish and was already on first-name terms with her.

'She invited me in for a cup of tea and told me all about her granddaughter, who's just starting medical school. Did you know Marina used to be a GP at the local surgery? I think she might have inspected my carbuncles once,' he said, scratching his stubbly chin, trying to remember. 'She knew Ivy too, from her haberdashery days, if you can believe it. We're living in a very small world, Juliette.'

It was a world that had just got infinitely smaller now that Alfie was in it. He'd already told me more about Mrs Lafleur than I was prepared to hear. Why couldn't he just sit quietly in the house and do the crossword, or fall asleep in front of the TV dreaming about his grave-digging days? Why did he have to be so interested in everything and everyone?

'I thought I might have a walk later, over to those gardens you told me about,' Alfie continued, as he boiled the kettle to make more coffee. He helped himself to Jamie's favourite mug from the cupboard, the one shaped like a Highland cow, the one I'd bought for him on a holiday we took to Oban, in the Scottish Highlands.

I reached across and grabbed it before Alfie could fill the mug, took another plain blue one from the cupboard and thrust it towards him, forcefully. 'Can you use this mug instead, please?'

'Oh, yes, sorry.' Alfie looked at the cow mug that I was still clutching in my hand, his confusion obvious. 'I didn't know that was a special one.'

He left a pause, expecting me to fill it with an explanation or a funny story. But I put the mug carefully inside my bag instead, and left the room before my breakfast could pop out of the toaster.

The mug is still sitting in my bag. I lean forwards as the Reverend Adebisi leads the mourners in a prayer, and cradle the ceramic cow horns in my hands. Jamie's favourite mug is one of the few things I've left around the house, like he's still taking up space there. So that when I open the kitchen cupboards and see his mug sitting next to mine, I can ignore the gaping hole he's left in my life, for a few precious seconds at least. But how am I going to protect Jamie's stuff from Alfie?

I spend a few minutes talking to the staff at the end of Isabelle Hart's funeral. When I leave the crematorium, there's a message on my phone from Poppy asking if I've made any progress with the half-sisters on my list of three. If I don't reply to her message, she'll just keep pestering me, or turn up on my doorstep. And I don't think I can face introducing her to Alfie.

I haven't found anything useful so far, how about you?

Two are a definite no. The third isn't on social media but I'll keep trying.

Me too.

So far, I haven't spent a single moment trying to track any of the half-sisters down, and I feel guilty for lying, but some bad habits have taken a hold.

How's life with Alfie?

I saw his knees this morning. He needs a longer dressing gown.

Lovely! If it all gets too much, come and stay with me and

Zarina for a few nights.

Thanks. I might take you up on that offer if he starts wandering around the house in his bare feet. Saw those too this morning, they looked like two dead fish.

Having a sandwich, thanks for the image.

You're more than welcome, any time xxx

I sit in my car doing a quick guilt search on the first Abigail Evans from my list, but nothing comes up. I should go home and sit quietly with my laptop, give this search the time and concentration it deserves. But I don't want to return to Raglan Road yet. I have a whole weekend ahead of me with Alfie. Just the thought of it brings on a strong desire to bite my nails, which I haven't done since I was a teenager. I'd already finished work for the day by the time I went to Isabelle Hart's funeral, and it's still only 5.30 p.m. So I drive to the office to make a start on the paperwork for Ravindra Singh's house clearance.

For once, I've got the whole place to myself. I sit in Loretta's chair, the most expensive and comfortable in the office, and put it through its paces, counting how many rotations it can do on a single spin – five is my record. I only stop when I start to feel sick and dizzy. If I throw up in Loretta's wicker rubbish bin, I'll never get the chunks out of the tiny holes. I return to my own desk and sharpen my pencils, arranging them in my drawer in order of size. I play solitaire on my computer after that, and watch some internet videos of ice-skating grannies in Alaska. I also marvel at an extravagant cake shop in Austria, where the butterfly buns are so big and heavy they need a reinforced cake stand just to carry the weight of the frosting. The cake shop instantly makes it onto my bucket list of places to visit before I die. And it's still only 6.54 p.m.

The novelty of being in the office alone quickly starts to wear off when I can no longer hear any sounds coming from other parts of the building. I lock up hastily and head to my favourite drive-through food place for a chicken coleslaw sandwich, a slice of carrot cake and a coffee. I eat it in the car park, listening to a podcast on my phone about hiking through the French Alps. But I can't stay here all night and my toes are starting to feel like a packet of frozen sausages, so I reluctantly drive home.

I've barely turned off the engine when Jamie appears in the seat beside me, making this the best part of my day by a long stretch.

'Did you save any carrot cake for me?' he asks. It's a long-standing joke between us, my weakness for any kind of cake and inability to set even a tiny sliver aside for him, despite all good intentions of sharing. 'Do you remember when I used to bring you slices of those exotic creations from the Three Cups Bakery?'

I haven't been able to visit the bakery since his death. Cake, as it turns out, is a very powerful substance for provoking memories.

'There was that mango and papaya sponge that you liked.'

'Until you said it looked like someone had minced up a finger and baked it into a cake.'

'There was a prune and caramel torte,' Jamie says, pulling a face at the combination of flavours. 'And your all-time favourite, the chocolate-orange cookie cake. I was lucky if I ever got a tiny taste of that one.'

Today, Jamie looks almost like his old self, apart from the fact that he's wearing the kind of sparkly, sequin-encrusted outfit that any Latin American dancer – entering a salsa competition – would kill for. It's ironic because in life, Jamie had two left feet. He also has a pink marabou feather woven through the front of his hairline, like a Roman Emperor wearing a laurel wreath crown. But his face is the face I remember, and I focus on his features.

'I've missed you,' I say.

'It's only been a few days. You can't have missed me much in that time.'

'It feels like months.'

He tries to take my hand but I feel nothing, not even a wisp of displaced air, or a faint sense of heat and I sigh with longing.

'I see you've been taking my favourite mug out for a walk,' he says, nodding at the face of the Highland cow, which is poking out of the bag that sits at my feet.

'I had to rescue it from Alfie. It felt wrong to let him use it.'

'He's definitely making himself at home, then. If he starts wearing my best jeans you have my permission to give him a severe talking-to.' Jamie is teasing me but he does it so kindly, I can't help smiling.

'So, how was the funeral of Isabelle Hart?' he asks, jumping from subject to subject more than he usually does when we talk.

I realise there's a slightly manic edge to his conversational style that was never present during his mortal life. He was the most laid-back person I'd ever met. If you wanted to talk for three hours about the pros and cons of butter, or who was the greatest rock band on the planet, he'd happily indulge that conversation, ignoring the pressures of time, work and expectation. But today, he seems more unsettled, and that's disconcerting in itself.

'The funeral was nice,' I tell him. 'There were ten of us there. She had some close friends at the home.'

'Ah, you've always liked Risley Manor. Have you got your room picked out yet?' he asks, sparkly outfit shimmering suddenly in the headlights of a passing car, which sends rainbows of pink, purple and gold spinning through the interior around us. It's like sitting in the middle of a mobile disco. 'Personally, I'd go for the room with the private roof garden, between those two twisted chimney pots. You can see for miles from up there, and the sunsets are amazing.'

'I like the rooms at the back, away from the driveway,' I say. 'They're really quiet, they've got the best light and doors that open out onto the gardens. I could grow some begonias or lilacs and put some ferns in a shady spot.'

'I can picture it now, love, it's just a pity you can't keep anything green alive. How are the plants in the dining room, by the way? Are any of them still clinging to life?'

'The ferns died a few months ago, but the ficus is still hanging on by a few green leaves. Sorry,' I add, knowing how much he loved looking after the plants. 'I think they miss you too.'

'Plants are clever that way,' Jamie says. 'They form attachments. I mean, it's not like having a cat or a lizard or a hamster or anything, but if you're pining away for me in that house, they'll be feeling it too. You've got to start making it your home, love. It needs you as much as you need it.'

'Do you remember the day we came to see it for the first time?' I ask, smiling at all the memories from that day, hoping to divert him from more talk of dead plants and home making. 'You loved this house the moment you set eyes on it.'

'And you needed a little bit of persuading,' his says, blowing a stray strand of pink feather out of his eyes. 'But you warmed up to it in the end. And I think Alfie likes it too.'

'He's definitely settling himself in,' I say, wishing he wasn't.

Jamie is suddenly gone. For a fraction of a second, I can see a faint afterimage of the marabou feather, but it fades all too quickly. I don't linger in the car today, it's too cold. And it's not until I'm taking off my coat in the hallway, that I realise Jamie didn't ask me to reimagine the life of Isabelle Hart, in any kind of musical genre. I stand for a moment trying to work out what it could mean. Is the spirit of Jamie getting bored with the games we used to play? Is he starting to forget all the rituals and routines that made our lives together so special? Or am I reading too much into what could simply be a one-time lapse?

I find a note from Alfie on the dining room table telling me he's gone down the pub. I feel a twinge of disappointment when I realise there's no casserole waiting for me in the oven, even though I was the one who insisted I didn't need looking after. A shop-bought sandwich, no matter how generous the chicken and coleslaw filling, is nowhere near as satisfying as a home-cooked dinner. I gather up my laptop and a bag of crisps and retreat to my bedroom, before Alfie can return from the pub, and start asking me questions about my evening.

I sit on my bed, laptop open, and revisit the Austrian cake shop while I nibble on the crisps. Then I decide to search for Abigail Evans. This time, I can rule out the first one on my list immediately, a photo on social media proves she's far too young to be Alfie's half-sister. You can't fake that amount of natural collagen in the skin. The second Abigail lives not far from Karratha, the last place there was any record of Joseph Evans. She spells her name slightly differently, Abygail with a Y, she also has a hyphenated surname, Evans-Hollister. She has a large social media presence, and I spend an hour scrolling through endless photos of family barbecues, trips to the beach, holidays in the hills. And apart from the fact that I am jealous of the outdoor, fun-filled life she's apparently living – in her pink flamingo patterned flip-flops, in the presence of near constant sunshine – I'm still no closer to working out if she is *the* Abigail Evans that we're looking for. There's no mention of an English dad. She has the same colouring as Alfie, but that description could apply to a tenth of the population of

Australia. The only way to know for sure is to send her a message, explain who I am – reassuring her that I'm not a stalker – and hope she responds.

It takes me half an hour, and many versions of my carefully crafted message, before I'm happy with the results. But my finger hovers over the send button for a long time. What if she really is Alfie's half-sister? Do I want to open up what could be a complicated can of worms? Do I want to deal with any potential fallout? What if I'm making the wrong decision? What if Alfie and Abigail don't want anything to do with each other, and all I'm doing is stirring up a hornet's nest of family trouble? I delete the message quickly before I accidentally send it, wishing I'd kept the existence of Abigail Evans to myself. Poppy never lets anything go and I suddenly feel exhausted, like I don't have the energy to deal with any of it.

I put the laptop on the floor and pull the duvet around my shoulders, snuggling down into my bed. Even if I don't do anything about Abigail Evans, I still have an entire weekend with Alfie stretching ahead of me. And I can't hide under my duvet for the whole of Saturday and Sunday, no matter how appealing it seems. Sooner or later, I'll need to eat or wash or leave the house for fresh air, and I'll be faced with Alfie's feet and knees once again. I turn my light out and pull the duvet all the way over my head, trying not to visualise varicose veins.

Juliette and Jamie
III
Confetti Blues

THE CONFETTI FELL IN pristine drifts of white all around me. Caught by a mellow summer's breeze, the cascade floated softly to the ground, where the white paper petals settled like cherry blossom. I closed my eyes, lifting my face to the sun, feeling the last of the confetti as it brushed past my nose and caught in my hair, claiming me.

'Juliette?' Jamie's voice sounded distant. If I opened my eyes, it would break the spell of this sublime feeling and I didn't want it to end, not yet, not until I was ready.

'What's going on, love? Are you having a moment out here all by yourself?'

I had no choice now. I'd have to explain the odd scene Jamie had stumbled upon. I opened my eyes and saw the confused expression settle on his face, as he took in the mutilated sheets of paper at my feet. The paper that I had torn up in a fit of anger, exasperation and frustration and thrown into the air around me, like confetti at the wedding I was trying to plan.

Jamie picked up what was left of the catering company information that I'd printed off the internet, with a slow smile of understanding.

'If you don't like the food these people are offering you, just say the word and I'll drag the barbeque out. We can have a burger themed wedding reception.'

It was almost enough to make me smile. The vision of Jamie lost in a haze of smoke and happiness, grilling on request. But the other emotions – the ones that had been simmering under the hood for weeks now, the ones that had led to my frenzied confetti moment – rose to the surface instead, and spilled out all over the backyard. Jamie put an arm around my shoulders and led me inside. He sat me down at the dining room table, as I sobbed into the sleeve of my sweatshirt leaving a snotty trail all around the cuff. Jamie rubbed my back making soft soothing noises, the kind you make for an inconsolable toddler when they've just dropped their ice cream at the beach. It felt like my ice cream had been buried under a sandcastle and a huge pile of dog poo. Nothing could soothe me out of that.

'What is it, Juliette?' he asked, when the tears had abated enough for him to be heard, and I'd found a tissue in the pocket of my jeans. 'Have you got cold feet about the wedding? If it's all going too quickly, we can slow things down if you want.'

'I haven't— got cold— feet,' I managed to say, between the lingering sobs that refused to stop.

'Are you sure, because this whole thing has been happening pretty fast, and I did kind of take you by surprise when I asked you to marry me.'

'It's supposed to be— a surprise,' I said, almost smiling at the glorious memory of the moment that would live with me forever.

Jamie had lured me to the bookshop, where he said he had a whole evening of stocktaking to get through. He'd promised me dinner at my favourite restaurant afterwards, if I agreed to help him. I rarely refused any request Jamie made. Spending time with him, whether it was going to the cinema, taking a walk along the beach, or just doing the washing-up, was time well spent. By the time I reached the bookshop that evening it was already dark, and only one light was showing somewhere deep in the interior of the building. Jamie found me as I stumbled through the History section, and steered me over to the counter. He knew the shop intimately. He could walk the entire maze of shelves with his eyes closed and know where he was at any moment.

When he flicked on another light, I was expecting to find piles of books, Jamie's laptop and a pot of freshly brewed coffee. Everything we needed to get us through the next few hours. But what I saw... the whole counter had been festooned with twinkling lights. Reading lamps had been gathered in from every corner of the shop, including the illuminated unicorn with the pink mane from the children's section, and the Moroccan mosaic beauties from travel. Strings of colourful paper lanterns had been hung between the bookshelves. A mismatched collection of tables and chairs, which I didn't recognise, had been arranged around an open space, like a restaurant with a dance floor in the middle. A trestle table was buckling under the weight of delicious-looking tapas.

'What's going on?' I turned a full three hundred and sixty degrees trying to take everything in. 'Have I forgotten your birthday? Or are we celebrating the anniversary of something important, like the first time you went to see The Eighteen in concert?'

Jamie watched me, enjoying the sense of awe and wonder he'd managed to create, turning the heart of the bookshop into something even more magical than it already was. When he took my hand and got down on one knee, I still didn't realise what was happening. Jamie liked to joke around. Asking my forgiveness (on bended knees) for forgetting to take the bins out when it was his turn, or apologising for staying out half the night with his friends, playing guitars and drinking beers. It was only when he took a ring out of his pocket that I finally understood.

'Juliette Jones,' he said, all joking now set aside. He took his commitments to the people in his life very seriously. 'I've been dreaming about this moment since the day you walked into my bookshop, and I finally understood what William Shakespeare had written about love, all those centuries ago. Will you do me the honour of becoming my wife?'

From anyone else it would have sounded corny, like the kind of proposal you get in a B-grade movie, performed by actors who couldn't get any other kind of work. But from Jamie, it was heart-stopping, a true reflection of his sentimental, sensitive soul. I didn't need to think about my answer, the decision had already been made on that same day in the bookshop. We were a sickening cliché, a retch-worthy display of love and affection. I was glad this moment was private; even I would have had trouble keeping my dinner down if I'd witnessed it from the outside. I pulled him to his feet, nodding my answer, incapable of actual words. And I hugged him so tightly his belt buckle popped under the strain. The ring was a beautiful emerald, set in twisted stands of white gold. Jamie had taken the idea to a jewellery-designer friend, it was a one-off creation and I loved it. He placed it carefully on my finger to seal the deal.

'Is that what all the lights and the food are for?' I asked, once I'd regained the gift of speech. 'Is this our engagement party?'

'I couldn't think of any other place I'd rather have it than the very spot where we first met.'

It was perfect, far more fitting than any impersonal restaurant. This place, right here by the counter, meant everything to us.

'I assume we're not the only people who'll be celebrating tonight,' I said, casting an eye over the food and drinks again. 'What would you have done if I'd said no?'

'Sold the bookshop and run away to Mexico.'

I grinned, trying to imagine Jamie in the heat and colour of Mexico City.

'Enchiladas give you heartburn,' I said.

'Then I'd be forced to live on tacos and burritos instead, and a fair amount of Mexican booze to help heal my broken heart.'

'You'd meet another Juliette, eventually.'

'But she wouldn't be the right one.'

The party was the best night of my life. Jamie had persuaded a friend with a Motown tribute band to play us into the small hours. My entire family, including my brother, his wife and kids, and several cousins I'd forgotten existed, had shown up to celebrate with us. Jamie's family were thrilled. His friends – fun-loving quirky souls who knew how to turn a good party into a legend – kept spirits high and the dance floor heaving. My friends had no idea what had hit them, and spent the entire night hugging me and admiring the ring. And Jamie never left my side. I loved that about him. He wanted to share every single second of it with me.

Since that night, almost twelve weeks ago, I'd spent every weekend trying to make wedding plans. Instead of enjoying a trip to the cinema with Jamie, or a leisurely meander around our favourite car boot sales, I'd been glued to my laptop. I'd spent hours scrolling through endless far-fetched visions of cliff-top ceremonies, vows recited to the strains of a choir, dresses made by elves from discarded fairy wings and moonbeams. I thought it would be a breeze to organise, a delight for the woman who was floating on an ocean of happiness in her own little pedalo of joy. The reality was far more prosaic. I had no innate ability to choose flowers, table decorations or bridesmaids' dresses that complemented each other, with or without the aid of a colour wheel. I had no idea what style of dress would suit me on the day, would allow me to breathe, to kick up my heels at the reception and still look good in the photos. Poppy had been on three heroic wedding-dress shopping trips with me already, and I was no closer to making a decision. And the catering companies, it was like they spoke a completely different language. Food wasn't just food when you were getting married. It was a statement, an atmosphere, a lifelong memory in the making. It also had the power to ruin your marriage, and heap generations of trauma upon your family, if you got it wrong.

The wedding was in eight weeks' time, and the only thing I'd managed to decide upon so far was the band for the reception. We had considered holding the reception here, in our new home. It looked positively cosy now that the dining room had a floor, the windows in the sitting room had been replaced, and the mould in the kitchen had been blitzed. The bookshop gave us more space, however, and it was the perfect venue for the low-key celebration that we both wanted. But low-key went against all the wedding tropes I'd been bombarded with, and I suddenly couldn't take any more of it. That's when Jamie found me in the backyard, surrounded by the confetti of my failed plans.

Jamie listened patiently, as I told him of my wedding woes. A pot of tea helped to restore a thin veneer of sanity.

'You should have told me what was going on, I could have helped you.'

'But I'm *supposed* to be the one who plans this, I'm *supposed* to be enjoying it,' I said, a few stray tears escaping me again as my hands tried to gesticulate my wedding pain.

'Juliette, love, you get stressed when we book a day trip to London on the internet. What on earth made you think a whole wedding would be easy?'

If he was going to get all logical about it, I might be forced to accept he had a point. Never, in a million years, did I think I'd be a victim of wedding fever. But here I was, in the grip of the illness and in need of immediate medical intervention.

'It's not that you can't cope with this on your own,' Jamie added sincerely, pushing a plate of custard creams towards me, 'it's more about the fact that you shouldn't have to make all these choices by yourself. This wedding belongs to both of us. It's as much my responsibility as yours.'

He took the peacock-feather patterned folder that had become The Wedding Folder and flipped to the first section.

'Right, the wedding cake,' he said.

Even the words were almost enough to start me crying again. Jamie hated fruit cake. A sponge seemed too light and fluffy for the occasion. But should I then order something gluten-free, dairy-free and vegan? For the first time in my life, cake had lost some of its appeal. That should have been a huge warning sign that the sickness was already taking hold, rampaging through my body and messing with my cake hormones.

'Okay, well this is an easy decision,' Jamie said, ignoring the incredulous look on my face. 'We'll go down to the Three Cups Bakery, tomorrow morning, order whatever you like the look of, and ask them to make it ten times bigger.'

'But what about all those people who don't like chocolate?' I said, imagining the disappointment on my mum's face when she saw the splendid creation I'd chosen, without a single scrap of white icing to be seen.

Jamie shrugged. 'Anyone who doesn't like chocolate cookie cake will have to find something else to go with their champagne. Okay, next, the wedding dress.' He turned to a new section in the folder and sighed. 'Why are you putting yourself through this torture, Juliette? Every time you've been out dress shopping with my sister you've come back in tears. I don't want anything about our wedding to make you cry, other than my dancing.'

I was already looking forward to watching his moves on the dance floor, they were rarely witnessed and dangerous to behold. Anyone foolish enough to stand within a ten-foot radius risked severe injury, or psychological damage at the very least.

'Why can't you just buy a dress you like and wear that? White makes you look like you've had a recent bout of food poisoning anyway. Unless that's the look you were going for, of course, and then I applaud your choice,' he said, backpedalling furiously as he registered the tortured look on my face. 'Pale and recently nauseated definitely makes a style statement.'

White, or any version of it, even with hints of peach or biscuit or gold, was the worst colour for my complexion. What I wanted to wear was a beautiful mossy-green velvet creation, with a boned bodice and long fluted sleeves that made me feel like a medieval princess. I'd already seen the perfect dress and dismissed it for not being bridal enough. But it was the dress that would make me happy. And Jamie was suddenly making a lot of sense. If we couldn't plan this wedding around what we wanted, fill the day with memories that would be special for us, why bother at all? And green would help show off my engagement ring to its best advantage.

Over the next two hours we decided on food – our favourite Italian restaurant also catered for parties. The only honeymoon we could afford was a weekend in Bath, buying a house was an expensive business. We'd design the wedding invitations ourselves. I even regained enough of my decision-making ability to forbid Jamie's idea of a karaoke cocktail hour. Jamie, left to his own devices, would have favoured a cowboy cake, burgers and fries for the wedding breakfast, and his favourite jeans and T-shirt for the ceremony. He'd already imagined the wedding as a World War II movie; a tank would take us to the church, my dress would be made out of a parachute, dyed green, and a 1940s jukebox would provide all the music at the reception. He'd also spent some time setting out his vision for a 1970s disco wedding, with a happy dance tune playing us down the aisle and every guest required to wear sequinned boob tubes and shiny flared trousers.

'Even the men?' I'd asked, trying to imagine his portly dad in a pink, glittery, chest-squeezing outfit.

'Especially the men.'

By the end of our planning session, I was looking forward to the wedding again. I was also annoyed that I'd allowed other people's visions of a picture-perfect wedding to bully me away from my own. Jamie always knew who he was and what he wanted and somehow stayed true to himself. I sometimes needed help, a gentle reminder that what I desired – even if it was messy, uncoordinated or came in unpopular shades of green – was already good enough.

Jamie swept up the confetti in the backyard as I cooked a frozen pizza for dinner, my mind fully occupied with the idea of our wedding as a romantic scene from a Regency novel. Jamie would make the perfect hero, with coat-tails and breeches, riding to the church in a tall hat and knee-high leather boots. My dress would be a simple cotton affair with a fake-fur-trimmed cape for modesty, my hair framing my face in pretty Regency ringlets. The dancing afterwards would be regal, elegant and dreamy in the soft candlelight. I could just imagine a string quartet playing popular songs from the era and (according to the internet) a Scottish reel or two.

I laid two plates out on the countertop wondering if it was too late to change our plans, if there was any possibility of finding a cheap, second-hand Regency chandelier online, with a matching cut-glass punch bowl.

Twelve

I SNEAK DOWNSTAIRS, EARLY on Saturday morning, and make myself a cup of tea. I pause briefly outside Alfie's door on the way back up to my bedroom, reassured by the soft snoring sounds coming from within.

By 7.32 a.m., I'm ready to leave the house. I creep quietly down to the hallway and hurry out the door to do the shopping. This time, I buy extra biscuits. Alfie clearly has a sweet tooth and has practically cleaned me out of digestives. I buy several healthy (sort of) ready meals for the freezer, and some carrots, onions, parsnips, potatoes, chicken and stewing steak that may find their way into a casserole. I usually avoid the coffee shop due to the intrusive presence of some of the other shoppers. There always seems to be someone who feels the need to ring their sister, mum, girlfriend or colleague from work, and describe (in lurid detail) the explosive diarrhoea their child has just experienced. Why do those conversations always carry so much further, on the circulated air of a supermarket, than any conversations about cute puppies or random acts of kindness?

Today, I find a quiet corner and hope for the best. And the only conversation I overhear is a charming interaction between two best friends, who are planning a weekend away in Berlin to celebrate a milestone birthday. By the time my peas have almost defrosted, I have no choice but to head home. How long can I keep this up for? How many weeks can I stay out of my own home trying to avoid Alfie? His presence is still so disquieting it's easier just to let him have the run of the place.

Alfie helps me with the shopping, when I finally return to Raglan

Road, putting everything away in the wrong places. Then he tries to give me some of his pension money to pay for his share of the food. But I won't accept the crinkled notes. He insists on making me a cup of tea instead, and then I'm caught.

'So, what do people do in this neck of the woods on a weekend?' he asks.

Mind their own business, leave each other in peace, hide.

'I'm not used to being this far out of town,' he says, glancing nervously out the window as if he might catch a glimpse of an African savannah, and a herd of giraffes strolling past.

It's thirty-five minutes to the centre of Sholtsbury, at a steady walk. We're surrounded by streets filled with terraced houses, so it's not exactly a rural idyll. Nonetheless, Alfie looks lost.

'Normally, I'd meet my mates down the Brown Sparrow for a spot of lunch and a game of pool, and leave you in peace,' he says, with a touch of longing in his voice.

'I'd be happy to drive you there,' I offer, my car keys already in my hand, but Alfie waves them away.

'What I was going to suggest was a nice walk to those gardens you told me about, and then a pasty from the bakery. I was chatting to Denzel, the owner.'

Does he never stop talking to people?

'He's making some special pasties this morning, from an old family recipe, and he's putting a couple aside for us in case it gets busy.'

'That's really nice of you, Alfie, but—'

'No buts, this is my treat, seeing as how you won't let me pay for my share of the food. And I'll be cooking all the dinners from now on, by the way.' He glances towards the freezer where he's just watched me stow my sad collection of ready-made chicken korma, macaroni cheese and savoury rice with beef. 'A hard-working lass like you needs a proper hot dinner at the end of the day.'

For some reason, a lump forms in my throat, and I find myself nodding. Five minutes later, I'm also putting on my coat and hat and leaving the house with Alfie, who seems happy to have the company. He prattles away about what people are growing in their gardens and how homely my neighbourhood is. And I realise that I haven't walked down my own street since the last time Jamie and I visited the bakery for some cakes. I've seen everything through the prism of my windscreen, as I come and go in my car. But now, thanks to Alfie, I am shown that the people at number forty have got a new extension at the back of their property – he's seen the builder's van coming and going. Mrs Lafleur, Marina, is preparing a flower bed so she can plant some yellow daisies for the summer. There are new residents across the road at number fifty-one, a young couple with a baby and a "daft dog that looks like an overgrown teddy bear." I hadn't even noticed the for-sale sign outside the house. I also have no idea who lived at number fifty-one before the new owners. The whole street has been complaining to the council for months about the potholes, according to Alfie, who heard it from Mr Buckley when he was in his front garden pressure washing his wheelie bin.

'You may live in the back of beyond, away from all the action, but I'll give you one thing, Juliette, you've got good neighbours.'

Neighbours I know nothing about.

He takes me to the rose garden. It's a small arrangement of muddy brown flower beds that I drive past almost every day, but have never actually visited. It's surprisingly peaceful, set back from the road with benches and some hedging to give it a more enclosed feel.

'I know it doesn't look like much at the moment,' Alfie says, as he leads me on a tour of the empty flower beds, 'but in the spring, this will be a riot of colour with tulips, hyacinths and irises. If you look closely, you can already see some of the shoots coming through.'

We bend down to inspect the earth and see the first green stirrings of spring daring to poke up above the frozen ground. At the centre of the gardens, where all the paths intersect, there's an impressive stone statue of someone called Florence Rose Bayliss. With her shirtsleeves rolled up to her elbows and a look of steely determination on her face, I've already decided she was either a prizefighter or a fish gutter, when Alfie puts me in the picture.

'Florence Rose Bayliss was the only child of a very wealthy industrialist. When she inherited her dad's fortune, she used it to build two schools, a swimming pool and the Royal Victoria Hospital.' The very one where Ivy's life began and ended. 'She gifted the whole lot to the people of Sholtsbury, along with a fund for their maintenance, and then built some fancy cottages for the workers at a local factory too. Quite the philanthropist was our Florence Rose.'

'How do you know so much about her?' I ask, looking at the statue with a new appreciation.

'I used to learn a lot about local history when I was digging graves. I remember there was one grave that belonged to Timothy Beckett. He designed all the public gardens in this town, including this one. He argued that people needed some green spaces they could use as their own, and he fought off a bunch of greedy property developers to ensure that Sholtsbury was greener than most.' Some things never change. 'Everyone in this town owes him a debt of gratitude. I reckon Timothy Beckett would be chuffed to bits if he knew that people were still enjoying those very gardens, to this day. And that earned him a few minutes of my time every week, just to keep his grave free from weeds. He would have wanted it kept neat and tidy.'

I glance sideways at Alfie. He's clearly enjoying giving me a guided tour of my own town, which I obviously know very little about. My knowledge extending to nothing more significant than the location of the cinema and the best place to get my curtains dry-cleaned.

'People these days seem to be in too much of a rush to notice what's around them. Graveyards are fascinating places to learn about your local history, if you take the time to look.'

We finish our walk at the bakery at the end of Raglan Road. I haven't been here since Jamie died and it changed ownership. The pasties that Denzel has set aside for us are hot and delicious, far superior to anything I can pick up in the supermarket. I take my time with the soft pastry and the rich meaty flavours inside, and when I thank Alfie, it comes from a genuine place. He seems happy that I've enjoyed my treat, happy to have done something for me. As soon as we get home again, he settles down for an afternoon nap in the chair he's adopted as his own.

For the first time since he moved in, I don't feel the urge to hide or leave the house. Instead, I (quietly) put all the food into the correct cupboards and do some washing. I water my ailing plants and politely ask them not to die this week. I even give them a fine misting of water just to show how much I care. Then I go upstairs to strip my bed. I'm not entirely sure when I did it last, and the sheets have started to take on a sewn-in-for-the-winter feel. I let myself into Alfie's room to put a clean towel on his bed. I don't know what I expected to find, but everything is neatly organised; bed made, curtains pulled back, window cracked open for ventilation. Alfie knows how to look after his environment. One of the photos I gave him, the one of Ivy standing outside Shimming's on her first day of work, is propped up next to the alarm clock on the bedside cabinet. The Christmas bauble that I sneaked into his suitcase now sits beside a collection of pill bottles. When Alfie finally gets his own place at Orton Lodge, he will have no difficulty making it feel like his own.

I take out my phone and calculate that the sheltered housing scheme is about twenty-five minutes away from Raglan Road, by car. I also find Abygail Evans-Hollister on social media again, type out a message explaining why I'm contacting her, and hit send before I change my mind. Alfie has a right to know if he has some family.

Alfie cooks vegetable curry for dinner, and we eat at the dining room table together. It's the first time it's been used for that purpose in more months than I can remember. The food is tasty. Alfie has a real flair for cooking. He spends most of the meal telling me about where he used to live in the centre of town.

'Fifteen years I lived in my old flat, knew everything about the building and the people. We had a magician, a plumber and his daughter, a lovely family who grew courgettes in their window boxes,' he says, spooning more curry and rice onto his plate. 'Although there wasn't a lot of the old crowd left by the time I moved in with Ivy. There was a friendly couple who lived on the floor above me, used to invite me round for a sherry and a mince pie, every Christmas morning. Then I took myself off to Ivy's for a turkey dinner with all the trimmings.' It's clear that he misses his home and his sister. 'And old Arthur Bassett, he was a character, played the trombone in a local brass band. He entertained us all during the first lockdown, with loads of lovely tunes, every night at seven o'clock on the dot. You could hear the clapping and cheering coming from every flat in the building. It brought the whole place together. And my old flat had its quirks,' he says, laughing, 'it was like a faithful old dog that liked having its belly rubbed and its ears scratched. And I miss it something rotten.'

The affection in his voice suddenly makes me teary-eyed, and I quickly have to pass it off as a reaction to the spices in the curry.

'But you've got a real cracker of a place here, Juliette,' he says, shaking himself out of his nostalgic mood. 'Have you been living in Raglan Road for long?'

I swallow a mouthful of curry. 'Almost two years. I haven't done much with it yet.'

'These things take time. You need to live with a house for a while to find out what you like about it, and what you don't want to change. You don't want to rush in and paint your room blue if it doesn't suit the lighting.'

There's not much danger of me rushing into anything. The real danger is that the house might stay this way forever. Even though the paint in the sitting room has always reminded me of regurgitated peas, how can I change it without moving on and leaving Jamie behind? What if ripping out the carpets removes Jamie too?

I go to bed early. Not because I want to get away from Alfie, this time, but because after spending a large portion of the day in someone else's company, I am worn to the bone. I have to get some clean sheets from one of my drawers before I can remake my bed, which involves moving several of the boxes that I've stacked against it. I push the bigger ones aside, grab one of the smaller boxes and instantly feel the bottom give way. Jamie's things tumble out all over the floor, things I haven't seen since I packed them away and shut them up in the spare room.

I run down to the kitchen for some tape and repair the box, trying to put everything back inside it without looking. But it's hopeless. My fingers are running over the smooth lettering on his favourite harmonica before I can stop them. He could never get a proper tune out of it. But it was what it represented to him that was important, it made him dream about sitting around a campfire, with nothing but the moon and stars for company. He was a cowboy out on the open plains when he played his harmonica. I hold it close to my body and then place it carefully back in the box. There's a pair of Wellington boots, still caked in mud from the last walk he ever took in them, through the woods on the outskirts of town. I flip open an address book and read all the random notes he wrote about the people he knew, right next to their contact information.

Gareth Shaughnessy, 75 Common Road, good bloke but don't lend him money when you're broke.
Poppy, 19 Park Street, don't forget her birthday again, she holds a wicked grudge!
Dave, 2 Mayflower Gardens, use for wedding photos, tell him not to do too

many close-ups of my dad, it makes him jumpy.

And then there's one word, written in blue pen along all the margins and across all the blank pages, *Juliette*. My name surrounded by hearts and fireworks.

I quickly gather the rest of his things: a fountain pen, books of easy guitar songs, a green neon lamp shaped like a cactus that always sat beside his bed at the flat. When I've sealed up the box, I push it into a far corner of the room where I can't see it. I don't even bother with the clean sheets. I climb straight into bed before the sadness that wants to swallow me whole can find me in the dark.

*

On Monday morning, I discover that Alfie likes to sing in the shower, loudly. I also discover numerous pairs of his underpants sitting in the laundry basket, waiting to be washed. And when I come home on Monday evening, I meet the same underpants again on a drying rack in the dining room. I am no stranger to underpants, but Alfie's are well-worn and saggy with a generous coverage across the seat. It's more than I want to know about him. Alfie's presence is beginning to spread through my laundry basket, kitchen and bathroom like a fungus.

I ring Jaya at the council, to see if there's any news on the sheltered housing front, but she hasn't had any updates. She warns me it could still take several months. I wonder if I should explain the underpants situation to her, if it would have any power to speed up the process. But I hesitate for too long, trying to find the right words first, and she ends the call before I can plead my case.

I also get a reply from Abygail Evans-Hollister. She tells me firmly that she isn't the person I'm looking for, that her dad was born and bred in Australia, and then she blocks me from seeing any of her social media accounts. In her shoes, I'd probably have the same reaction; suspect that the person who had contacted me out of the blue was trying to pull some kind of scam. And I'd warn all my friends (real and imaginary) not to engage with the crazy person. It leaves me with just one Abigail Evans on my list. But I have no desire to go through the whole messaging process again, so I shelve it for the time being.

If Poppy asks me how the search is going, I'll have to tell her that Alfie is occupying most of my time, which makes me sound like a much better host than I'm being. Since Saturday, I've spent most of my free time eating crisps in bed. Nowhere feels like a refuge after my encounter with the box of Jamie's stuff. My bed is the only safe island in a rough sea of troubles.

By Tuesday, Alfie is starting to feel like a full-time job. I have a list of prescriptions to pick up from his usual pharmacy, which is now too difficult for him to reach. There are blood pressure pills, cholesterol pills and a dubious-sounding cream called FungalSoothe. I try not to obsess over the very graphic images on the side of the box, because those fungus-ridden toes have made contact with my kitchen floor. I have to focus on my work instead.

I'm at a new flat in Albany Close, which belonged to a lady called Iris Chambers. She had a large collection of books and hundreds of old travel magazines. At some point in their history, the magazines have suffered a catastrophic coffee spill, and the pages – crinkled and glued together – are fit for nothing but the recycling centre. Iris had a fondness for nutty chocolate bars, judging by the number of empty wrappers I find stuffed down the side of her bed. But she also kept a photo of someone called Teresa under her pillow.

At the end of the afternoon, I'm just starting to load up my car with some of Iris's possessions, bound for a local charity shop, when I get a call from a woman at a supermarket. She asks if I know an Alfie Evans.

'Yes,' I say, hesitantly, wondering if he's been caught shoplifting, although that's not really Alfie's style. And I instantly feel guilty for even entertaining such an uncharitable thought.

'He asked me to phone you because he can't remember how to get home, the poor lamb,' the woman explains. 'He doesn't normally come to this supermarket, his usual one is on the Western Road, and he can't remember your address.'

I have a vision of him sitting forlornly in a lost property department with a tag around his neck – *If Found, Please Return to Raglan Road*. I drive to the supermarket and find Alfie in the coffee shop, enjoying a free pot of tea. He's chatting with a fellow shopper about the best washing powder to buy on a budget.

'Juliette!' He waves me over when he spots me. 'I couldn't

remember if you lived on Raglan Road or Rawlins Street. And when I asked the bus driver for help, he got all shirty and told me to get off his vehicle because he had a schedule to stick to, and I was causing a queue.' He suddenly looks embarrassed. 'I'm sorry you had to drive all the way over here. I would have found the right bus eventually, but what with all the extra walking about, my knees started acting up.'

All my irritation dissolves. Alfie is seventy-seven years old, and sometimes he needs a bit of help. When I'm seventy-seven, I might also need someone to come and collect me from a supermarket, and it would be nice if that person didn't give the impression that I was a burden. I pick up his bags of shopping and can't help noticing they contain all the ingredients for a fancy dinner, including a nice bottle of Spanish Rioja.

'I got all turned around,' Alfie explains when we hit the road, and join a long line of rush-hour traffic moving slowly through town. 'I thought I knew where I was going.'

'Alfie, it's okay, I don't mind coming to pick you up.'

He nods and stares off into the distance for a few minutes, uncharacteristically silent.

'You never think you're going to get old, but it just sort of creeps up on you when your back's turned, like a sneaky little bugger. And then one day, you can't manage the same stairs you've been climbing like a mountain goat for the last fifteen years. Or you fall asleep in the middle of your favourite TV programme, and wake up with your false teeth sitting on your chest.'

The image is one I will never be able to forget, no matter how many hours of therapy I can pay for.

'There's not a lot of dignity in aging. And then you forget where you're living, and have to be picked up like a small child from the school gates.'

'I'm sorry those things have happened to you,' I say, keeping my eyes on the road. 'But you also make an excellent chicken casserole.'

Alfie hoots with laughter. 'I can't be completely over the hill yet then. And just you wait until you taste my beef bourguignon. You're in for a real treat, Juliette.'

Alfie settles into a more contented silence, smiling quietly to himself.

By Friday, my noble feelings towards Alfie have all but evaporated.

In his first call of the day, he wants to know how to put the washing machine on for an extra spin, because his socks still feel wet and he doesn't want them dripping all over my dining room floor. His second call, thirty-eight minutes later, is to ask if I've got any sticky tape, and where he can find it. By the third call, I'm beginning to lose my patience and answer curtly, with the minimum of words. He asks where the sticky tape is again because he got distracted by something on the TV, and has already forgotten what I told him the first time.

When the phone goes for a fourth time, I don't even bother checking the screen. I can feel by the automatic elevation in my pulse rate that it's Alfie.

'What is it now, Alfie?'

'Sorry to bother you again, Juliette, but I forgot to tell you earlier, I accidentally put one of your white T-shirts in with my washing.' Meaning it has touched his underpants, they have shared the same water, done the dance of the dirty laundry. 'And some of the colour has come out of my socks and turned it a bit blue, I'm afraid.'

I count to fifteen but irritation still surges through me. 'Which white T-shirt exactly?'

'It's got a little emblem on the front. It looks like a black sheep wearing a woolly hat.'

'How blue is it?'

'You know those blueberries you bought at the weekend, it's a bit bluer than that.'

I hang up on him before I say something that I ought to regret, but may not be kind enough to feel bad about afterwards. That particular white T-shirt, the one with the black sheep on the front, has been my favourite since Jamie bought it for me, on a trip to Northumberland. It's handmade, one-of-a-kind, totally irreplaceable. And now it's the colour of fruit. I set my phone to aeroplane mode. If Alfie has a supermarket emergency in the next few hours, somebody else will have to attend. I will not be held responsible for any actions I may take against him, with a bag of carrots, if I'm summoned to pick him up from the vegetable aisle.

My anger is still maturing nicely by the time I get home. I frown at my formerly white T-shirt as I pass it on the drying rack, just inside the sitting room door. All of Alfie's clothes have miraculously repelled the blue dye from his troublesome socks. My T-shirt is the only casualty. The smell of beef bourguignon hits me before I've even hung up my coat, and it draws me towards the dining room. Alfie has already laid the table with real napkins and my best non-paper plates. The light from two candles throws a mellow glow over a pot in the centre of the table, the source of the incredible smell.

'You shouldn't have gone to all this trouble,' I say, dropping my bag at my feet, as he emerges from the kitchen holding two glasses of wine. He's wearing smart black trousers with a salmon-pink shirt. 'I'm sorry I was so rude on the phone. But that T-shirt was very special, I've had it for years and—'

The doorbell rings.

'Hold that thought, Juliette,' Alfie says.

He puts the glasses of wine on the table and hurries past me into the hall, without making eye contact. A few seconds later I hear voices, and Alfie returns to the dining room with Mrs Lafleur. She's dressed in a floor-length black dress, with a shawl to keep her shoulders warm, a hint of sparkle in her eyeshadow. And that's when the penny finally drops. The beef bourguignon isn't for me. This is not Alfie's way of apologising for ruining my shirt. He's got a date with my next-door neighbour, Mrs Lafleur.

'Juliette, it's lovely to see you, dear.' Mrs Lafleur grasps my hand in both of hers, and covers her confusion at my presence with a warm smile. 'Alfie said you were going to be out until late this evening, something about going house-hunting with a friend who needed the company?'

I'd totally forgotten about my fictitious plans with Vanessa, mumbled hastily under my breath as I left the kitchen that morning. I had been intending to spend an hour or two with a podcast and some fries, in a quiet car park somewhere. But Alfie's phone calls had pushed all thoughts of it out of my head, and I'd come straight home by accident.

'My friend had to cancel at the last minute, family emergency,' I say, not looking Mrs Lafleur in the eye.

'Well, we can take our dinner next door to my house, so we don't disturb you, dear.'

She's already reaching for the oven gloves that Alfie has left on top of the pot on the table.

'No, Mrs Lafleur, please stay here and enjoy your meal.'

Alfie smiles nervously at me from the doorway.

'I was going to have an early night anyway.'

I hurry into the kitchen where the smell of beef bourguignon is even more delicious. I grab a packet of biscuits from the cupboard, scoop up my bag with my free hand and close the door behind me as I leave them to it. Unfortunately, I can still hear the muffled sounds of their conversation coming up through the floor in my bedroom. Mrs Lafleur seems to be finding Alfie hilariously funny, and it's impossible not to catch the odd word, even though I'm doing my best not to listen. My name crops up more than once, followed by a low rumble of words that are trying not to be heard. I can't tell if the words come from Alfie, Mrs Lafleur or both.

I have to hand it to Alfie, he's a fast worker. Seven days after moving into my home and he's already romancing one of my neighbours. At the age of seventy-seven, he hasn't given up on the hope of companionship, or possibly even love. I can't say the same thing for myself. At the age of forty-five, I'm still too attached to my dead fiancé to consider any other love. My life slammed to an abrupt halt when Jamie left this world and took most of me with him.

The sounds of companionable conversation coming from the dining room are suddenly too much to bear. I don't want to hear another second of their date. I change quickly into my most comfy sweatpants and a jumper, creep quietly downstairs and let myself out the front door.

Thirteen

I DRIVE TO THE nearest shop for a packet of cheese crackers, and then return to my parking spot outside the house to wait. I'm determined not to leave my seat until I've had a conversation with Jamie. And today, he does not keep me waiting. He's sitting beside me before I can even start to settle myself down. He smiles, and I feel my whole body let go of the tension I've been carrying around for days.

'I needed to see you,' I tell him, wishing more than ever that I could reach out and touch the warm skin on his hand, not the empty space where his hand should be.

He gently brushes my cheek with the tips of his fingers, and I try to convince myself I can actually feel it. He's wearing a very old and scruffy pair of jeans with a plain black T-shirt. His feet are bare, for some reason, but I'm relieved that they look nothing like Alfie's. They are strong and familiar, slightly hairy-toed. I can see the crooked little toe that he broke on the day we moved into our house, when he tripped and fell down the last three stairs in the hallway. His eyes seem to have changed colour, from their normal warm hazelnut brown to a deep and all-seeing green, which makes him look like a character from a sci-fi movie. I try to ignore the tiny ruby that is stuck to one of his front teeth, although it's hard not to launch into a series of pirate comparisons. Pirate seems to be his most common theme just lately. I'm thankful there's no parrot sitting on his shoulder.

'So, Alfie Evans has a date,' he says, raising his eyebrows at me. 'I bet you didn't see that one coming.'

'I should have, he's been engaged thirteen times.'

'Thirteen?' Jamie whistles, impressed by Alfie's tally.

'I should probably warn Mrs Lafleur,' I say.

'She can take care of herself. Besides, warn her about what? Alfie's a decent old man just looking for a bit of company.'

I know he's right, but I also feel a bit defensive because I have a sense of what's coming next.

'So, are there any fellas out there catching your eye?'

'How can you even ask me that?' I'm instantly incandescent. I can hear angry blood pounding through my ears at the injustice of his question. 'How could I ever look at anyone else, or think about anyone else?'

'Because I'm nothing but dust, Juliette.'

And there it is. The truth that I refuse to face.

'I mean, I enjoy these talks as much as you do. But you can't spend the rest of your life in this car chatting with a ghost, or whatever it is I am.'

'Right now, you look like a pirate,' I tell him, and he grins, toothily. The ear pounding starts to subside, but I'm still feeling on guard.

'Well shiver me timbers, I would have made a great pirate,' Jamie says. 'A life on the high seas, swigging grog before nine o'clock in the morning, shouting *ahoy* at every passing seagull, I can picture it all.'

He's trying to make me laugh, to ease me out of the mood I'm in, but I refuse to feel any better. He's got no idea how this feels. He never had to deal with being the one who was left behind, still carrying all our hopes and dreams. I carry our unfinished business around with me everywhere I go. How could I just let it all seep away, when everything we did together was based on the assumption of a long and happy future?

'I know it's been hard, love,' he softens, trying to take my hand. 'I know you didn't ask for any of this, and you didn't get to say goodbye, that was harsh. But I'm not coming back.'

'What? No, I'm not ready. I need to talk to you!' I'm panicking now in case this is the last time I'll ever see his stupid face.

'No, I didn't mean that, I'll be back for more of our chats,' he reassures me quickly. But the tears have already come, and it takes me several minutes to get myself under control again.

'I'm sorry I'm not doing better without you,' I say, sniffing, wiping my nose on my hand. I should have tissues stuffed into every single one of my pockets. I'm getting tired of wiping my nose on my own sleeves and hands, like an eight-year-old.

'You've got nothing to be sorry for. If the tables were turned, I'd have eaten myself into some extremely large pants by now. Poppy would have to threaten me with an evening at one of her yoga classes, just to get me to take a bath, once a month. My hair would be down to my navel and as greasy as a chip-shop counter from the 1970s. You've got nothing to be sorry for,' he repeats earnestly, 'but none of what you're doing can ever bring me back.'

'You don't know that,' I say, sounding like a sullen child.

'I'm pretty sure there's no lightning-bolt resurrection miracle in my future. And I'm worried that you've stopped living your life.'

'It's not much of a life without you. Anyway, I don't know how to start living it again without losing you completely. I don't want to lose you.'

All my cards are finally on the table, if he didn't understand before, there's nothing left to hide now.

'Is that why you've been mooning over my old trainers, like they're some special archaeological relic?'

I can't help smiling. 'When I see your old trainers, I remember all the times you wore them, when we went out shopping for geraniums, or walking on the beach. Or that evening we went to listen to your friend's poetry reading, at the church hall in town.'

'Worst poetry I've ever heard in my life,' Jamie says, shaking his head, but his smile is broad and genuine.

'It was so terrible you had to stuff your sweatshirt into your mouth to stop yourself from having hysterics.'

Jamie nods, remembering. 'It was when he started reading that ode to his bellybutton fluff that I really lost it.'

'And I had to kick you in the shins because people were staring.'

I don't tell him I have a copy of "Ode to My Bellybutton Fluff" on my phone, so I can read it whenever I want to remember that night.

'Nothing can remove those memories, Juliette, love. But you don't need to hug my stinky old trainers to keep me close. And as for getting on with your life, I'm not expecting you to sign yourself up for a tango class at the community centre, or go on a singles-only cruise to the Caribbean. Just let yourself live a little, be in the world. It's a better place when you're in it.'

'That's so corny,' I say, frowning. 'You never used to say things like that when you were alive.'

'Death changes you.' He's smiling again. 'I've become very wise, here on the other side, and you have to listen to everything I say and follow my excellent advice.'

'Or you'll do what?'

'I'll turn up here next time speaking nothing but Spanish.'

'It'll make a nice change from all the gibberish you usually talk.'

My joke raises nothing but an exasperated sigh from Jamie.

'I'll get my hair cut into a mullet then, and take to wearing orthotic shoes.'

Just the thought of Jamie in orthotics...

'Your first task is to toss out those ratty old trainers that you've grown so fond of, and then you should think about getting a new carpet for the sitting room.'

'But we were going to do that together, get some samples, paint the walls and find a new sofa.'

'You've got to start doing some of those things by yourself now.'

'I can't. You know how hopeless I am at making decisions. I can't do it without you.' It's a lame excuse, and not exactly true, but I'll grasp at anything to stop this conversation from moving any further in a direction I don't want it to go. 'Do you remember that time we went to buy a new kitchen floor, and it took me two hours to pick between a black and white checkerboard lino, and those laminated boards? You went to buy a sandwich and a birthday present for your mum because I was taking so long. And when you came back, I was standing in exactly the same position as the one you left me in.'

But Jamie is gone. He never normally leaves while I'm in the middle of reminiscing. He loves those memories too, but not enough to stay with me today. I sit in the car for another forty-five minutes, summoning up all the will I have to leave him behind. Alfie and Mrs Lafleur are still chatting away in the dining room, when I go back inside. The door is closed. I tread silently up the stairs and shut myself in my room. I try to picture myself throwing Jamie's trainers in the bin, but it seems like an impossible action to take. It's easy for him to say it's time to move on, but move onto what? Every moment I spent with Jamie – even the ones where we were arguing about who to invite to the wedding – were a hundred times better than all the moments

I've had since he died. And throwing away his trainers won't change that.

I meet Alfie the next morning in the dining room, which has been cleared of all evidence of his date with Mrs Lafleur. He's halfway through a round of toast, an array of jams and spreads placed on the table before him.

'How was your evening with Mrs Lafleur?' I ask, trying to hit a breezy tone.

'We had a very pleasant time, thank you.' There's a faint blush to his skin as he says it, and a miniscule hint of smugness, but he's also fidgeting awkwardly. 'I'm sorry about kicking you out of your own kitchen last night. I thought you were going to be out all evening.'

'Don't worry about it, Alfie. I'm just glad you and Mrs Lafleur are getting along so well.'

'She's an interesting woman, knows all sorts of things about the world. Did you know she lived in Japan for a few years?'

The only things I actually know about Mrs Lafleur are that she lives next door to me and she owns a casserole dish.

'Anyway, she's making me dinner next, on Sunday evening, so you'll have the place to yourself for once.' He shifts uneasily again. 'She, um, told me about your fiancé last night too.'

That stops me dead. I can't turn away from him or run for cover, I am a fly caught in sticky amber about to be suffocated. My face has already frozen in an awkward expression. It feels like a cross between a grimace and a plea for mercy.

'I had no idea, I'm really sorry. If I've said anything or done anything to upset you...'

'You haven't,' I hear myself saying.

'It sounds like he was a smashing fella, your Jamie. I'm sorry he's no longer with us.'

I mumble something incomprehensible under my breath and turn around, leaving Alfie with his toast. I'm not ready to have any conversation with him about Jamie. He'll say all the things that have already been said, by my own family and friends, time and time again. And I don't want to hear any of it, not here in my house.

Whatever plans Alfie has for this day, I don't want to be a part of them either. No cosy walks to the rose garden, where the intimacy of talking can open the door for questions about Jamie. I don't know what Mrs Lafleur has told Alfie about Jamie and me, but I don't want to hear my own tragic story told back to me. As soon as I'm dressed, I grab my coat and stuff my scarf, hat, gloves and laptop into a bag. I head for my car before Alfie can emerge from the dining room.

I drive into town and park right in the centre. I love the bustle of Sholtsbury on a Saturday and the power it has to distract me from my own thoughts. I wander aimlessly for some time, barely noticing the shops I drift through, or what they're selling. It's the buzz of sound, the collection of murmuring voices that soothes me. It carries me up escalators and through chains of shops, the maze of racks and shelves burying me deeper the further I venture inside. The back of any shop, where most people don't linger for long, is surprisingly comforting. I welcome the claustrophobia, the feeling of being a long way from any exit or entrance. I want to feel buried by the clutter of scatter cushions and vases full of fake flowers. I'm a budgie under a cage cover, and that's exactly what I need.

Eventually, I let my feet take me out of the central shopping area and follow a familiar route to Jamie's shop, a reliable source of good memories. But when I reach the shop, the door is firmly locked, even though it was supposed to open over two hours ago. I cup my hands over my eyes and peer through the windows, but there are no lights on inside, no signs of life. For a Saturday, this is unheard of. It's the best day of the week for sales and for customers who want to sample bookshop coffee and homemade cakes.

I linger for twenty minutes marching up and down the pavement, trying to keep my feet warm. But nobody turns up with a set of jangling keys and apologies, or stories of emergency trips to the vet with a sick dog. And I finally retreat to Rosemary's Cafe, on the opposite side of the road, from where I can still see the bookshop. I've never been locked out of Jamie's shop before. I don't know how to relieve the pressure that's building behind the wall in my chest. The man behind the counter in the cafe doesn't know why the bookshop is closed either. So I buy a cheese and chutney sandwich, a latte and a slice of rhubarb cake, and settle myself at a table in the window for what could be a long vigil.

I'm on my second latte when I decide to do a bit of searching for Abigail Evans. Poppy has turned up nothing, and I need something else to think about. The last Abigail Evans on my list is difficult to track down, with a very sketchy social media presence. All she's posted on any of her pages is a few photos of sunsets and flowers in her garden. I try a wider internet search instead, but it appears she's never been in any local papers for growing prize-winning marrows, or complaining about a new highway being built next to her house. She's never won any kind of award. She doesn't belong to any clubs or societies that post photos of their annual fundraising fairs or fancy-dress balls on their websites. I try a couple of family history sites but I can't get very far without setting up a membership, and I am definitely not in a membership kind of mood today. And I come to a sudden halt.

Maybe Ivy had the right idea by contacting an agency to do the searching for her? I'm not sure I want to go down that route either, what if Abigail Evans doesn't want to be found? I decide to carry out another search for Joseph Evans, just to pass the time. The only other occasion I tried to find Alfie's dad was at the very beginning of my quest, with no success. But this time, I use a different search engine, and I'm a little surprised when the results come thick and fast.

I can discount most of the people straight away. The one Joseph Evans that I'm left with appears in many of the photos on a particular website, for The Friends of Galton Hall. And it couldn't be anyone but Alfie's dad. I enlarge one of the grainy images and stare at Joseph Evans, shocked by his sudden appearance on the screen of my laptop. He's a lot older than he was in the only other photos I've seen of him, but Alfie has clearly inherited his dad's thick hair and broad nose, even their expressions are similar. I wonder what Alfie would make of the likeness. According to the website, Joseph Evans was one of the benefactors who helped fund a total restoration of Galton Hall (between 1959 and 1970), which was an historic community building not far from Karratha. He was a much wealthier man in Australia, apparently, than he'd ever been in England. He died in 2002.

I scroll through the gallery of photos on the website and one of them in particular catches my eye. Joseph Evans attended a Christmas dinner-dance at Galton Hall in 1968, and standing close beside him, wearing a pretty yellow dress, is a young Abigail Evans. The photo is dark and blurry but Joseph Evans is leaning down, saying something to his daughter. Abigail's smiling, holding onto his hand. They are the family that Alfie knows nothing about. I hope Joseph Evans didn't abandon them too. And I suddenly feel angry on Alfie's behalf, but I can't let it colour my view of Abigail. None of this is her fault. And if she and Alfie meet and find they have some common ground...

I send an email directly to The Friends of Galton Hall, explaining that I am an acquaintance of the Evans family. I tell them I'm trying to trace Abigail with some news, if they could pass my details onto her. That way, it's Abigail's decision if she wants to contact me or not. I send a quick message to Poppy, filling her in on my progress. She replies instantly with a thumbs-up emoji and the promise to talk soon. She and Zarina are currently out shopping for a new mattress. This is a very serious business, according to Poppy, that has so far caused two minor disagreements and one more heated discussion – requiring the healing balm of an expensive lunch at Zarina's favourite bistro to smooth things over. I glance around the tables in Rosemary's Cafe. I'm not sure about any healing balm, but the rhubarb cake isn't bad. I don't recall Jamie ever coming here when he owned the bookshop, but he had a regular lunch order delivered from Olivetti's – pastrami and avocado on wholemeal bread (no seeds). So Rosemary's Cafe never really had a chance of being noticed.

I peer across the road for any signs of activity, but the bookshop is still dark and lifeless. And the maximum time allowance on my parking space is about to expire. I pack my laptop away and trudge back to the centre of town, coat collar turned up against the bitter easterly wind, casting a disappointed glance at the bookshop as I pass it. I don't like it with the lights off, the shop looks dead, beyond resuscitation.

When I return home, I find a note from Alfie. He's gone to visit some old friends at their retirement home and won't be back until this evening. I wonder if he's gone out deliberately to give me a bit of time alone in my own home. Whatever his reasons, I'm grateful for the solitude. I take a cup of tea into the sitting room, remove Alfie's socks from the sofa, and put my feet up on the footstool. It's been several days since I've even entered this part of the house, and it looks different to me today, almost like I'm seeing it for the first time. The late afternoon sun highlights the cracks in the coving, and the yellowing paintwork that was once white. Jamie and I had planned to redecorate the entire room, starting from the top down, or the bottom up, depending on the state of the floorboards under the horrible nylon carpet. The carpet that gave me friction burns the first time I ever crawled across it to retrieve a discarded slipper. Jamie wanted to paint the room a dusky blue-green colour to make it cosy. He also had big plans to strip and polish the floorboards and restore the fireplace to its former glory. My ideas for a wood burner were shelved when we discovered the cost. But I suddenly remember that my vision for the room involved a soft wool carpet (no more friction burns), and walls painted in neutral shades to allow for colourful paintings and pictures. Neither of us could stomach the idea of beige or grey. But what do I want now?

Jamie was always steadfast in his choices, sure of his own taste in everything. The best band in the world was The Eighteen. The best restaurant meal to order on any birthday or anniversary was rib-eye steak with proper thick-cut chips. The right time of year to visit Cornwall was in January, when we could wander through the narrow, deserted streets at our leisure, or stand on the beach and lean into a howling gale, like a couple of crazy people. But if I had to decorate this room right now, if I had to choose, I'd want it to feel like a warm hug of a room, with natural elements like wood. Isn't this what Jamie wants me to do? Move on, live life, imagine a future without him?

I take my tea and hurry out of the room like there's an angry rhinoceros charging after me. Too many things have been unsettling today: Alfie talking about Jamie, the bookshop being closed. I cannot cope with redecorating the sitting room as well, even if it's only an imagined makeover. I'm not willing to trade the faded, ugly wallpaper and my memories for the pleasure of freshly painted walls. This whole day has been unnerving and I want it to end.

*

By Sunday evening, I've managed to go a whole thirty-six hours without seeing Alfie. At 7 p.m., he leaves the house to have dinner with Mrs Lafleur. The smell of his aftershave slowly seeps under my bedroom door as he passes, alerting me to his departure.

I make myself some proper dinner, vegetable stir-fry and noodles, and sit to eat at the dining room table. Unfortunately, Mrs Lafleur's dining room is on the opposite side of the wall, and I soon become aware of the muted sounds of their second date. This time, there's the quiet beat of some music, and my imagination quickly fills in the blanks: candlelight, easy conversation, a tiny frisson of romance, Mrs Lafleur serving up stew and dumplings as they share the details of their days. Hot tears are suddenly rolling down my face and into my noodles, adding unnecessary salt to the soy sauce. I feel more alone than on any weekend where I've spent the entire two days in my own company, speaking to no one. I take my plate into the kitchen and finish my dinner with my back pressed to the outside wall, where I can hear nothing but my own sniffing.

Monday morning can't come soon enough. I have a new house clearance job to start at Willow Tree Flats, in the centre of town. I'm grateful for the familiar routines it brings. I'm tired of thinking about my own difficulties. It's exhausting. The flat that I've been sent to clear occupies the whole top floor of the building, and it's filled from floor to ceiling rafters with things that belonged to Jim Ravenshaw. I dive straight into the sitting room with a roll of bin bags. Judging by the black viscous grime that covers every surface, this room hasn't felt the touch of a duster, or been disturbed by a vacuum cleaner, for over a decade.

Halfway through the morning, I get a call from Loretta informing me of the date of Ivy Edward's funeral. I'll have to pass the news onto Alfie, nobody else knows he exists. At lunchtime, I also get an email from The Friends of Galton Hall telling me that they no longer have any contact details for Abigail Evans, as she moved to England some years ago. I stare at the email, making sure I've read it correctly. If Alfie's half-sister is living in this country, it would explain why I've struggled to find any trace of her life in Australia.

'I wonder if she even knows that Alfie exists,' Poppy says, when I meet her after work, in the Toad and Fiddle.

We're sitting in a quiet corner of the bar, working our way through heaped plates of fish and chips, and I'm more than happy to spend time with someone other than Alfie. The only downside is that Zarina has joined us for a change, meaning all reminiscing about Jamie is off the table. The disappointment sits heavily in my stomach, along with the chips, making me feel queasy.

Zarina loved Jamie too. They used to engage in regular bouts of friendly sparring over their totally opposite views on life, in almost every area conceivable. It never descended into any kind of argument.

They just enjoyed challenging each other. But I don't feel comfortable letting Zarina catch even a glimpse of just how Jamie-centric my thoughts are. I'm also a little intimidated by how attractive she is. Poppy is appealing in the same way that a fairy at the bottom of your garden might capture your imagination and fire your delight; she's slight, wispy and eccentric looking. But Zarina has a fierce kind of beauty that blazes through her brown eyes, and seems to illuminate her entire being. Sometimes, it's hard to look directly at her.

I pull my bobbly old cardigan around my body, covering up the stains on the shirt I've been wearing for work. If Zarina could see the true state of my fingernails, she'd probably faint.

'So, what's your next step, you two?' Zarina asks, skewering a chip and pointing it at me. 'Are you going to have another go at finding Abigail Evans, now you know she's an English country gal?'

'I think Juliette should do it,' Poppy says.

'But you're better with people,' I argue.

It was much easier to handle the idea of Abigail Evans when she was a vague concept, on the other side of the world, with the buffer of social media to prevent any real contact. But now that I'm faced with the real possibility of having to talk to her on the phone, I'm not so keen.

'No one's arguing with the fact that I'm better with people,' Poppy says.

Zarina and Poppy both stare at me knowingly, like they've had many private discussions about the state of my mental health, and everything I'm now saying just confirms their assessment.

'But you're the one who discovered that Abigail Evans existed in the first place,' Poppy says.

'And you're currently living with her brother,' Zarina adds, finishing her own chips and leaning over Poppy's plate to help herself to some more. 'If she doesn't know anything about Alfie, she's in for a hell of a shock.'

'Or she could have been trying to track him down for years.'

Zarina nods. 'Maybe poor old Abigail's got a big family tree pinned to the wall of her home office.'

'And she sits and stares at the name of her only brother, every night, and cries herself to sleep because she doesn't know where he is,' Poppy says, pretending to wipe tears from her eyes.

'Can you two stop doing your double act thing, please?' I say, rolling my eyes. I know they're just joking around, but I'm really not in the mood.

'Sorry,' Zarina gives me a sheepish smile. And just to prove she means it she helps herself to some of my chips as well. 'But how many people in this world have the power to reunite a family that was broken more than half a century ago? She might be able to offer Alfie a home, or some nieces and nephews. He'll have someone to visit at Christmas, and people to throw him a surprise eightieth birthday party.'

'Okay, okay, I'll try and find her,' I say, finally giving in, 'but if she turns out to be dead, or wants nothing to do with Alfie, I'm coming straight round to your house, so I can sit on the sofa and complain about it for hours.'

Poppy smiles and gives my knee a friendly squeeze. 'So, how is life with Alfie?'

'He's had two dates with my next-door neighbour.'

'Not Mrs Lafleur?' Zarina asks, with a chip suspended on her fork, midair.

I stare at them both, stunned, wondering if everyone in the entire town knows more about my own neighbours than I do. 'How do you know her name?'

'She's that sweet old lady who used to be a GP,' Zarina says, matter-of-factly.

'If you two are about to tell me you've been round to her house for tea...'

'She came out to ask us if you were okay once,' Poppy explains, 'not long after Jamie. We'd been round to see you and she wanted to know if there was anything she could do. She was kind, nice.'

Zarina nods. 'I liked her. Alfie could do a lot worse. And at his age, having someone who knows her way around a stethoscope, well, it's got to be an attractive prospect. It must be a bit like meeting someone in your twenties and discovering they've got a family holiday home in the Mediterranean.'

'I think we should meet Alfie,' Poppy says. 'We've heard so much about him, I feel like I practically know him.'

'You could invite Mrs Lafleur round for dinner and we could all make an evening of it,' Zarina says, really getting into the idea.

'I don't want to make an evening of it.'

'We could bring the food if you don't want to cook,' Poppy offers. 'I want to hear all about Alfie's grave-digging days.'

'I want to know if he's serious about Mrs Lafleur,' Zarina says. 'It might give me some hope if Poppy ever dumps me, and I find myself back on the market again when I'm seventy-seven.'

'Nobody is bringing any food,' I say more loudly than I mean to, scaring the people sitting at the table closest to us. 'I am not having a dinner party,' I add, lowering my voice a fraction. 'You're not meeting Alfie, and I'm never coming to this pub with you two, ever again.'

'So, that's a no then?' Poppy can tell she's pushed me too far and the teasing stops. She shovels half a dozen of her own chips onto my plate as a peace offering, which I graciously accept.

Zarina starts telling us a tale about two of her co-workers who were caught in a cupboard at work, doing a very unconventional stocktake. I let the conversation drift over me until my appetite returns and I finish my fish. Once upon a time, long ago, the idea of having Poppy, Zarina, Mrs Lafleur and Alfie round for dinner would have been fun. But that three-letter word has been absent from my life for such a long time now, that I no longer have any concept of what it means. I have no idea if I'll ever have any fun again.

'Let me know if you find out anything about Abigail Evans,' Poppy says, when we're saying our goodbyes in the car park, an hour later.

'She probably moved back to Australia years ago,' I say.

'Or she might be living twenty miles down the road. Come round for dinner next week?'

I smile in a noncommittal fashion. I'm not sure I can take another round of them ganging up on me, or trying to force dinner parties on me that I don't want to throw. It's an exhausting job, keeping them both at arm's-length. But I'm also grateful for their lively company. Since Alfie moved into my house, I've hardly spent any time with anyone else, including my imaginary friends.

Juliette and Jamie
IV
Mrs Juliette Matthews

'JULIETTE, LOVE, ARE YOU awake yet?'

Jamie brushed a stray hair off my face and kissed me softly on my forehead.

'Go-way, I'm s-leep.'

'Juliette.' Jamie jiggled my elbow gently, trying to bring me back to the surface.

But I'd been having such a lovely dream about the wedding and I didn't want it to end. We'd decided to move the ceremony from the local town hall to a meadow in the middle of nowhere. It was filled with wild daisies, buttercups, cornflowers and the gentle humming of fat summer bees. Half a dozen tables had also been arranged under some shady oak trees, ready for a feast afterwards, with white tablecloths billowing dreamily in a warm breeze. I wanted to skip barefoot through the meadow because all the wedding guests had just decided to roll down a steep slope at the far end of the field, and I didn't want to miss out on the fun. And that's when Jamie had tried to wake me up.

'Juliette, do you know where my keys are? It's nearly seven thirty and I've got to go to work.'

Jamie always left earlier than me to deal with his morning commute through busy traffic. He never put his keys down in the same place twice, and was incapable of finding them without help. Sometimes, however, I had a suspicion he knew exactly where his keys were and he just enjoyed watching my struggle for consciousness in the mornings.

'Juliette,' he whispered close to my ear this time. I tried to push his stubbly chin away from my skin, but he nibbled my neck softly, refusing to let me fall back into my dream. 'I've made coffee and toast, if you tell me where my keys are, you can have breakfast in bed.'

He wafted a mug of coffee under my nose. I opened one eye.

'Your keys are in the fruit bowl on the dining room table.'

Jamie smiled and kissed me on the lips this time. 'Is there anything I'm supposed to do for the wedding today?' he asked, as I turned over onto my back, rubbing sleep out of my eyes.

'You said you were going to pick up those cactus-shaped place names from the printers, the one next to the guitar shop on the other side of town.'

The place names for the reception were Jamie's idea. I would have been happy with a classic design on a plain ivory card, but I didn't want to spoil his fun.

'I'll do it before lunch. My mate, Doug, is coming into the shop this morning. He won't mind looking after the place for an hour. See you for a sandwich at Olivetti's, at midday?'

I nodded, trying to fight the urge to close my eyes again.

'You can tell me all about this new place you're clearing out.' Jamie propped an extra pillow behind my head, so I could drink the coffee he'd brought up on a tray.

'Don't forget to tell your mum that we can't come over for lunch this weekend, after all,' I said, as the long list of Things to do Before the Wedding slowly began to drift into my consciousness, nagging to be done.

'She'll be as angry as a goat with its head stuck in a bucket. You know how much she likes showing off my good looks and natural charm to all the neighbours.'

'And don't forget I'm going to the florist's after work. She needs to know if we've decided on the white roses for the table decorations, or the mixed woodland display. So I won't be home until later.'

'You can remind me yourself at lunchtime,' Jamie said, tucking my hair behind my ears and kissing me on the top of my head.

He took a sip of my coffee, stole a slice of toast and closed the bedroom door on his way out. I listened to him going down the stairs.

I could always tell what kind of a mood he was in by the way he tackled the descent. He often took them at a gallop, keen to get out on his motorbike if it was a sunny morning. Other times, he jumped the last four steps, like a kid showing off to his friends. But today, he was slow and steady, due to the toast.

I got up ten minutes later, cursing Jamie as I tripped over the trainers that he'd left directly in my path to the door. I'd asked him hundreds of times to leave them somewhere else because for some irritating reason – that defied all the laws of reason and justice – he never tripped over his own shoes. Or mine. Even when I deliberately kicked them off on his side of the bed, he still managed to pick his way through the leather-booted minefield, denying me the sweet nectar of a point well made.

I got ready for work in a vaguely grumpy mood, reminding myself that we'd only been living together properly for four months, that these were the kind of kinks that would work themselves out over time. And there were probably things I did that drove Jamie nuts too, although infuriatingly, he hadn't mentioned any of them. I had nagged him repeatedly about the trail of orphaned clothes he left all over the house, as if they had no home to go to. His habit of leaving oily bits of motorbike strewn across the dining room table and the tired old kitchen counters, which had now developed the patina of a mechanic's workbench. I'd also made my thoughts clear on his habit of grabbing my clean underwear, from the drying rack, and using it to wipe up any accidental spillages in the kitchen. I was already way ahead of him in the nagging stakes. But it was hard to stay mad at Jamie for long. He'd rub my feet, or clean the kitchen, or buy me a cake from my favourite bakery, and my irritation would melt like the chocolate icing on my tongue.

There was no chance of me ever living in a clean and orderly house now that I was living with Jamie, I realised, making my way past a heap of his discarded clothes on the stairs. But there was also every possibility that after a year or two of this kind of happiness, I might not care. Living with Jamie in our own home had been like the best kind of camping holiday. We toasted marshmallows over the hot coals in the fireplace, made dens in the sitting room with blankets and chairs – so we could stay warm when the heating broke down, and ice formed on the inside of the windows. It had been the best few months of my life, and in six weeks' time, we'd be married. I couldn't wait to find out what would happen next.

I was working that morning at a house not far from the bookshop. Jamie had persuaded me to meet him at Olivetti's for lunch. It was one of our regular haunts because of the happy tomato-red plastic chairs, and the sheer size of the portions. One sandwich from Olivetti's contained enough calories to keep anyone going for the rest of the day. Jamie had already sent me several texts, trying to decide between two of his favourite choices. The meatloaf sandwich was a foot long and could be nibbled for several days afterwards. And the Mexican burrito was so spicy it required a gallon of milk as a chaser, but the doughy softness of the tortilla made the ensuing heartburn worth it. When my phone rang at 11.02 a.m., I was expecting it to be him.

'I tripped over your shoes again this morning,' I said, trying to sound stern. 'You owe me another "sorry" cake from The Three Cups bakery.'

There was an uncharacteristic pause.

'Excuse me, but am I speaking to Juliette?' The voice was unfamiliar, uncertain.

The tips of my ears burned with embarrassment. 'Sorry. I thought you were someone else. This is Juliette, how can I help you?'

'My name is Doctor Berry, I work at the Royal Victoria General hospital, and I'm afraid I'm phoning with some difficult news.'

I don't know how anyone is supposed to react to those words, but my first instinct was to think that any difficult news must be destined for someone else. There was nothing about my day that could be tainted by the words of a doctor.

'I'm sorry to tell you that Jamie Matthews was involved in an accident earlier this morning,' the doctor said. 'He was brought to the Accident and Emergency Department here at the hospital, and he's in a very serious condition. We found your contact details on his phone, under Wife.'

I'd had several discussions with Jamie about his habit of referring to me as his wife, before the day of our wedding. I'd said he was tempting fate, asking for trouble, inviting all the gods of mischief and mishap to rain their chaos down upon us. We'd be cancelling the ceremony due to freak snowstorms in August. A national shortage of wedding cakes would force us to celebrate our union with a budget swiss roll from the supermarket. A direct hit from a lightning bolt on the shop that was altering my dress, two days before the wedding, would see me walking down the aisle in an ill-fitting, off-the-peg monstrosity. But in none of those discussions had a doctor from the Accident and Emergency Department ever appeared.

I have no memory of how I drove to the hospital. Poppy was climbing out of her own car as I arrived. Apparently, I'd phoned her with the news. We stumbled into Accident and Emergency together, clinging to an unspoken hope that this could still be a terrible mistake. Jamie's phone might have been stolen, along with his motorbike, by a joyriding opportunist. The real Jamie might still be at work, entering a delivery of new stock onto his catalogue of books, oblivious. As we waited at the reception desk for Doctor Berry to be called, I remember noticing the smell of doughnuts, and seeing a sugary paper bag hurriedly pushed out of sight by the receptionist. I remember a picture on the wall, a crimson flower, single stem, with absurdly large petals. It looked like a daisy, but not the kind you'd ever see in real life. And it was as if a part of my brain was trying to keep me away from the cliff edge, by noticing the unimportant, the mundane details of life.

When Doctor Berry appeared a minute later, I could tell from his face that Jamie was in real trouble. He took Poppy and I into a room, away from the curtained areas and the beeping of machines, away from wherever Jamie was. He did it quickly and gently, there was no avoiding of eyes or flinching away from the terrible job that was his to carry out. Jamie had swerved to avoid a deer that had run onto the road and, according to several eyewitnesses, had then hit a pothole and lost control of his motorbike. His injuries had been severe, and although they'd done everything they could to save him, his heart had stopped beating and he could not be resuscitated.

'I'm very sorry, Mrs Matthews, I know this is extremely difficult news to hear. Is there anyone else we can contact for you?' the doctor asked.

It was the first and last time I would ever be called Mrs Matthews. I remember Poppy shaking her head and thanking the doctor. Tears were already strangling her words; grief already vibrating through her body. I was still holding her hand and I could sense it coming through her muscles and bones. All I could feel in my own body was disbelief, it quickly shifted to numbness as I stared at the doctor's name badge, slightly wonky and in need of a good wipe. The words couldn't touch me yet, not as long as I stayed above their meaning and focused on the daisy paintings, doughnut bags and name badges of the world.

'Would you like to see Jamie?'

'Yes.' I knew I needed to do it, to see for myself that he was dead, or there would always be some part of me that would never fully believe this day had happened.

A woman from the Mortuaries and Bereavement Team led us to another section of the hospital, away from the urgency of the still living. We followed her through countless sets of doors, and into such a warren of corridors that I couldn't even tell which way we were pointing. The glimpses I caught of the town through the windows made no sense. We headed down into the basement of the hospital, into the still of the afterlife. The mortuary was cold, scrubbed, with stainless steel tables set at regular intervals. A bank of matching steel drawers reminded me of Loretta's filing cabinets. We were steered into a private room, off to one side.

And then, Jamie's body.

I'd never seen him so still, not even in sleep. He was always twitching and fidgeting, but there was no life left in him here. His face was grazed and cut, sliced open by the accident, his mouth lopsided. He looked like a grotesque version of the Jamie I knew, as if a mortician had already tried to mould his features into a death mask. I wanted him to open his eyes, just one more time, so he could see how much I loved him. Poppy clung to my hand, crushing my fingers in a painful vice. She sobbed loudly, taking great gulps of air, trying to breathe through the trauma of seeing her beautiful brother on a slab. I wanted to touch his toe, just to remind myself what it felt like, before I'd never be allowed to touch any part of him again. His skin was icy with none of the fleshiness I was so used to feeling. They were no longer Jamie's feet, even though just hours before, they'd been pressed against mine, in bed, warm and full of life.

Afterwards, Zarina took Poppy home, her face solemn, determined to hold it together for the sake of Jamie's sister. They went to deliver the news to Jamie's parents, who were still unaware. In the world they inhabited at that moment, Jamie was alive. I drove myself back to Raglan Road and quietly entered our house, checking every room just in case Jamie had somehow found his way home. Then I lay down next to his shoes on the bedroom floor, going over and over our last conversation, the everyday words we'd spoken to each other. The last glimpse I'd ever caught of him closing the bedroom door. I tried to etch that image upon my brain so I'd never forget a single detail. The cheekiness of his smile, the spot where he'd cut his chin while shaving, the frayed hems on his jeans, the fresh laundry smell he left floating in his wake.

There had been no sudden premonition of things to come, no red haze of warning in my semiconscious state, no reprieve from the fate awaiting him. If I'd just called him back, said his name, forced him to turn towards me for a few seconds. If I'd called to him before he'd reached the bottom of the stairs, demanding more toast, more hot coffee, then maybe the deer wouldn't have been in the road. It would have run to safety and disappeared into a field, before Jamie and his motorbike had ever made an appearance on the same stretch of tarmac. Jamie would have been a vital ten seconds away from death, a close call, but nothing more. And none of us would have known how near he'd come.

Over the next two weeks, Poppy and Zarina spent a lot of time in my house cooking meals, making tea. Poppy needed something to do, she said, something to engage her hands because they shook when she stood still for more than a second. She arranged the funeral without any help from me. Staring at walls, doors, floorboards and chimney breasts had become a new full-time occupation that required my undivided attention. I did very little else. If tears found their way to the surface, I shut them down ruthlessly, before they could settle in and rip me apart from the inside. Poppy offered to cancel all the wedding plans for me, the food, the band, the flowers and the dress. But I needed to make those calls myself. The ceremony that was supposed to bind Jamie and I even more closely together could only be undone by me. Only I had the power to say those words.

The funeral was like a sequence from another dream. I couldn't focus properly on anything that was happening, and the day appeared before me in confusing, disjointed fragments, colours, sights and sounds. My family formed an unofficial guard around me, only letting those people who needed to approach with their condolences through the barricades. I remembered being surprised by their sudden compassion and understanding, like it was a side to them I'd never experienced before. Poppy clung to my arm through the whole service, weeping as quietly as she could. But she still managed to drown out the Reverend Adebisi when she mentioned something about Jamie's love for his family. Mine was the only dry eye in the house. Shock had taken me so far beyond tears I couldn't find a single one anywhere. I wanted to stand up and tell the other mourners that it wasn't a stiff upper lip, I wasn't being strong for anyone, or showing respect for the dead. I was simply in dry-eyed denial. Jamie was the only person who would have understood it, and we were now separated by the lid of a polished wooden coffin. I knew the order of the service inside out. I'd already been to what seemed like hundreds of other funerals. But I wanted nothing to do with this one, and I couldn't wait for it to end. And after it was over, after the sandwiches and the hugs from his mother, after the duty rounds to thank everyone for coming, I sat in the car outside our house, not wanting to be there either. Not knowing how to get through the next two hours without Jamie, never mind the rest of my life.

Another two weeks later, and I'd fallen into a routine. I'd already gone back to work; there was no point being at home alone when I could bury myself in the end of other people's lives. I found the routines soothing, something I could hold onto, finding refuge in the busyness. But at the end of each day, I'd sit in the car outside our house still reluctant to go inside. The empty rooms that waited for me were a constant reminder of what I'd lost. Sitting in the car as I nibbled on a packet of crisps, or listened to a talk show on the radio about kidney stones, was a better alternative.

Jamie was a constant presence. I was already having one-sided conversations with him inside my head. I saw no reason to stop talking to him just because he was dead. At times, those conversations became more verbal. And then, one Tuesday afternoon, I was in the middle of telling him about a Californian road trip that Poppy and Zarina had decided to take – where they planned to scatter some of his ashes – when it suddenly happened.

'Make sure Poppy goes to my favourite shop in Oakdale, the one where I bought my boots, that's a very important place to visit on any road trip.'

I dropped the crisps I was eating on the floor, shocked by the unexpected sound of his voice. In all the conversations I'd started with him since his death, he'd never once spoken back to me. He sounded so close that I turned to look at the seat beside me.

'Jamie?'

He was in the same clothes he'd been wearing on the fatal day that he'd left for work and never come back. His face was no longer cut and grazed. His skin was almost luminous it looked so perfect. His hair seemed thicker and shinier than normal, like he'd been through some sort of celestial upgrade, a buff and puff for the dead. But it was definitely Jamie, down to the mole on the side of his neck and the crow's feet around his eyes, although even the crow's feet seemed less deep and craggy than I remembered.

'Do you know you're sitting out here in the dark, love, talking to yourself again?'

I stared, frozen, all the wind knocked out of me. I waited for him to disappear, assuming he was a momentary blink, a glitch in my grasp on reality, fuelled by a serious lack of sleep.

'But what are you doing here?' I asked when I finally started breathing again. He was still in the seat beside me, smiling softly at my bewilderment. 'I mean, are you real?'

I reached out to touch him, but I already knew there was nothing corporeal there, no body to generate heat, no lungs to breathe from, no beating heart. My hands found nothing but air.

'I think I'm only here because you miss me, Juliette, love.'

It was like calling the Grand Canyon a ditch, comparing the Sahara Desert to a sandpit. I didn't just miss him, most of the time I could barely breathe because his death had punched such a huge hole through the very centre of my chest. So if my despair was big enough to cause this glorious hallucination, I was wholeheartedly glad, and the tears finally came.

Jamie sat patiently, letting me cry myself out. It took some time before the biggest sobs subsided into a more manageable flow of quiet tears.

'I'm sorry for leaving you,' Jamie finally said. 'Did I have a good funeral, at least? Did Poppy cry the loudest?'

I nodded, half-smiling through a fresh wave of tears.

'She was just the same when she was ten and she lost her pet rabbit,

Stew. She cried for three days straight, made all of us go to his funeral in the back garden. My dad bawled like a baby.'

'I was the only person who didn't cry at your funeral,' I told him, wiping my eyes, trying to clear my blurred vision so I could concentrate on his beautiful, beloved face.

'Well, someone had to listen to what the Reverend Adebisi was saying about me. Did she mention my guitar playing, my love of books and my unfulfilled potential as a rock star?'

'She even told the story about the time you almost fainted on the shoulder of the drummer from The Eighteen.'

'Just as long as she didn't mention the time I stole Aiden Quail's girlfriend at college, not my finest hour as a human being. Aiden didn't turn up to the funeral, did he?'

'I don't know. There were so many people there, I didn't recognise everyone. This is weird, talking to you about your own funeral.'

'I think we plunged straight past weird when I turned up in your car.' Jamie grinned, a shiny white halo emanating from his teeth, a heavenly sparkle. 'I'm glad my funeral wasn't a disappointment. We both know a good one when we see it. So, if you had to grade mine on a scale from one to ten, would it be a seven or a nine?'

I paused for a second to consider my answer, and he'd gone. I sat in the car for some time trying to figure out what had just happened, but it was impossible. All I knew was that a version of my Jamie had returned, and I was going to hold onto him as tightly as I could. If I allowed grief to enter my life and work its way through me, in the natural course of things, Jamie would disappear. I was certain of it. There was no decision to make. My life, with any rendering of Jamie in it, was worth a thousand lives without him. All I had to do was stop myself from fully feeling, just like I'd done at the hospital, at the funeral, at home and everywhere else. It was as if I'd been holding myself together until this miracle of delusion could swoop in and save me. And now that it had, I was determined not to let anything take it away.

Fourteen

ABIGAIL EVANS PROVES TO be just as elusive in England as she was in Australia. Several trawls through social media brings up very little, not enough for me to determine which part of the country she might be living in. And none of her accounts have been added to for over five years. Either Abigail Evans decided not to engage with social media, long ago, or she now uses a different name on a different account. Either way, it's going to be difficult to find her. She could be dead, of course. She'd be about sixty-three years old by now, if my rough calculations (based on her approximate age in the photo from The Friends of Galton Hall) are correct. And unexpected things happen. I know that better than anyone.

I try some more general internet searches – when I should be cleaning out the pantry at my latest clearance job – hoping that she might have become part of a wild-swimming club, a banjo-playing group, or a rambler's association. But after two hours on my laptop, I've got nothing to show for it. And I return to the dried pasta and desiccated coconut in Jim Ravenshaw's kitchen cupboards.

I'm going to need a new strategy. I could attempt to track down any old acquaintances of Joseph Evans, or the descendants of those acquaintances. Maybe Alfie's dad stayed in touch with someone after he moved to Australia. But I'd have to ask Alfie for some names, and that would involve a lot of explaining that I don't want to engage in yet. I do know someone who works in the Births Marriages and Deaths Department at the council. If I ask nicely, they might carry out some investigations for me, at least that way I'd know if Abigail Evans is still in the land of the living. But I also decide against that, it feels too intrusive.

I'm still up to my elbows in tins of processed peas and corn, when I realise my best option is to join a family history site after all. It's the one place where a large body of information is already gathered. And if Abigail Evans is also a member, she's more likely to be open to someone contacting her out of the blue. I chose the most well-known site, MyHistoryThroughTheAges.com, and spend my lunchtime going through the membership process, and then looking for Alfie's half-sister in earnest. Several options appear as immediate possibilities and I decide to message all of them. If no one replies, or none of them are the right Abigail Evans, I'm out of options. One way or another, I'm getting close to the end of my hunt for Alfie's half-sister.

I can't help wondering what she looks like, now that she's all grown-up. Does she resemble Alfie, Ivy, her dad? What does she do for a living? Does she have her own family? I've spent so much time trying to track her down I'm undeniably curious, and I find myself hoping she's also a member of MyHistoryThroughTheAges.com.

My thoughts wander frequently back to Abigail Evans throughout the afternoon, when I should be concentrating on Jim Ravenshaw's flat. It's a large home and Mr Ravenshaw made serious efforts to fill every square inch of it. This house clearance is going to take a long time. I'm just making a start on the main bedroom, which is filled with boxes and boxes of old clothes, when my phone rings with an unknown number.

'Am I speaking to Juliette Jones?' an unfamiliar voice asks, when I answer.

'Who is this, please?'

'This is the Accident and Emergency Department at the Royal Victoria Hospital.'

For a moment, I think someone is playing a sick joke. It's such a carbon copy of the conversation I had almost two years ago, that I suddenly feel like it's happening all over again.

'I have an Alfie Evans here who asked me to call you,' the person explains.

'Alfie?' Who should be at home, reading the newspaper or inspecting his bunions, not doing anything that could land him in Accident and Emergency. 'Is he okay? What's happened?' I ask, panic slowly rising.

'Mr Evans is absolutely fine,' the voice tries to reassure me. 'He hurt his knee and needed some help, and someone called for an ambulance. He's got some badly strained muscles but nothing too serious. Your granddad's all fixed up and ready to go home, in fact, if you'd like to come and collect him.'

In the background, I can actually hear Alfie chortling. It's that sound more than anything that allows me to let go of the tightly gripped muscles in my stomach.

This time, I'm fully aware of my drive to the hospital. It's only as I walk through the doors of the Accident and Emergency Department that I start to feel my gut clenching again. This is the only time I've been back here since the day that Jamie died. This is the place where Jamie's life left his body, where his toes became cold and alien to me, and I suddenly can't get any air into my lungs.

The same woman is standing at the reception desk and I cannot even approach her for fear of completely losing it, passing out, having some sort of hysterical meltdown. I find an empty seat in a quiet corner, away from everyone else and close my eyes. But all the deep breathing in the world isn't going to help me now. Every emotion that I routinely refuse to acknowledge is trying to push its way to the surface, but I can't let any of it out. Alfie needs me and he's already been waiting for ages. I'll have to face the crimson daisy and the receptionist one more time.

I approach the desk focusing on a patient safety notice on the wall, reading its instructions for good hand washing and mask-wearing procedures. I'm on my fourth silent recital of *now rinse your hands for a minimum of twenty seconds* by the time the receptionist tells someone that I'm here. A nurse leads me to a curtained area, where Alfie is lying on a bed looking small and old. There's such an air of fragility about him that I'm surprised I've never truly sensed it before, he's a bird with a broken wing.

'Juliette!' He smiles with genuine warmth and affection when he sees me, and it almost tips me over the edge again. I have to bite my lip just to hold everything together. Alfie instantly stops smiling. 'Bloody hell, I thought I was the one who'd been through the wars, but you look worse than I do. What's happened?'

'Nothing, bad headache, migraine,' I lie, quickly silencing his concerns. 'So, how did you end up in Accident and Emergency?'

If there's one thing I know about Alfie by now, everything comes with a story.

'I went to see one of my old mates in the graveyard, where I used to work, old Harry Blenkinsop. He was a good friend, Harry, and I like to visit his grave once or twice a year. Only this time, I got my foot caught between Harry's headstone and his nearest neighbour, and when I tried to tug it free, I twisted my knee something rotten. I couldn't stand up after that,' he says, pulling a pained face as he touches his bandaged leg. His left trouser leg has been rolled up above his knee, making him look like a holidaymaker bound for a paddle in the sea. 'I was lucky there was someone visiting a grave not too far away, and they called the ambulance. Otherwise, I'd still be there now, getting ready to join old Harry in his grave, bit too cosy, if you ask me,' he says with a shudder, 'too many worms for my liking.'

Which is ironic, considering he used to work in Sholtsbury's parks and gardens, and worms would have been a prominent feature of his daily life.

'Mr Evans will need some looking after for a few days.'

A doctor enters through the curtains behind us, it's not the same doctor who delivered the news about Jamie, and I'm relieved. But she's clearly under the impression that I'm Alfie's carer. She helps him sit up, swinging his legs over the side of the bed like a pendulum.

'He'll need plenty of rest, and he also needs to keep his leg elevated as much as possible, until the swelling goes down.' She turns to Alfie with a stern, doctor's expression. 'No gymnastics or riding unicycles for at least a week, and keep putting ice on that knee for the next few days. But there's no permanent damage, Alfie.' The doctor helps him off the bed, making sure he's steady on his feet before she hands him a walking stick that he's already been fitted for. 'You'll be back to kicking up your heels in no time, but you'll need to see your own doctor if there's any lingering stiffness or pain. It's been nice chatting with you, Alfie.'

'Don't take this the wrong way, Doc, you've been terrific, but I hope we never see each other again,' Alfie says.

'The feeling's mutual, Alfie, you take care of yourself.' The doctor gives me a knowing smile as she leaves.

Alfie talks non-stop on the way home, telling me about the ambulance crew and the flashing lights and the fuss that everyone made of him. He goes into great detail about the laugh he had with the nurses, and the miraculous powers of the painkillers he's been given. Not only have they stopped his knee from hurting, they've also temporarily cured the pain in his lower back, and the mysterious stabbing sensation he's been getting in his ears, for the last few months. He also swears blind the painkillers have improved his eyesight, shifted a "hefty bung of earwax" and increased his IQ by at least twenty points. I'm grateful the medication has made him even more talkative than usual, although it also makes him giggle at his own jokes like a mischievous schoolboy. It's been such a big day for Alfie that he barely notices my muted response to his story. He's so exhausted from the whole experience that he goes to bed at 8.41 p.m., and instead of staying up to enjoy the peace and quiet, I'm in my own bed twenty minutes later.

The next morning, Wednesday, I phone Loretta and tell her I'm taking three days off work, annual leave, to deal with a family issue. She doesn't ask any questions. Thankfully, Alfie can get himself up and dressed. I help him down the stairs and settle him in the sitting room, bringing him some toast and coffee.

'Would you mind popping round to tell Marina what's happened?' Alfie asks, making himself comfortable with cushions, blankets and the remote control for the TV. 'She'll be wondering why I haven't been to see her.'

I've never *popped* round to see any of my neighbours before, but I can't just leave Mrs Lafleur on the other side of my walls, worrying. When she sees me at the door, she gives me such a friendly smile, and I know I've done nothing to deserve it. In the two years that I've been living next door to her, I've never once enquired about her health/garden/granddaughter. I'm not even sure I've ever stood this close to her before, close enough to notice the incredibly soft brown of her eyes, and the delicate gold chain with a bumble bee pendant that she wears around her neck.

She refuses to let me hover on the doorstep and leads me into the back part of the house, into her own dining room. It's a cosy, lived-in room with pictures of her daughter and granddaughter covering every flat surface. Books, plants and cushioned chairs give it a homely feel. It's nothing like the barren wasteland I've created in this room's twin, on the other side of the wall, separated by nothing but a thin row of bricks and a solid shield of grief.

I tell her about Alfie's fall and his trip to the hospital, and she's genuinely concerned for his welfare.

'I told him to be careful if he was going to be clambering about that old graveyard, but Alfie's always got ideas of his own.' She shakes her head, like she's known him for years, like she's fully aware of this particular foible of his – acting like a man half his age. She disappears into the kitchen and returns with a plate of freshly baked cookies. 'Would it be alright, dear, if I take these round to your house and tell him what a silly old fool he is?'

'Be my guest,' I say, smiling at the affection in her voice.

'When you get to our age, you've got to be careful not to twist anything, or break anything. It all takes so much longer to heal. That's why I do my yoga twice a week, and the karate keeps me nimble.'

'You do karate?' I say, hoping she doesn't take the surprise in my voice as an insult to her physical abilities.

'There's a class at the local community centre for all ages. The man who teaches us thinks a bit too much of himself, he spends half the time checking his hair in the mirrors. But he knows his karate.'

I have obviously been fooled by the layers of homely knitwear that Mrs Lafleur usually wears, and by my preconceptions about her age, because, apparently, she's a ninja. And she can definitely give Alfie Evans a run for his money.

Alfie is as pleased to see Mrs Lafleur as she is to see him. I stand on the sidelines as she satisfies herself that he's okay, and has been well taken care of by the staff at the hospital. She insists on removing the bandage and inspecting his knee.

'I'm not sure I'm ready for you to see my knees, Marina,' he says, pretending to be coy. 'Just the sight of my bare legs might transport our relationship to a whole new level of intimacy.'

Mrs Lafleur shakes her head at him. 'I think I can control myself. I've seen thousands of knees in my GP's surgery, and yours are nothing to write home about, a little too much on the skinny side to win any prizes worth having.'

Alfie roars with laughter, as Mrs Lafleur gently flexes his knee in different directions. Then she reties the bandage with dextrous fingers, which I now know have been trained by yoga and karate. Only then is Alfie allowed to take one of the cookies, he makes little noises of appreciation as he drops crumbs down his jumper and onto the carpet. They're so engrossed in their conversation, and their doctor/patient role-play, that neither of them notices as I slip silently out of the room, feeling like an intruder in my own home. But I can't avoid Alfie for long.

By midmorning, he's got me planted in the sitting room, by the fire, and we're both listening to Mrs Lafleur talk about her work as a GP. And I can't help it, I'm hooked. She's led such an interesting life and she knows how to tell a good story, it's an irresistible combination. I can see why Alfie likes her. She steers clear of mentioning Jamie. But she shows such a genuine interest in my work, that I find myself telling her and Alfie about the time I discovered the proceeds of a jewellery heist. The thief, an eighty-seven-year-old accountant, had stashed the jewels under his bed inside an old pillowcase. He'd also saved several articles from the local paper showing the very jewels I'd found. I tell them about war medals and citations for bravery. And about one woman's collection of plastic shopping bags, stuck to the walls in every room of her house, like rustling, undulating wallpaper. It was the strangest homage to supermarkets I've ever seen. And I spent that entire clearance job craving sausage rolls from Sainsbury's. I don't mention what I found among Ivy's possessions and the evidence of Alfie's half-sister.

Mrs Lafleur prepares carrot and coriander soup for all of us at lunch, with freshly baked bread that she must have got up at dawn to prepare. Then we all sit and watch an episode of Alfie's favourite antiques hunting programme. By the time Mrs Lafleur leaves to run some errands of her own, I've been lulled into such a sense of ease that it almost feels wrong. The numbness that I experienced at the hospital has also thawed. The whole house seems warmer because of Mrs Lafleur, and for the first time in eighteen months, it feels lived-in.

By the following morning, Alfie is bright and perky and restless.

'I can't just watch TV for the next five days,' he says, when I've cleared away his breakfast things and built up a good fire to take the chill off the air. Even with the heating on, the room still feels wintry. Why have I never noticed how unpleasant that is before?

'You could think about what you want to say at Ivy's funeral,' I suggest. 'I can help, if you like.'

'What with everything else that's been going on, I keep forgetting about the funeral. I mean, I haven't forgotten about Ivy,' Alfie explains unnecessarily, 'it's just I'm not a big fan of funerals. When you've been to as many as I have, it all starts to get a bit too depressing, and prophetic.'

I can't argue with that. I must have attended many more funerals than Alfie and I understand what he means. But Ivy's will be different. She will be properly mourned and remembered, even if it's just by me and Alfie.

'Anyway, it feels a bit daft, standing up and talking about Ivy in front of all those empty seats.'

'I'll be there,' I say, wondering if I've actually mentioned that fact to Alfie before now.

Alfie's eyes moisten and he needs a few moments to compose himself.

'Thank you, Juliette.' His voice is husky, he dabs at his eyes with a handkerchief. 'I'm glad it won't just be me and Ivy. She deserves better than that. And Marina insists she's coming too.'

'I'm sure Mrs Lafleur would like to hear all about Ivy. I know I'd like to know more.'

'Well, me and you can do that anytime, we don't need a funeral to talk about my sister.'

Just for a moment, I feel like I must have really known Ivy, when she was alive. I picture her as she was in her photos, full of life and energy and hope.

'And if you ever want to talk about your Jamie...' Alfie hesitates, studying me before he continues, judging whether it's wise to finish his thoughts or not. 'I mean, I don't want to pry or anything, but I know what it's like, losing people you love. Sometimes you just want to say their name out loud. It feels good, like they're still here with you. Nobody warns you that's one of the things you'll miss the most when they're gone, just saying their name and having them answer. It's such a simple thing and everyone takes it for granted. But when it's gone, it can break your heart.'

I'm so winded by his words that all I can do is study an old stain on the carpet. And I realise that I do want to tell Alfie about Jamie, but I cannot risk it. What if talking about Jamie, with somebody who didn't even know him, dilutes my own memories, or interferes with my ability to see him in my car?

The silence stretches out between us until Alfie clears his throat, shifts in his seat and picks up the slack again.

'Did I ever tell you about the time Ivy saw someone stealing a pair of top-notch dressmaker's scissors from the haberdashery at Shimming's? She chased the thief through the whole store, pelting him with cotton reels. She was so quick off the mark she almost broke the women's hundred metres world record, by all accounts.'

I smile at the picture Alfie is creating in my head.

'She had a damn good aim too, our Ivy, caught me on the side of the head with a ball of socks once. She lobbed it from twelve feet away, when I threatened to drop her favourite doll into the garden pond. Mind you, I was only seven years old at the time, so you can't judge me too harshly.'

We sit for the rest of the morning talking about Ivy and her life, and how much Alfie already misses his big sister.

Fifteen

ALFIE HOBBLES AROUND TO see Mrs Lafleur in the afternoon, so they can do the crossword together, and he can "let her talk about her knitting creations." I drive to the supermarket to do a shop for the coming week, and when I get home and park outside the house, Jamie suddenly appears. Right away, I know something is wrong. He's always materialised in a solid-looking state, not ghost-like or spectral. He's always been three-dimensional, visually at least. But today his whole body has a slightly see-through quality, like he's only half here and half somewhere else.

'What's wrong, why are you so faint?' I ask, reaching out to pat his arms and legs, like I can make them more substantial again. Even his clothes are fading in and out, his blue jeans and a plain black T-shirt like some kind of shimmering mirage in the desert.

'I don't know what's going on but something feels different.' His voice is faint and faraway and I have to strain to catch his words. If he was a computer, he'd need a reboot. But there's nothing I can do, no button I can press, no service I can call for help – not without being examined by a doctor for the state of my mental health.

'Please don't leave me.' I am pleading with a ghost but I'm suddenly terrified that if he disappears now, I'll never see him again. Is some part of my subconscious trying to cut me off, to shut these wonderful visions down?

'It's okay, I'm not going anywhere,' Jamie says, but his face flickers and wobbles like the picture on an old analogue TV, that's about to lose its signal. 'You and Alfie have been getting along well,' he says, trying to change the subject, to calm things down. 'And Marina is adorable. Why didn't we make friends with her when I was still around?'

'There wasn't any time,' I remind him. His grip on the timeline of his own life often gets muddled. But that's not the only kind of time we're talking about.

'I want to tell you something,' he says. He can see that I'm close to tears so he tries to rest his hands over the top of mine. 'I don't know what's happening to me, I don't know if I'll get another chance to come and sit with you.'

'Please don't say things like that.'

'You were already thinking it yourself, Juliette. We always knew this couldn't last forever.'

'Why, is there somewhere more important you have to be right now?'

'Well, I was thinking of trying to track down some interesting people, while I'm here, William Shakespeare, or the first Queen Elizabeth perhaps. We could have a little chat about life, or the Spanish Armada. I might even spend some time polishing my halo.'

The thought of Jamie with a halo, it's enough to temporarily pull me back from the edge. Even if his halo did have a certain celestial quality, he'd still manage to get his grubby fingerprints smudged all over it, or drop it on the floor and dent it, like an old saucepan.

'The point I'm trying to make is that we may not be able to take the same path forever. At some stage, you're going to let life back in again, and that's nothing to be afraid of.'

I'm suddenly snivelling, all thoughts of his halo gone. There's nothing I can do to stop the tears.

'Are you— trying to say goodbye to me?'

'No, Juliette, love, I'd be happy to sit in this car with you and talk for all eternity, or longer, if that was an option. I miss you just as much as you miss me.'

'Not possible,' I sniff, wiping my nose on my sleeve again and not even caring how sticky and gross it is this time. 'I had to pick Alfie up from the Accident and Emergency Department yesterday.'

He nods and his smile fades. 'That was a hard one. I'm sorry you had to go through that alone. But Alfie is there for you, if you need someone to talk to. He's seen it all at the graveyard so he knows what you're going through. And Marina's shoulders were just built for crying on. In fact, she'd probably consider it an insult if you didn't wipe that snotty nose of yours on her jumper, at least once.'

'I don't want Alfie or Mrs Lafleur, I want you. What's wrong with talking to you?'

He considers his answer carefully before delivering it. 'There's nothing wrong with talking to me, except we both know I'm not really here. Right at this moment, in fact, your new neighbours from across the road are watching you talk to yourself, wondering if they should call someone.'

I resist the natural urge to turn my head and look. Jamie could disappear in the blink of an eye. I need to focus on him and nothing else.

'You feel real to me, I don't care what anyone else thinks. Isn't that all that matters?'

'What matters to me is that you live a good life. I don't want you hiding in the shadows until you're a little old lady, with only your cats for company.'

'I haven't got any cats.'

'It could be mice then, or frogs or budgies. The point is if I don't come back—'

'Stop saying that!'

'Then I want to know that you'll be okay. You're the love of my life, Juliette Jones. I want only good things for you. And if I keep turning up in this car, I'm worried that's not going to happen.'

'If I promise to see some of my real friends and paint the sitting room, will you promise to keep coming back?'

I've never tried bargaining with him before, but it's a good offer and if it works...

'You know I can't make any promises, love, I'm not really in control of what's going on. I don't make a conscious decision to come and see you, it just sort of happens, and then I'm suddenly here.'

'So, where do you go when you're not here?' I ask, wondering why I've never questioned him on this subject before.

'It's difficult to describe. It's only when I'm talking to you that I have any real sense of consciousness. The rest of the time, it feels like my head is filled with cotton wool, like I'm standing on a lonely moor with mist swirling all around me.'

I have a vision of him dressed in a long cape and knee-high boots.

He's holding a lantern to light his way as he stumbles across a damp and boggy moor, the howl of a feral beast carried on the night air around him.

'That doesn't sound very nice.'

'It's not really anything. I can't feel the cold, I never think about food or fall asleep, I'm just sort of there.'

'I thought you might have made some friends by now, or joined a choir or something.'

That makes him laugh out loud. For a few seconds, he's my Jamie again, with just a hint of transparency in the centre of his chest, where his heart should be. But it doesn't last and he fades again like a candle burning the last of its fuel, guttering before it dies.

'If this is goodbye, then you should know that I'll never get over you,' I tell him.

'Now there's no need to be all dramatic. No Romeo and Juliet stuff, remember? If I get even the faintest hint that you're yearning to lie down in any old tombs...'

'Stop trying to make me laugh, it's impossible to cry when you keep saying stuff like that.'

'You never were any good at multitasking.' Jamie grins. 'Do you remember that time you almost fried my favourite leather belt, because you were trying to cook dinner and tidy up at the same time? I nearly ended up with a string of chipolata sausages through the belt loops on my jeans.'

'That never happened. You just like teasing me about it.'

There was a moment, when my hand hovered over the frying pan with Jamie's belt, and he walked into the kitchen and saw what might have been. It quickly got written into our folklore. But this is Jamie at his most insufferable, there's nothing more infuriating, because he has somehow made me smile again. I want to tell him how angry I am, but what I want even more is to talk about the old times, our times.

'So, this life that we lived together,' Jamie says, before I can distract him with a really good memory, like the one of our first date, when he came round to my old flat to cook dinner. 'If you had to reimagine it as a musical, what genre would you chose?'

'Don't do that, don't say that.'

'But we've done it with all the other lives you've witnessed.'

'It just sounds so final, like something you'd do at the end, and this is not the end of us.'

'Let me tell you what I'd do then. Because I've got this great song in my head for the day you walked into the bookshop, with that confused look on your lovely face, and changed my life forever.'

'It better not be anything by The Eighteen,' I say.

And he's gone. Panic rises quickly inside my chest until I'm struggling to breathe. What if that was the last time, what if he never comes back? What if the last words I'll ever say to him are The Eighteen? I can't bear the thought of never seeing him sit beside me again.

I'm back inside the house and running up the stairs. I drag the boxes filled with Jamie's stuff away from the walls and empty every one of them. I place each of the precious objects around me on the floor until I'm literally surrounded by everything I have left of him. I've missed seeing these things so much that I almost can't go through with it. I almost pack everything away again immediately, so I don't have to feel any of the piercing pain that goes along with this.

I pick up his wallet before I chicken out. The leather feels smooth and soft from years of being handled, and from accidentally going through the cottons cycle on the washing machine, more than once. His bank cards and driving licence are still stuffed into the little pockets, but I set it aside. I need to start with something easier. His big red woolly jumper was a stalwart in winter. It's full of holes, patches and repairs, but he refused to get rid of it because of the memories it held for him. I pull it over my head, catching just the faintest trace of Jamie's everyday aftershave. I hug the jumper to my body letting it warm me.

The next thing that draws my attention is Jamie's watch. He wasn't wearing it on the day of the accident. Poppy and I found it sitting on the counter in the bookshop, next to a pile of change and some well-matured pocket fluff. The watch is vintage, and like lots of things that Jamie owned it was pre-loved, with a history of its own, long before it ever found its way onto his wrist. He cherished the old face in deep, crackled, green enamel and the way it gained time every day. He said it had a mind of its own. Why have a watch that keeps perfect time when you can have one with its own personality? I slip it onto my wrist where it dangles loosely like a chunky bracelet. At some point during its recent confinement, it has stopped ticking and there are no signs of life when I wind it gently. Maybe it too is mourning the loss of Jamie.

'Your watch has stopped working, so you'd better come back and help me fix it,' I say out loud. Jamie has never appeared anywhere but the car, but maybe he can still hear my voice. Maybe my words will cut through the misty moor he's currently wandering across, and lure him back? 'And your red jumper has got even more holes in it than before. I may be tempted to unravel it completely and wind it back into balls of wool, unless you convince me not to. And it better be a really good argument to save your jumper this time!'

I look through an assortment of Jamie's socks. He had what seemed like hundreds of pairs because he never threw any of them away, even when they developed holes and got shoved to the back of a drawer. His absolute favourite pair was thick, woollen and knitted on a Scottish isle. I pull them on over my own socks, and reach for the pair that he always wore at Christmas. Jamie had no concept of tacky. If the socks played Christmas carols at every other step and made him laugh, then he didn't care what anyone else thought.

I lay all his pairs of jeans out on the bed, like a faded patchwork quilt of denim. Every single pair has seen more life than it ever had a right to expect, and still be fit for wearing. Jamie was merciless with his jeans. He wore them to extinction. He said they didn't really start to feel good until they were threadbare through the knee or the bum, and that was when they entered the comfy years, when they gave up having a plan of their own and shaped themselves to his body instead. In the back pocket of his most beloved jeans, I find a business card from Olivetti's with a new lunchtime special scribbled on the back.

'Hey, Jamie, Olivetti's is going downhill without you,' I tell him, talking loudly to the curtains and the carpet and the cupboard doors. 'They stopped selling the triple cheese and pastrami baguette, and now they do avocado and vegan mayonnaise.'

In another pocket, I discover a tiny conker, aged and wrinkled now that it has lost its woody lustre. I remember the day I gave it to him, on our second date, when we took a long walk through one of Alfie's favourite parks. The leaves were turning and the ground was scattered with conkers. I had no idea he'd kept it, in the pocket of his most worn, most loved jeans, a token. I slip it into my own pocket and have to leave the room just to pull myself together. This is much tougher than I thought it was going to be, and I knew it was going to be a challenge to my sanity. But now that I've found the second-date conker, now that I know Jamie kept it with him...

I sit at the top of the stairs, trying to breathe deeply, but all I manage to do is give myself the hiccups. I lay flat on my back on the carpet until they eventually subside. I have to keep going, it's not just about goading Jamie into another car visit anymore. I genuinely want to see his stuff. I've missed seeing his things around the house and even his battered DIY gloves, with all their rips and tears, feel like old and cherished friends.

I move onto a pile of Jamie's music books and it's all his little notes, comments and doodles that keep me glued to the pages for over an hour. He was incapable of reading any book, magazine or newspaper without adding his own words. When I move onto his favourite books, it's even worse: Jamie has stuffed so many things between the pages that some of them are twice as fat as they were originally, and others have cracked their spines under the strain. I could never figure out why he used books to store concert tickets, shopping lists, scribbled down addresses and shop receipts. But each book is like a history of his life at the time he was reading it. And he always had a book with him, as if running a bookshop wasn't enough. He read more than a hundred a year and could talk in detail about every single one of them. His capacity to absorb their words, digest their value, meaning and worth was like a superpower. Some of the best books I've read in my life, the ones that have truly left their mark, were recommended by Jamie. He could read my moods as easily as the books he loved so much, and he always gave me something to ease the aches and pains of my soul, or lift my flagging spirits. And it wasn't just for me, he could perform the same miraculous service for anyone, if he knew them just a fraction. It was one of the things that made his bookshop great. The books were only part of the story. It was Jamie's appreciation of their merit that raised the whole building to the status of a reading temple.

'Jamie, I need a really good book to read,' I say to the room around me. 'I haven't read a single one since you left me, and I don't know what to choose. I might accidentally read a trashy romance or a saga, if you don't come back and pick out something special for me. Or I might lose my way in the bookshop on the High Street and wander into the New Age section.'

He refused to have anything in his own Top Reads stand that wasn't written by a bona fide Dalai Lama. I listen for a second, but there are no mysterious sounds or sighs of impatience to charge the air around me.

I sort Jamie's books into neat piles and move onto the shoes and boots. Collected over the entire course of his adult life, and rarely thrown away, they form quite a gathering of old friends. I find the matching pairs and line them up neatly, until they look like they're about to perform a bodiless line dance. By the time I move onto the contents of his old laptop, my energy is starting to wane, and I realise it's now dark outside. I'm hungry and my legs are aching from sitting on the floor like a teenager. I go downstairs to make a sandwich. There's no sign of Alfie, but I can still hear the rumble of voices on the other side of my wall. I flick the heating on and water my ailing plants just to move around and loosen up the muscles in my back.

When I return to the bedroom, the first thing that strikes me is how much it looks like one of the houses that I'm so used to clearing out. Only this time, I'm sorting through Jamie's things: his memories, his precious possession and treasured finds, his everyday evidence of a life lived. If I was clearing out his house, this is what it would look like. I take off his jumper, fold up his jeans and place everything back in the boxes, feeling like Jamie has tricked me into this. All those times he tried to persuade me to go through his stuff and that's exactly what I've ended up doing, except I'm not about to dump anything. The only thing I keep out is a book he was reading when we went to Paris. It's filled with ticket stubs to the museums and galleries we visited, with postcards, cafe receipts and the splendid memories of the four days we spent there together.

I carry, haul and drag each one of the boxes down the stairs, stacking them against the dining room wall. I have to get them out of my room because now that I've opened them once, I know I'll be tempted to keep dipping in for another look, and then another. And I'm not ready to perform a house clearance on Jamie's life. I need to encourage him to come back and visit, not give him solid reasons to stay away.

Sixteen

'JOCELYN WEBSTER WAS AN avid county-cricket fan, and could often be found sitting contentedly in the Mary Hutton Stand at her local club, supporting her favourite team.'

I'm at the crematorium, trying to block out the voice of the minister, Amos Stickythorn. This was not a funeral that I was planning to attend. I'm now way behind on clearing out Mr Ravenshaw's flat. Loretta has already sent me several snarky messages, asking if I need to be booked onto a refresher course for the basic principles of filling a black bin bag. But I have to ignore Loretta. I need to follow the rituals. I need to know if Jamie is ever going to visit me again and this is the surest way of finding out. He's never failed to turn up after a funeral before, but since yesterday, when he was so faint and uncertain, I need some speedy reassurance.

Today, I'm the only mourner at the funeral. So it should be easy to think about Jocelyn Webster and everything I learned about her life while I was sorting through her things. But I'm finding it hard to focus. The minister seems to be taking twice as long as usual to deliver the service, his voice twice as irritating and monotone. He could be reading from a car-parts catalogue, not talking about a woman who played in some national chess competitions. She was also a woman who hadn't cooked anything but baked beans and microwave pot pies for years, judging by the stack of tins and cans I found in her kitchen cupboards. She had a lovely crochet blanket for her knees, and she fed the birds in her tiny strip of garden, where I found three feeders and a birdbath. It's important to remember the details, not only to honour the memory of the woman I never met – but know so much about – but also because it's the details that Jamie relishes. I need to concentrate, to give him an incentive to come and sit with me again. I know he'd love to hear about the time Jocelyn kayaked around the coastline of Cornwall. I've seen the photos, and I found an old paddle propping up a broken shelf in her cupboard. Jamie is going to love helping me reimagine that particular event in Jocelyn's life as a mini opera, or in the style of a pop song. He won't be able to resist. But I have to do this right. Focus on Jocelyn Webster now, and not the thought of seeing Jamie.

When the service is finally over, I try to drive home at my normal speed but it's hard not to put my foot down, take all the shortcuts, sail through all the orange lights. That's not how I normally drive though, and it feels important to do everything right. I can't let Jamie pick up on my desperation to see him again. I can't risk it. I don't want to jinx anything.

I'm nervous as I drive up Raglan Road. I have to park further down the street than usual as a delivery van has taken up the space outside my house. I turn off the engine and wait. Sometimes it takes a few minutes for him to appear. I try to breathe deeply, but I can feel a tremor in my hands and I can't help glancing at the seat beside me every few seconds. As the minutes begin to stack up, my palms start to feel moist with fear and I can't seem to get any air into my lungs. I have to rest my head on the steering wheel just to stop the dizziness that's making everything in the car spin. Fifteen minutes crawls by and there's no sign of Jamie. But I'm not willing to give up yet. Thirty minutes and Jamie is still absent. I've bitten off every one of my nails and developed an irritating twitch in my left foot. I play with the second-date conker, nestled in my pocket. I keep it close at all times now. The air is so chilly it feels like it could snow inside the car, but I have to wait. After another hour, however, I know he's not coming. It's never taken him this long before, and the car is cold and lifeless. For the first time since I lost him, he hasn't come to hear about a funeral, and I don't want to think about what that means.

I know I should go inside – I'm shivering with cold and I need to use the bathroom – but leaving the car would make everything more final. I start the engine instead and ease out of my parking spot, deciding to give Jamie another chance. I have to drive somewhere before I can return and repeat the whole process. I head into town and have some lunch at a familiar cafe, eating a sandwich without noticing what's in it, wondering how long I should leave it before heading home again.

I check for any messages on my phone, just to fill in a few more minutes, and notice an email from someone called Abigail Armitage-Evans. She's read my message on the family history site and is curious to know which branch of the family I'm enquiring about. She gives nothing else away. But there are a string of company logos and contact details at the bottom of the email, and it's obvious she's messaged me from her workplace – Cycle Climb Kayak, an outdoor clothing store. I type the name into my browser... the store is only an hour's drive from where I'm sitting right now. If she's *the* Abigail Evans, I could get a sneaky look at her for myself, see if there's any family resemblance, without having to explain anything to anyone. By the time I drive home again, it will be dark, and that might increase my chances of being visited by Jamie. He always seems more comfortable talking to me in the dark.

Cycle Climb Kayak sits in a large shopping centre on the edge of a sizeable town. The centre, shaped like the spokes of a wheel all connected to a central hub, has an impressive glass domed roof. When I eventually find the store where Abigail works, I walk in and pretend to look through the racks of down-filled walking jackets. There are two staff members on the shop floor. A young, fresh-out-of-school teenager, refolding all the T-shirts on a shelf, and a more mature woman behind the counter. I edge a little closer to the counter, picking up some hiking boots and studying the grip on the soles like I'm a seasoned boot-buyer. I try to get a proper look at the older woman, and I can quickly tell that she's not Alfie's half-sister, she's also too young. Maybe it's Abigail's day off, maybe she works in the office and never ventures down to the shop floor. I feel foolish for thinking I could just walk in and study her from a safe distance, like she's a tiger at the zoo.

I make my way through the maze of rails towards the shop exit, and almost trip over someone crouching down next to a box of shiny water bottles. She straightens up to her full height, and I'm suddenly standing face to face with a female version of Joseph Evans. It's all there, the broad nose, strong eyebrows and thick head of hair. Her mouth is a different shape, her neck is longer. But there's no mistaking that she's an Evans. If she and Alfie stood next to each other they'd look like two peas in a family pod.

'I'm so sorry,' she says, placing a hand on my arm by way of an apology. 'You gave me quite a fright, are you okay?'

'You're Abigail Evans,' I say, before I can think about the consequences of saying anything at all. The name on her badge simply says *Abi*.

'Do I know you?' Her smile is beginning to falter as she senses something uncertain in the air, her shop manager demeanour vanishing.

I have no choice but to explain. 'I contacted you on the family history site, you sent me a reply.' I show her hastily on my phone so she knows I'm not a shoplifter or a stalker.

'You're Juliette Jones?'

I nod. 'I saw the shop logo on your email and since I was already in the area...' It's only a tiny lie to confirm my lack of craziness.

She calls the other woman over with a wave of her hand, and for a moment, I think she's about to have me ejected from the shop. Instead, she tells Mina (according to her name badge) that she's going up to the office for a while.

'Have you got time for a chat?' she asks, already leading the way towards the back of the shop and a door marked private. It's only now that I'm starting to hear hints of her antipodean accent, which has obviously been changed by her years spent living in England. And it's now a unique hybrid of northern English and Australian.

The office is a pokey, airless cupboard with no windows and a strong smell of disinfectant.

'Are you researching your own family history?' she asks, closing the door for privacy.

She offers me a coffee from a machine. I stir in two sugars to help calm me down.

'Actually, I'm not even related to you,' I say. 'I'm a friend of Alfie Evans.'

There's no flicker of recognition on her face. I suddenly wish I'd gone to Jamie's bookshop, instead of driving all the way out here to land myself in it.

'Is Alfie related to my dad?' she asks, as we sit on the only two chairs in the office, which are hard and uncomfortable, designed to make a guilty person squirm. 'I don't know much about Dad's family, he never talked about his parents. I don't even know if he had any brothers, sisters or cousins. Did Alfie ask you to track me down?'

She's eager for details and I'll have to give her some.

'He's quite an elderly gentleman. I wanted to see if I could find you before I said anything to him directly. I didn't want to raise his hopes too high.'

Or stir the hornet's nest. This is the worst possible way this could have happened. I'm totally unprepared for this conversation. And it's obvious that Abigail knows nothing about Alfie, or her dad's former life.

'So, is Alfie my dad's brother?' Her face is excited. 'I moved here years ago, after Dad died, but I've never managed to track down any of his family. It seems they all scattered to the winds. That's why I was so interested when I got your message. It's the first time I've had any contact from someone who knew my dad's family, here in England.'

'Alfie is definitely related,' I say, working up to it, half-hoping she might guess the truth herself, but she's clueless. 'In fact, Alfie is only about fourteen years older than you.'

She takes a sip of scolding coffee and frowns. 'I don't think I understand.'

'Did your dad ever talk about what he did before he emigrated to Australia?'

'He worked in the shipyard, but he never said much about it. I think he grew up in the Sholtsbury area. I only know that because I overheard him talking to Mum once.'

'He actually lived in Grange Road for a few of those years. And that's also where he got married to Frances Mary Reed. Alfie is their son.'

I watch the words sinking in slowly, twisting her excitement into something else.

'He was married to someone else before Mum? But that doesn't make any sense, why would he move to Australia if he already had a family?'

I can see she's working up to suggesting this is all a case of mistaken identity, so I take the photo of Joseph, Frances, Alfie and Ivy out of my bag and hand it to her. 'That's Alfie, and his older sister,

Ivy. They were five and two when your dad left.'

'He left?'

She's flawed, I watch the shock and disbelief forming on her face and I'm ashamed of causing her this much pain. It's not my place to deliver anyone with this kind of news about their family.

Abigail stares at the photo for a few moments, tracing the face of her dad with her finger.

'So, you're saying that my dad was already married when he moved to Australia. He had two children, and Alfie is my half-brother?'

'After your dad emigrated, he cut all ties with his English family. He never contacted them again. Alfie has no idea that you exist.'

'But I thought you said you were here on Alfie's behalf?' she says, looking even more confused.

'I am, sort of,' I explain, deciding I need to tell her everything. It's the least she deserves. 'Ivy died a few weeks ago. I was sent to clear out her house and found Alfie and some letters from an Australian agency. Ivy wanted to understand what had happened to her dad. I only found out about you when I started looking. Alfie's not very interested in his dad, but he's got no one else. And I thought if there was any chance that he still had some family...'

She is struggling to take it all in, to process the overload of information. She looks close to tears and I still have no tissues in any of my pockets. I decide against offering her a used paper napkin from the cafe where I've just had lunch. It would only add insult to injury if she ended up with carrot cake smeared across her face.

'I'm so sorry,' I say, reaching out to touch her arm, and then thinking better of it. 'I didn't come here intending to do this, it's just that you looked so much like the photos of your dad, and it sort of leapt out of me before I could stop it.'

'It's okay, Juliette.' She looks anything but okay. 'I always knew Dad must have had a past. I think Mum might have known everything. She said things to him when they argued, things I didn't understand. And later on, when she was starting to lose her memory, she used to talk about someone called Frances Mary. I had no idea that Frances was Dad's first wife.'

'If you don't want to meet Alfie, I promise he'll never hear about any of this from me, he'll be none the wiser. It's the least I can promise after ambushing you at work.' This is not one of my finest moments, and I'm desperate to salvage something out of it for everyone. 'For what it's worth, Alfie's a real character, he's worth getting to know, and I think you would have liked Ivy. I've learned a lot about her over the last few weeks, and it sounds like she was a lovely person. She enjoyed baking Victoria sponge cakes.'

'That was always my dad's favourite,' Abigail says, another piece of her family puzzle slotting into place.

'And she clearly wanted to track your dad down. I don't think anyone ever goes to all that effort just to give someone a piece of their mind. I'd put money on the fact that she was thrilled when the Australian agency told her she had a half-sister.'

Abigail's unsure, the doubts and unanswered questions are written all over her face in big, bold, metaphorical marker pen. She's curious about Alfie but mostly she's still in shock, because of me.

'I'm sorry,' I say, for what feels like the hundredth time, wishing there was more I could do to prove I meant it. 'I know this must be really difficult.'

'I just don't know why he would have left his family.'

This is the part that's bothering her the most, the realisation that her dad wasn't perfect, that he made mistakes, hurt other people. And that there's at least one person in the world (Alfie) who thinks very badly of the dad she loved.

'I can understand why Alfie's so angry. If Dad had done that to me and Mum…' she shakes her head, and continues to stare at the photo as if she's seeing her dad properly for the first time. 'Do you think there's any chance Alfie will want to meet me?'

Even after everything I've just told her, she's still curious. I think Alfie would like that strength of character in her.

'I can't be sure,' I say, trying to be as honest as possible. 'He's been staying at my house for a while now, so I've got to know him better. And I think it would be a shock at first, but he wouldn't blame you for what your dad did. And I know he misses Ivy. He's a good brother.'

She smiles with very watery eyes. 'It would be nice to have a brother. I'm sorry I never had a chance to meet Ivy. I'm not sure I could have been as forgiving as her.'

She tries to give the photo back to me, but I stand, leaving it in her hands.

'Send me a message if you decide you want to meet with Alfie.'

She says nothing as she lets me out of the door at the bottom of the stairs and escorts me all the way to the front of the shop.

'Thanks for coming, Juliette. I'll tell you what I decide about Alfie, either way.'

She shakes my hand, back in full managerial mode now that she's out on the shop floor, as much on display as the hiking poles and blister-proof socks that we're standing next to.

I feel like I want to apologise again, but she's accosted by the youngest member of staff with a jumper-folding crisis, and I'm left standing on my own with nothing but my guilt for company.

The journey home is an uncomfortable one. The mess I've made of things seems to grow bigger with every mile that I drive. I should have arranged to meet her properly and then broken it to her gently, not gone crashing into her life like a wrecking ball. But the cat is out of the bag now and there's no way of forcing it back in. Before I can even make it home, Abigail sends a message. I pull over to the side of the road to read it.

I want to meet Alfie. He's the only family I have left too. Can you talk to him for me, Juliette?

I message back telling her I'll do my best to arrange it, and drive the rest of the way home wondering how I'm going to tell Alfie.

I've already got my key in the front door before I realise that I didn't even wait in the car, after I parked it, to see if Jamie would appear. Normally, nothing has the power to pull me away from him, but I've made such a mess of things with Alfie and Abigail that I can't think of anything except how to fix it. One thing's for sure, I cannot drop a bombshell on Alfie, not after everything he's already been through.

I find him in the dining room. He's sitting at the table reading a newspaper, his foot propped up on a stool and the remains of his dinner on a plate before him.

'I've saved you some chicken pie and roast potatoes, it's in the oven,' he says cheerily, when I dump my bag on a chair. 'Have you been somewhere nice?'

It's an innocent question, he's being polite, but I can't lie to him.

'What's with the boxes, by the way?' Alfie continues, before I can answer, nodding towards the pile of Jamie's things against the wall. 'Been having a good clear-out?'

'Something like that, yes,' I say, not wanting to explain about Jamie's stuff right now.

'I've got something exciting to tell you,' Alfie adds, before I can get a word in edgeways.

'Alfie, I've got something to tell you too, and I've got to do it right now.'

Any lie I tell him about where I've been and what I've been doing will fester overnight into something monstrous.

He finally stops firing questions at me and folds his newspaper. 'That sounds serious. Am I in trouble again?'

'It's nothing you've done. I need to make a confession, and I don't think you're going to like it.'

So much for breaking it to him gently, but there really is no easy way of doing this, I realise. Cups of hot tea and gentle enquiries into how he feels about surprise family reunions would only make him suspicious.

'Okay, out with it then.'

Alfie can tell I'm serious and he's unafraid. I'm the one who's feeling sick with nerves. I take the chair on the opposite side of the table, my fingers fumbling with anxiety.

'I found something when I was clearing out Ivy's stuff. It happens quite a lot, family secrets, things the deceased never told anyone else, but normally there's no one left to pass anything on to.'

Alfie's forehead creases. 'Go on.'

I take a deep breath. 'Ivy tried to find your dad, years ago. It seems he emigrated to Australia.'

'I wondered if the old bugger had scarpered somewhere.' Alfie's arms are now folded tightly across his chest. 'You're not about to tell me he's still alive, are you, because if he's ended up in a retirement home and he needs some money from me, he can whistle for it.'

'No, he died years ago. I'm sorry, Alfie, I know you said you weren't interested in what happened to him, and if that was the only thing Ivy had discovered, I wouldn't have bothered telling you. But she found something else.'

Alfie says nothing this time, so I carry on. 'Your dad got married again to a woman called Elizabeth.'

'I hope for her sake she had better luck with the old bastard than we did.'

'Well, it seems they had a child.'

The look on Alfie's face is indecipherable.

'Her name is Abigail Armitage-Evans, she's your half-sister and she's still alive. You were so upset at losing Ivy, and I just thought that if you still had some family left, you'd want to know.'

'Did you now?' Alfie struggles to his feet and there's suddenly nothing unclear about how he feels. He can't even look me in the eye he's so angry. 'Well, I'll thank you to stay out of my personal business. You've taken me in and looked after me, and I'll never be able to repay you for that kindness. But that doesn't give you the right to go poking about through my life, as well as through Ivy's.'

For a man with a damaged knee, he moves with surprising speed as he leaves the room and heads down the hall.

'Alfie, wait!' I follow him up the stairs as he climbs more slowly. 'She's a lovely woman.'

'You've spoken to her, then?' He stops and turns to face me, one hand gripping the banister so tightly his knuckles have turned white.

'Actually, I've met her, this afternoon. It was sort of an accident, but she didn't know anything about you. She was shocked that her dad had another family, really upset.'

'It seems you've upset more than one person today then.'

Even though it's true, I'm still wounded by Alfie's words. I follow him all the way to his bedroom door.

'She'd like to meet you, Alfie. But it's totally up to you, if you don't want to—'

'What I want is for you to leave me alone.'

He slams the door in my face, and I hear him swearing and cursing as he hobbles across his room. It's the second disaster of the day. I sit at the top of the stairs feeling like a one-woman catastrophe. In fact, everything is falling apart so beautifully, it's like my life has suddenly turned into a stage play. And if someone made a musical of my life right now, it would have to start with a song called "Oh What a Mess You've Made Catastrophe Juliette." I'd be sitting in an old-fashioned saloon bar with my head in my hands. A troupe of dancing cowboys would be singing on a stage behind me about my terrible words and deeds, and a sheriff would be rounding up a posse to run me out of town. I'm so out of practice at life – the messiness of everyday human interactions – that I have forgotten about the potholes and how easy it is to fall headlong into one, or two. Alfie deserves better. But what can I do to fix it? And if Alfie doesn't want to meet Abigail, then she would have been better off not knowing of his existence at all. I should have told Alfie first, taken my cues from him, not plunged ahead regardless of his feelings – feelings he'd already expressed to me in the clearest terms. What made me think I knew him better than he knew himself? And what if Alfie doesn't want to speak to me again? The thought makes me more upset than I expected. I know I didn't want him in my house in the first place, but I don't want us to part on bad terms either. He's more like a friend than anything else now.

I tread softly down the stairs and leave Alfie in peace, with the opening bars of "Oh What a Mess You've Made Catastrophe Juliette" forming themselves inside my head.

Seventeen

I DON'T USUALLY WORK on Saturdays, but after taking time off to look after Alfie, I am way behind schedule on Jim Ravenshaw's flat. Someone needs to finish the job before the client starts asking questions. I linger far longer than usual in the kitchen, before I leave for work, but there's no sign of Alfie. I lay out some bread and condiments for his habitual toast, and prop up a note next to the kettle, telling him again how sorry I am. I know this isn't over though, and there's still the question of Abigail to resolve.

At work, I try to immerse myself in Mr Ravenshaw's flat, to keep my thoughts occupied. He deserves as much of my attention as anyone else I've done this for. I have to empty out the drawers in his bedroom and sort through some boxes I find in the wardrobe, which contain dozens of copies of a wildlife photography magazine. I'm certain I can find someone who will treasure them as much as Mr Ravenshaw clearly did. They are full of amazing photos of tiny frogs, hummingbirds in flight, Scottish red squirrels scampering up trees. The old pairs of leather shoes lined up at the bottom of the wardrobe, however, have been squashed beyond salvation. I check my phone twice as much as usual, but there's no word from Alfie.

By the end of the day, I've finally finished clearing out the flat. I've also vacuumed all the carpets and cleaned the kitchen floor, just to fill in some time. I'm waiting for Otis and his van to come and pick up some of the bulkier items of furniture, as arranged. By 5 p.m., he still hasn't appeared and his phone is turned off as usual. I contact Loretta, who is also putting in some overtime at the office, but she can't get hold of him either. I'm in no mood for Otis and his disappearing act today.

I close the door at 5.39 p.m. and make my way home, still fretting about Alfie and the trouble I've caused him. As I pull into a parking space outside the house, I see Otis' van disappearing up ahead of me, turning right at the end of Raglan Road. Hobson's House Clearance is clearly displayed on the side of the vehicle; it's definitely him. He's never been to my house before. But whatever excuse he's got for not turning up at Jim Ravenshaw's flat, it can wait until Monday. I'm not going to chase him down now.

As soon as I enter the house, I hear voices in the dining room. Mrs Lafleur is paying Alfie a visit. The atmosphere changes when I walk into the room, we have unfinished business.

'How are you, Juliette?' Mrs Lafleur asks, just as kindly as she always does.

'I'm a little tired,' I tell her honestly. 'I'm glad to be home. What have you two been up to today?'

'Just the usual,' Alfie says, not quite smiling, but at least he's speaking to me again. 'There's some tea left in the pot if you want a cup.'

'Thanks.'

If it's a peace offering, I'll gladly take it.

I head towards the kitchen to get a mug and that's when I notice the boxes. Or the space where the boxes (filled with Jamie's things) should have been sitting, piled against the wall. But the boxes have gone.

'That Otis chap called from your work,' Alfie explains, seeing the puzzled look on my face. 'He said you needed him to get rid of some stuff, and you said yesterday that you'd been having a good clear-out, so I told him to come right over and take it all.'

'He took *those* boxes?'

The world, and everything in it, seems to pause.

'Is there something wrong, dear?' Mrs Lafleur asks.

'Those were the wrong boxes. That was everything I had left of Jamie.'

I'm already grabbing my bag and flying towards the door. Alfie has messed up on a cosmic scale. Otis has got his wires crossed again, and now all of Jamie's things are on their way to the refuse centre, like a pile of junk that nobody wants. I jump into my car and phone Otis, while I pull out and speed down the road as fast as I dare. Predictably, there's no answer. I put the phone on speaker and call the office, but Loretta has now gone home for the day. And if I can't catch up with Otis...

The only way to reach the refuse centre is through the middle of town, and the traffic is tortuously slow. Hopefully, the same traffic has also slowed Otis to a crawl. I try to concentrate on the roads, thinking about nothing except staying in the right lane and stopping when the lights turn red, which by some cruel twist of fate, seems to happen far more frequently than usual. I try Otis' phone again, but he's got it turned off and there's no option to leave a message. How could this have happened? Why didn't Alfie phone to check with me first, before letting Otis take all of Jamie's stuff? Some days, I can't get him off the phone, but he obviously didn't want to talk to me because of last night's argument. And now the worst of all possible happenings has come to pass.

As soon as I've cleared the town centre, the traffic eases, and I make good time. Otis drives like there's a compulsory fifteen mile per hour speed limit on every road. If I can just make up some of the ground between us, there's still a slim chance I can save Jamie's stuff before it hits the bottom of a skip.

When I finally pull into the refuse centre, I see Otis' van driving away in the opposite direction, he's already unloaded everything. I don't waste any time trying to flag him down. I need to find someone who can help me. I have to explain what's happened, the catastrophic error that's occurred. Maybe some things can be fished out of the skip before they're buried and lost forever. I pull into a bay directly in front of the household-waste bin and rush to see if I can spot any of the boxes that I know so well, but the skip is almost empty. I find a man called Derek and drag him back to the scene of the crime.

'That one was full, it's just been collected by the waste management company and taken away, that's why you've got a nice empty skip there now,' he explains slowly, like I'm baffled by the complicated concept of emptying a skip when it has reached its capacity to hold junk. 'Just chuck your stuff into that one, there's plenty of room.'

'No, I'm not trying to get rid of anything. I want to rescue some boxes. Can't you call the waste management company and ask them to bring the other skip back? Or if I know where they're heading, I can meet them there.'

'Once it's left the site, it's out of my hands,' Derek says, with a more-than-my-job's-worth shrug of his shoulders.

'But none of this stuff should have been taken away, it was a huge mistake.' The pitch of my voice is rising to panic level. I have to resist the compulsion to grab his yellow high-visibility shirt and mangle the importance of my words into his chest. 'Please, can't you do something to help?'

'That skip's halfway to landfill by now, and there's nothing I can do to bring it back, sorry,' he says, already turning away from me to help someone with a load of wooden floorboards.

I hurriedly track down another high-visibility worker and ask them where the skip has been taken to, with the same negative results. I do a frenzied search on the internet, but it's impossible to find out what I need to know. Jamie's stuff – virtually everything I had left of him – has gone.

I sit in my car for so long just staring into space that Derek eventually has to ask me to leave. I'm blocking the parking bay and other customers need to use it. I'm in no fit state to drive all the way home. I'm so numb I can't tell my indicator from my elbow. I need to stop somewhere and gather myself together. The only place I can think to go is the bookshop; it's ten minutes away.

The building is in darkness, when I park outside, even though it's supposed to be open until 7.00 p.m., every Saturday. It's the second time I've come to visit only to find the shop closed. On the door, there's a handwritten sign announcing that the shop has now closed down, and I realise that the windows are empty of displays. I press my face to the glass door and peer inside. The interior of the shop has been stripped. All the bookcases have gone. The counter has been ripped out. The entire heart of the shop has been gutted and there's nothing left. There's just enough light coming from somewhere in the back for me to see that the whole place is being refurbished, newly plastered walls and ceiling. I squash my nose hard against the glass, trying to see different areas of the shop from various angles, but it doesn't matter where I look, I can no longer see any trace of Jamie. Everything he ever touched, fixed or broke has been torn out and cast away. Apart from the day that he died, this has been the worst twenty-four hours of my life. I've lost almost everything, apart from one book from Paris, a Highland cow mug and the second-date conker, which is still sitting in my pocket. And is now even more precious than it already was. All the photos, letters and keepsakes have been lost for all eternity. Every last one of his shoes and pairs of jeans has gone. It's such a huge hole I'll never be able to fill it.

I slump into the seat of my car. There's a message on my phone from Alfie, but I can't talk to him now. I'd only say something I'd never be able to repair, and I don't want that on my conscience as well as everything else. I also don't want to explain this latest tragedy to Alfie or Mrs Lafleur. I can't face either of them, I can't go home. There's only one place where I can seek refuge.

'What are you doing here?' Poppy smiles as she opens the door, paintbrush thrust through her hair like a pin. 'Oh god, we weren't supposed to meet in the pub, were we? I've had one of those weeks where everything has gone wrong, and I...'

Her words trail away as she registers the look on my face. She steers me softly into the house, guiding me down the hall so I don't bump into the walls.

'Juliette, what's happened, what's wrong?' She sits me on the sofa in the kitchen. Her voice is filled with fear, I have to say something to ease her anxiety, but the words are impossible.

'Is it something to do with Jamie?'

'The bookshop,' I manage to say, after several failed attempts where no words come out. 'It's gone.'

Poppy frowns. 'What do you mean, gone?'

'It's closed down, everything has been gutted from front to back. All of Jamie's things have been taken away.'

'But you can't mean the bookshelves?'

'They're gone. The counter's gone, the boot print on the wall, nothing's left. It's all in a skip somewhere.'

Poppy's face melts with sudden sadness. She loved visiting the bookshop too. She helped her brother decorate the children's section, with beautiful paintings of fairies and glow worms, moons and stars. We haven't just lost a shop we've lost a whole chunk of our history.

'I knew this might happen someday,' she says, wiping her eyes, 'but I was hoping that some of it might survive, like mosaic floors at a Roman villa, or footprints captured in wet clay tiles.'

I eventually manage to explain about the boxes, about Otis with his van and my pointless dash to the refuse centre. But I'm still so frozen it feels like I'm describing a puncture I've just repaired on a bicycle wheel.

'So, it's all gone too, there's nothing left?'

Poppy grabs my hands and holds them. She understands how devastated and unhinged I should be feeling at this moment. Her grief is powerful enough for both of us, and she doesn't even notice that my face is impassive, unyielding. I wait patiently as she sobs all over her apron, blowing her nose on the pocket. As soon as she's cried herself out, she leaps up from the sofa, and when she returns, she presses something into my hands.

'You need this more than I do.'

It's Jamie's old scarf, made with leftover wool from all the knitting projects that Poppy started but never finished. It's soft and familiar, a crazy patchwork of clashing colours. I press the wool to my face and sit motionless, feeling blank, unable to identify or process a single emotion.

The rest of the evening has a strange dreamlike quality, and hours of time seem to pass in a matter of minutes. Poppy cooks us some dinner, a glass of wine sits untouched beside me. Then I'm following her up the stairs to the spare room, where she's insisting that I spend the night. She hugs me for a long time, but I can't wait for her to leave me alone. And finally, I'm in the dark, clinging to Jamie's scarf in case that too disappears. I let sleep take me down quickly.

In the morning, numbness is still the only thing I can feel. Poppy makes me a bacon sandwich for breakfast. But the greasy texture turns my stomach and I end up playing with the rind instead of eating it. She also gathers together a small survival box containing a few precious things that belonged to Jamie, so I can take him home with me again. There's a book of maps (filled with scribbled notes) that Jamie used whenever he planned his road trips, and his favourite childhood teddy bear, Growler. Growler is worn down to the threads on one side of his body, where Jamie used to trail him along the floor, a trusted companion on all his adventures.

I tell Poppy I'm grateful, even though these things have more meaning for her. They don't belong to the Jamie I had in my life. I promise to call her when I get home and if I need someone to talk to, but I know I won't do either of those things. I don't even care about seeing Alfie. I just want to go home now. I'm too exhausted to go anywhere else.

Jamie doesn't appear when I pull up outside my house, but I didn't expect him to and I don't linger in the car. Alfie is nowhere to be seen. He's left a note on the dining room table, along with a bag of fresh cakes from the bakery at the bottom of the road. The delicious smell fills the room like a sugary flower in full bloom.

Juliette, I'm very sorry about the boxes. I had no idea what was in them, and I should have phoned you first. Marina's hopping mad with me for being so careless with your things. But not as angry as I am with myself, I've been a prize idiot. I really hope you managed to catch up with Otis and his van.

I never got a chance to tell you my news, the other day. Jaya, from the Council Housing Department, phoned to say a place had unexpectedly opened up at the sheltered housing scheme. It has already been cleared out (we both know all about that part of the process) and I can move in straight away. So that's where I've gone, and I'm finally out of your hair.

Thank you for your kindness, generosity and hospitality. I'll never forget living here with you, and I hope that you might consider coming to my new home for a visit soon. You'd be more than welcome, anytime.

Love, Alfie

It's only then that I realise there are no signs of Alfie anywhere: no underpants on the drying rack, folded newspapers or discarded socks. The house has a stillness that hasn't been present for what feels like months. It is finally mine again. And I have never felt so alone. All of Jamie's things are gone, the bookshop has gone and the visitations in my car have come to an end. Jamie has gone. For the first time, the full weight of it hits me and I sit on the floor with my back against the chimney breast. There's nothing to keep me from facing my grief. The tears come in painful, full-body sobs that I hope Mrs Lafleur is too deaf to hear, because it is a frightening sound, and there's nothing I can do to hold it in. I have lost the love of my life and I'm finally letting myself feel it.

The next few days pass in a haze. Poppy calls at regular intervals to make sure I'm eating and sleeping. She also calls the office and tells them I won't be coming in for at least two weeks, and for once, I don't argue. I can't face going through anyone else's stuff when I've just lost all of Jamie's. I spend a lot of time just lying on my bed, or on the sofa, or on the floor at the top of the stairs. Grief pins me to the carpet while I make a study of the ceiling above me. All the cracks and imperfections are strangely absorbing. I take Jamie's ashes out of the airing cupboard and carry them around with me, trying to feel his presence through the jar, but it's hopeless. So I put him back in the cupboard again.

I think about Jamie, constantly. The heartbreak comes in waves, some with the power to uproot trees and lift solid brick buildings from their foundations, others are more gentle and they release a stream of memories I cannot suppress. But he is gone. I'll never sit with him in my car again. All the conversations we have from this point onwards will be painfully one-sided. The awful, crushing sadness is present as soon as I wake up in the morning – like it's been hovering over the bed all night long, just waiting for me to open my eyes – and it stays with me through every minute of the day that follows. There is no relief.

At some point, Mrs Lafleur calls round with a beef stew. I answer the door in my pyjamas and dressing gown. She runs her professional eye over my dishevelled hair and the blotchy skin on my face and takes charge for a few hours. I'm incredibly grateful. She runs me a bath and it's so soothing I never want to get out. She combs through the knots in my wet hair afterwards, and says nothing as the tears roll down my face. I'm like a river in full flood. She listens to some beautiful piano music on the radio, as I eat the stew, and lets me cry on her shoulder when the sorrowful sounds become too much. The music seems to have been written for me and my grief, inviting me to mourn in ways I don't fully comprehend until I feel the heartbreaking melodies resonate through the bones in my chest. Melodies that then sink straight down into the aching muscles of my heart. She tucks me up in bed before she leaves, and I want her to stay forever. But I know that at some stage, I will have to get myself dressed and pick up the pieces of my life, shattered as they are.

When I wake up the following morning, I know I need to get out of my house. I need some relief from myself, from Jamie. For a few hours at least, I have to think about something else. I put on some semi-clean clothes, pull my hair back with a tie and drive all the way across town to Orton Lodge. Even at this time of year, the gardens at the front are immaculate. I've never seen such well cared for shrubs. The flats are arranged in groups of twos and threes around little courtyards for sitting in. It's one of the nicest housing schemes I've been to.

Alfie's flat, 3B, is on the ground floor. He says nothing when he opens the door. He just guides me over to a comfy chair and lets me cry.

'Get it all out, Juliette,' he says, placing a box of tissues on the coffee table in front of me, and I suspect he's been talking to Mrs Lafleur. 'There's no point trying to hold it in. When you've lost someone you love that much, the only thing you can do is to feel it. And there'll be plenty more where that came from, but, eventually, it'll get a little easier.'

That's impossible to imagine, my tear ducts have found dozens of new connections to my heart and it feels like it will never stop. How could there possibly be any end to it? But I do manage to gain control over my own prolific waterworks, for a short while at least.

'I'm glad you've come to visit. I wanted to say sorry in person. I had no idea what was in those boxes, and I wish I'd had the sense to call you before I let Otis take them. I wish I could go back and change that.'

'Me too,' I say, dabbing at a small leakage from the corner of my eye.

'I'll be sorry for the rest of my days, Juliette.'

He's obviously been beating himself up about it, but I don't want him to punish himself any longer. Alfie is kind and good and loyal. He just made a mistake.

'It was an accident, Alfie, I don't blame you,' I tell him sincerely. And for a moment, I'm not sure which one of us needs access to the tissues more urgently.

I take a long look around the room we're sitting in. It's only been a few days, but Alfie has already managed to make it feel like his own. I realise I've never seen him in his own place before, first he was staying with Ivy and then with me. There's a photo of Alfie and Ivy in a frame on the coffee table, and another picture of some deer in a pine forest is hanging above the fireplace.

'That belonged to Ivy,' I say, remembering what Alfie said about it being a birthday present from their mum.

'I grabbed it from Ivy's sitting room before everything got taken away, and took it round to my mate's place for safekeeping. I couldn't let it end up in the hands of a stranger.'

It was the right thing to do. It's one of the only family heirlooms that Alfie owns.

'The furniture was here when I moved in.' Alfie points at the tiled 1970s coffee table and the high-backed sofa, in a questionable shade of lavender. 'Not my favourite colour but it's comfy, and all things considered, I think I've landed on my feet here.'

'It's a great flat, Alfie,' I say.

It's been given a fresh coat of paint. The carpet is soft and there's a gas fire burning. A long window looks out over a square of garden that will be beautiful in the spring and summer. In the winter, he'll be able to watch, from the comfort of his own armchair, as high winds blow through the trees in the distance. Alfie shows me around the rest of the flat, there's a small neat kitchen with plenty of cupboard space, the bathroom is properly tiled with a pale pink suite that gives the room a soft glow. There are fitted wardrobes in the bedroom, and a thick carpet that is much warmer and friendlier on the feet than the cold, hard laminate flooring I find in so many flats and houses. Everything here is homely. They're a good fit, Alfie and his new flat. He'll be happy here.

'Marina has already been for a visit,' he says, boiling the kettle and making us both a coffee. 'She can get here on the number eleven bus, if she doesn't want to drive, and there are no ridiculous rules to stop visitors from staying over,' he adds with the faintest blush. 'There are a couple of grand charity shops close by, and we're going to go hunting for some cushions and lampshades, make the place feel a bit more my style.'

'This place really suits you already,' I say, helping myself to a chocolate biscuit.

He smiles and it's obvious that he feels it too.

'I'm sorry about going behind your back to find your half-sister,' I say.

'Don't you worry about that, you were trying to do the right thing, and I've been a daft old bugger. It's not Abigails's fault either. I've been thinking that I'd like to meet her,' he says, nodding approvingly to himself. 'It's what Ivy would have wanted, it's what I want.'

Alfie's words bring on a fresh batch of tears, and I know it's because he has a chance at completing the missing pieces of his own story. Maybe Alfie and Abigail can help each other; form one little family from the remnants they've both been left with.

'Will you contact her for me and make some arrangements?'

'I'd be happy to, Alfie.'

He spends some time telling me about the other residents, the old friend he discovered living in another flat on the complex.

'I thought the old miser was dead and that's why I hadn't seen him for the last two years, but it turns out he's been living it up here. And there's a lovely Jamaican lady across the hall, her family comes to visit several times a week. I've already been over for more coffee and cake than someone my age can handle,' he chuckles.

'You're more than welcome to come and visit me, if you ever want a night away. I'll keep the spare room ready,' I tell him.

'No offense, Juliette, but I've had my fill of spare rooms, for the time being. But I will be coming to see you and Marina, of course. I'll cook us all a nice roast one Sunday. Now that I know my way around your kitchen, it would be a shame to let that go to waste.'

The thought of Alfie and Mrs Lafleur coming round for Sunday dinner is enough to active my tear ducts again. For the first time since Jamie, I feel properly seen. Poppy is wonderful, I'd be lost without her. But having Alfie and Mrs Lafleur – with their total lack of connection to Jamie – is what I need more than anything. The land of the living, maybe I'm not quite done with it yet. And this is a small step back towards the outer edges, at least.

'I reckon I would have liked your Jamie,' Alfie says, offering me another chocolate biscuit. 'How did you two meet?'

I tell Alfie about the curious twists and turns of fate that led me to The Wise Old Whale Bookshop, and the way Jamie's beautiful soul was even more attractive than his deep brown eyes.

'It doesn't hurt though, does it,' he smiles, 'having someone nice to look at.'

He's a good listener, prompting me for more details when I dry up, helping me bring Jamie into the room, so he's a part of this visit too. It's such a kind thing to do that I work my way through another quarter of the tissues before I'm dry-eyed again. Alfie makes us some lunch, and I stay the whole afternoon as we watch one of his favourite programmes on TV. Then he shows me how to keep a lettuce fresh in the fridge, by chopping out the stem, patting it dry with paper towels and storing it in a ziplock bag. I resist the urge to look in his cupboards, but I have a feeling everything will be neat and orderly inside.

By the time I get home, it's already dark. I sit in the car for a few minutes with my eyes closed, saying a silent thank you to Jamie for all the times he kept me company in our little bubble of togetherness. And it isn't quite as devastating as I feared it would be.

'Wherever you are now, Jamie Matthews,' I say the final words out loud, 'I hope the singing's good and the company's even better. I wish only good things for you.'

The house feels cold when I let myself inside. I flick the heating on and go upstairs to find my slippers. The room is a mess and I have to crawl on my hands and knees, stretching my arm under the bed to retrieve them. But my slippers are not the only things I find.

Juliette and Jamie
V
Reprieve

JAMIE WAS IN DEEP trouble and he knew it. I almost felt sorry for him as he tried to make it up to me. But I couldn't hide my upset, it was sliding down my face and onto my T-shirt without restraint.

'I can't believe I forgot your birthday,' he said, for the tenth time since he'd got home, running a hand over his face, as if it might wipe the slate clean. 'I was going to get you this great book about Victorian cake recipes that I knew you'd love. But we had that flood in the bathroom above the shop two weeks ago, and then we moved into Raglan Road the next day, and it went clean out of my head.'

'It's okay,' I said, even though I was crying like he'd committed a truly heinous crime. 'This is ridiculous.' I wiped the tears away with the back of my hand but it just encouraged more to come. 'I don't know why it's upsetting me so much.'

'It's because this is your special day, love, and you deserve a fuss. A man who'll turn up with a cake and a bunch of flowers, and sing to you so loudly that all the dogs in the neighbourhood would be joining in with the chorus.'

He shook his head, disappointed with himself, then took my hand and led me into the dining room and sang a rousing chorus of "Happy Birthday." My tears finally dried up. I'd been waiting all day for a card, or a delivery from The Three Cups Bakery or even a phone call wishing me a Happy Birthday. Except for our engagement, surprise parties weren't his normal style; he couldn't keep a secret when he was excited about something. He'd wake me up, in the middle of the night, just to tell me about a cabin in the Lake District he thought we should book, because it sat just a rabbit's hole away from where Beatrix Potter used to live. So I wasn't expecting any surprise celebrations. But when he eventually arrived home at 7.30 p.m., empty-handed and asking what was for dinner...

'Let's go out to that lovely little Italian place down the road, we'll order the biggest tiramisu they've got and eat the whole thing between us.'

He was already tugging me towards the hall, but I pulled back.

'I can't go to Antonio's in my pyjamas.'

'Then you've got five minutes to change into something with enough elastic in the waistband to allow for reckless tiramisu consumption.'

On a Tuesday night, we were virtually the only people in the restaurant. A log fire burned in the corner. The smell of fresh basil and garlic bread was almost enough to make us believe we were sitting in the Umbrian countryside, not squashed between a pet food store and a Chinese takeaway on the main road into Sholtsbury. True to his word, Jamie ordered a large tiramisu that came to the table with birthday candles blazing. Later, at home, when I was too full to move – and we sat on the sofa surrounded by the unopened boxes from our recent move to Raglan Road – I realised it had been one of my favourite birthdays, after all. No expectations, no organisation or big build-up. Just a spur of the moment dinner that seemed to possess magical qualities, even though all I could find to wear at short notice was an old pair of stretchy jeans and a jumper that was covered in bobbles. Even though there was no card or present, no grand gestures. But when I told Jamie he was forgiven, he shook his head wearily and sighed.

'You're far too quick to let me off the hook, Juliette. I should have written myself notes and posted them all over the bookshop, in my shoes, next to my toothbrush. Forgetting your birthday is a crime and I'm truly sorry. I wanted to do something special.'

'If you ever forget it again, that's it, I'm throwing you out of the house,' I told him, shifting positions so I could breathe more easily.

'I can't argue with that. One forgotten birthday might be forgiven, if I'm lucky, but two forgotten birthdays—'

'Especially if they occur within five years of each other,' I stipulated, smiling.

'If they occur within five years of each other, I'll be throwing myself out of the house, you don't have to worry about that.'

'And I'm applying the same rules to myself, if I ever forget your birthday—'

'But you'd never do that.'

'You're right,' I said, knowing it was true. 'There's no way I'd ever forget your birthday, unless we got invaded by aliens, and they sprinkled the clouds with a memory suppressant that rained down on everyone.'

'But if that happened, I'd forget my own birthday as well, so I wouldn't even know you'd forgotten to buy me a present.'

'This is getting way, way too complicated,' I said, closing my eyes and snuggling down into his side. 'Tiramisu is not an aide to clear thinking.'

Jamie struggled off the sofa, before I could get really comfortable. I was too full to ask where he was going and stretched out instead, my overstuffed belly propped up by some well-placed cushions. When he finally returned, with his hands hidden behind his back, he was looking very pleased with himself, like a man redeemed.

'I suddenly remembered I did buy one thing for your birthday, almost a year ago.' He dangled a plain brown knitted sock in front of him, like he was gifting me the Taj Mahal. 'Happy Birthday!'

'Thank you?' I took the sock dubiously and could instantly feel the weight of something heavy stuffed inside it. 'No wrapping paper?' I guessed.

'Another thing I forgot. But I found what's inside that sock in an antiques shop on Whipple Street, just down the road from that crafting place you love.'

I felt the outside of the sock, testing for lumps and bumps, like a child in possession of an oddly-shaped Christmas present trying to prolong the mystery and intrigue. If it turned out to be a lump of coal, or some kind of birthday joke, we'd be having words. I worked my way down to the bottom of the sock with my fingers, finding something cold and smooth, and carefully extracted a beautiful enamel box.

'Jamie, it's absolutely gorgeous!'

It was decorated with tiny red dragons on a deep sea of mossy green, and I loved it instantly.

'You haven't heard what I'm going to do with it yet. You'd better get comfortable because it's quite a story, and I don't want you falling asleep on me halfway through. I know what you're like when you've had dessert.'

I sat up, looking alert, playing the game, and tried to ignore the pressure the upright position put on my stomach. I now felt like I'd swallowed a cantaloupe melon.

Jamie took his place beside me, one arm wrapped around my waist, helping to support my birthday belly.

'I once read about an old tradition from somewhere exotic and interesting, I can't remember where.'

'But you always remember everything you read. Are you just making this up because you forgot my birthday?'

'I swear, I read it in a book about these old Norwegian traditions that almost everyone had forgotten, or it could have been Swedish traditions, or possibly Chinese.' His forehead wrinkled as he tried to remember. 'Anyway, the tradition came about because these fishermen, or sailors, or whoever they were, worked in rough, dangerous seas and every time they set sail, there was always a chance they might not come home again. So they wrote the thing they loved the most about their beloved on a piece of paper, and held it tightly in both hands, thinking about that person. Then they sealed the paper quickly inside a box, so none of those special thoughts and feelings could escape.'

Jamie drew a small piece of folded paper from his pocket, my name already written across the front in his long looping scrawl. He held it in both hands and closed his eyes. His face was a fascinating mix of twitches, smiles and a curious single raise of his eyebrow. I would have given anything to know what he was thinking at that moment, what it was about me that he treasured the most. But I could not interrupt the ritual. When he finally opened his eyes, he stuffed the paper inside the box and snapped it shut.

'And now, for the best part.' I could tell something good was coming by how much he was enjoying himself. 'According to the tradition—'

'Which could be Norwegian, or Swedish or Chinese.'

'I've got to hide this box somewhere so it can't be easily found.'

'What?' I was off the sofa in a heartbeat, cantaloupe belly or not. 'But why bother giving me a present if you're just going to hide it? That's mean!'

Jamie smiled. 'It's not mean. The fishermen hid the boxes in case they perished at sea and never came home again.'

'You are not a fisherman or a sailor.'

'True, but I'm hiding it because someday, when we're old and grey and I've forgotten your birthday again, that's when you'll need it the most. You'll find it, open it and feel just how much I love you. For the fisherman and sailors, it was one small way of letting their womenfolk know how they truly felt.'

'If you perish at sea, I'll never forgive you.'

'Okay, I promise I won't board any boats or seafaring vessels without wearing at least three life jackets.'

'Also, if you refer to me as womenfolk again, I'll batter you with a cushion and walk out of this house forever, and you'll never see me again.'

'Personally, I would never refer to you as womenfolk, not even if my life depended upon it. It was purely for the purpose of historical reference, you understand.'

It was such a beautiful idea, so romantic and old-fashioned, the perfect representation of Jamie himself, and everything I loved about him. If any other person had tried to pull that one on me, I would have been convinced it was an attempt to mock any such rituals, and that when I eventually opened the box, I'd find nothing inside but a childish knock-knock joke. But Jamie was just being himself. A big-hearted romantic. The man who wanted to love someone so much he'd feel the way Romeo felt when he thought his own Juliet was dead. How could I make fun of that?

'Do I have to close my eyes and count to ten so you can hide it, or do you want me to go and stand in the backyard?'

Jamie considered the problem for a second. 'You're in no fit state to stand anywhere, not after the amount of tiramisu you've consumed tonight. I'll put some music on instead, so you can't hear what I'm doing. I already have the perfect place in mind. But you have to promise to forget about the box for a while, don't go looking for it as soon as I've left the house on Monday morning, or it won't work.'

'I promise,' I said, my hand on my heart for dramatic effect.

I lay down on the sofa again, listening to the unromantic strains of The Eighteen. The music hid any noise that Jamie was making, I had no idea which room of the house he'd disappeared into. Although I was already planning ways I might accidentally stumble across the enamel box, in the course of an extra vigorous spring-clean, which would involve shifting some furniture and taking a crowbar to the floorboards, if necessary. He took so long he could have been digging a hole under the foundations of the house, with his bare hands. When he eventually returned – with no sign of any dirt lodged under his fingernails – he looked extremely pleased with himself.

'Now, if you're wondering what to get me for my birthday,' he said, settling down on the sofa again, feet up on the stool, 'I can point you towards an alternator and starter motor for my motorbike that I've been lusting after. It's all any man could ever want from his one true love.'

'Can't you give me one little clue about where you've hidden it?' I asked. 'It is my birthday, after all.'

'I cannot. But one day, when you do find it, you'll know that I may have forgotten your birthday once, but...'

'You're never going to finish that sentence, are you?' I nestled into his warm body again, closing my eyes.

'Not even if you put a shiny new camshaft cover in my Christmas stocking. My lips are sealed forever on the subject.'

Eighteen

I WRIGGLE FORWARDS ON my stomach until I'm a little further under the bed, and my hand finds something solid and hard. It's definitely not a slipper. I sit back on my heels, when my head has cleared the bedframe again, and stare at the familiar object like it's a gift from the gods, Jamie's fortune-telling snowglobe. He bought it on a road trip down the Pacific Coast Highway in America, and it was one of his favourite things. He consulted the oracle of the snowglobe almost daily. Should he get the pastrami sandwich or the potato salad for lunch? The snowglobe had the answer. Was it going to be warm enough to take the motorbike out for a ride to the coast? Don't bother consulting the weather forecast, what does the snowglobe say? It was all done in a very light-hearted manner. He didn't believe in horoscopes, tarot cards or anything else you could find in a New Age gift shop, but the snowglobe was a part of his history. He loved the heaviness of it in his hands, and the sloshing noise it made when he shook it, so that the tiny written nuggets of wisdom floated around the snowy scene inside the glass, answering any question he had. And it has inexplicably found its way to the space under the bed.

Jamie was never careless with the stuff he cared about. I may have found his dirty socks in all sorts of odd places – inside a vase, hanging from a hook in the kitchen where the soup ladle should have been – but he never would have let the snowglobe roll loosely around the room. And then I realise, the globe must have been inside the box that I moved, the one that gave way and dumped its contents all over the carpet. It rolled under the bed all by itself. I'm so absurdly happy to see it again that I sit on the floor and shake it, asking it a series of my own questions. The answer I like best is *you'll never be truly alone.* I haven't lost everything of Jamie's after all. Fate has delivered me with his precious fortune-telling snowglobe, which is ironic in itself, and something Jamie would have found highly amusing.

I set it down on the carpet and crawl onto my belly again, trying to see what else might have rolled under the bed from the same box, escaping a fateful end at the refuse centre. It's too dark to see much, but my fingers find something smaller this time. I pull it out into the light. It's one of Jamie's silver rings, the one that never left his finger. It was given to me by the funeral home, but I'd put it away like almost everything else that reminded me that Jamie was no longer here. I hold it tightly in my closed palm just feeling the cool smoothness of the silver, picturing Jamie wearing it. I set it down next to the snowglobe and scramble even further under the bed this time, using the light on my phone to guide me.

There's just one more escapee. A beautiful cherry-wood sphere with foxes, holly leaves and winter trees carved into the surface. A present from Poppy, Jamie used to sit and play with it absentmindedly when he was trying to figure out a problem at the bookshop, or how to help a friend in the grip of a career/relationship/financial crisis. I'm lucky that all three objects had the sense to roll a good way under the bed, so they weren't visible from any position other than the one I'm currently lying in. Otherwise, I would have scooped them up and added them to the lost boxes. I'm also fortunate that I do not routinely feel the need to vacuum under my bed. If I'd stored any boxes in this space, it would have prevented this dreamlike event from happening. I have regained three treasured possessions, three pieces of Jamie that I can keep forever.

I reach out to grab the wooden ball, but a notch in one of the carvings has got stuck on a tuft of carpet, and I have to tug it several times to pull it free. The tugging also lifts a neatly cut square of the carpet itself. I know for a fact that it was not cut when the carpet was laid because Jamie and I inspected the job when it was done. It was one of the few things in the house that we changed as soon as we moved in. The black and white geometric patterns of the old carpet did strange things to my eyes – it was like walking into a migraine every time I entered the room. It had to be replaced. So this square of carpet, I realise, as I inspect it by the light of my phone, has been cut deliberately, after the fact.

I shuffle my way backwards and then move the entire bed, inch by inch, lifting one leg and then another, until the hole in the carpet is fully exposed. When I kneel down beside it, I discover the underlay has also been neatly cut. At the bottom of the excavation, I find a piece of plywood, two inches by two inches, screwed down onto the floorboard. I race downstairs and root around in the storeroom in the backyard until I find one of Jamie's screwdrivers. The screws come up easily, they're not old, not part of any repair carried out decades ago. When I lift the plywood patch away, it reveals a hole, inside which sits a black velvet bag, and just the sight of it causes my heartrate to skyrocket. I extract the bag, being careful not to catch it on any splinters, and then sit cross-legged on the floor. My hands are suddenly trembling because I know what this is.

I untie the cords on the bag and find a familiar enamel box inside, the one that Jamie bought for my birthday and then hid in the house. But it wasn't supposed to happen like this. I wasn't supposed to be as desolate and bereaved as the women in the tale, the ones who had lost their husbands at sea. I was supposed to be old and grey, my teeth no longer my own, my earlobes as long as my chin. It gives me the shivers to think of the jokes we made about this very special gift.

I'd made several lacklustre attempts to find it over the last eighteen months: clearing out cupboards, searching through the Mason jars in the kitchen, shining a torch into the vanity unit under the basin in the bathroom, looking for any secret holes in the walls. But it never crossed my mind to look for signs of a mutilated carpet. There's no way Jamie could have guessed that the snowglobe would eventually lead me to it, he would have loved that.

I sit with the box in the palm of my hand. Now that I've finally found it, I'm not certain I want to read whatever's written on the piece of paper inside. I'll only ever get to read it for the first time once. A part of me wants to save it for a really dark day, one where I can barely get myself out of bed. But the rest of me is too impatient to wait.

I open the box slowly. But there's no Disney-esque puff of fairy dust, no ghost of Jamie's love rushing out to envelop me, no flickering of lightbulbs. The piece of paper that he held in his hands is neatly folded inside, with one partial oily fingerprint embedded on the far righthand corner. He'd been working on his bike the day before the accident. I caress the fingerprint gently, it's another treasure I'll gratefully hold onto.

I open the note, feeling slightly sick with the anticipation, and stare at Jamie's words, a true message from beyond the grave.

Juliette, I love so many things about you, but the one thing that's in my heart right now is the way you hug me. It's never half-hearted, you commit with your full body and soul and try to squeeze everything you're feeling into me. I love that about you. You give the best hugs ever.

If you're reading this note and I'm no longer with you, know that I expect you to live a full and happy life without me. And don't be getting some notion in your head about honouring my memory by hanging onto all my records, and my stinky old trainers. I know what you're like. You have to promise me to carry on and listen to my wise words.

I loved you, always, my Juliette.

Jamie xxxx

I hold my breath for so long that it hurts when I finally breathe again.

How did he know?

Why write something about a life without him, something so prophetic that it makes me feel doubly sick with confusion? Why not just rattle something off about my sense of humour instead, or the way I made him hot chocolate before bed, with the good marshmallows?

I was supposed to find the box when we were old and grey and still happily living our lives together. But there were so many layers to Jamie. Maybe he had a sense, never fully conscious, that he wasn't destined to live a long life.

I read the note again and again trying to see anything hidden in the meaning, any last secret I can extract from his words. But I will never know what made him write about himself in the past tense, or why he talked about his stinky old trainers. There's no way he could have known that they would become such a focus of our conversations in the car. How could he have foreseen it? Coincidence seems like an insult to the message he's left behind. But I have no other explanation, maybe I never will.

When I've committed the note to memory, I fold it safely into the box. Then I replace the plywood and the carpet layers, before moving the bed back into its usual spot. I position the enamel box on the bedside table along with the snowglobe, the silver ring and the wooden sphere, arranging the precious finds until I'm happy with the way they look. This is my personal shrine to the man I loved, something to greet me when I wake up in the morning.

Another thing that grief teaches you – never take anyone for granted. We hear that phrase so often in life that it loses all meaning and impact, forgotten in a second. But if I could have Jamie back, just for an instant, if I could do anything with him right now, even if it involved unclogging drains, I'd take it gladly and be grateful for that time. If I could do something as ordinary as sit on the sofa with Jamie, watching the six o'clock news... Just to hear his voice, or let my foot fall lazily across his, or share a knowing smile...

I've had a lot of time to think about it, over the last eighteen months, and I know that if I could have my time with Jamie again, I'd be more present every day, through all the six o'clock moments.

Nineteen

I ARRIVE AT THE crematorium car park thirty minutes before Ivy's funeral begins. The place is empty, except for a few cars parked in the spaces reserved for staff, and there's just one other vehicle. I recognise it from Raglan Road, it belongs to Mrs Lafleur. I'm very glad that I won't be the only mourner.

I sit in the car composing myself until I'm ready to go into the crematorium. It's the first time I've left the house in three days. Mrs Lafleur has been round for a chat, but the rest of the time I've been wandering around the house by myself, sitting in all the rooms, letting memories of Jamie slowly surface. It's been hard. I've fought for so long to keep everything at bay. I've been through whole boxes of tissues, living in my sweatpants, letting my slovenly streak take the reins for a while. I only had a shower when I realised the blocked-drain smell that kept stubbornly following me around was coming from my own body. But it hasn't been all sorrow and sweatpants. I've also watched the sparrows in the backyard washing their feathers in the birdbath, the meticulous way they go about it, giving themselves over to the task entirely. I've done some research into how to care properly for my house plants, now that I'm their sole guardian. I am very slowly allowing myself to start living in my house again. Making choices about how I want it to be now there's no Jamie to share it with. It's what he's been trying to tell me all along. Life moves on, if you let it. And that's a normal part of grieving.

Next week, I'm going back to work. Loretta has already lined up a nice flat in Cromwell Park for me to clear, nothing too overwhelming. Loretta might be many things I don't understand, but she was devastated when Billy, her French bulldog, had to be put to sleep last year, so she has a sense of how I'm feeling. Love comes in all shapes and sizes, with two legs and with four. There's nothing to be gained from grading loss on a scale.

I've also been looking at new duvet covers online, something to freshen up my bedroom, but I haven't managed to hit the buy now button yet. It might still be too soon for that. I've got a long way to go before I can even contemplate stripping wallpaper in the sitting room, or ripping out the old plumbing in the kitchen. But there is a chance that the day will come. I've also made an appointment to see a bereavement counsellor. I'm still not sure I've done the right thing. I don't know if I can talk about losing Jamie with a total stranger, but I think it's worth a try. Poppy went to see a counsellor for a few months after Jamie died, and I could see the positive changes in her. Up until now, I didn't want anything to change. But change has found me anyway in the shape of Alfie Evans. Alfie Evans, the most unlikely angel, if you believe that some people take that form on this earth. And I'm not sure what I believe after Jamie's uncannily accurate note. Maybe it doesn't matter what I believe. I'm just grateful that Alfie has entered my life, and stuck with me like a limpet to a battered salty rock by the sea.

Alfie, Mrs Lafleur and I are all set for a big Sunday roast in two weeks' time, and I'm looking forward to it. My house already knows the sound of their voices. I've also deleted my fictitious friends from my contact lists. I've got real people to think about now. Perhaps it's because Alfie and Mrs Lafleur have been through losses of their own, but I find their company easier to handle than that of my old friends. Alfie and Mrs Lafleur are unafraid of grief; they know how to let it take its own course, its own time. They don't try and measure my progress, or give me a verdict on how I'm coping. And for that, I will be forever thankful.

I still ache whenever I think about Jamie – the absolute love of my life – with a longing that is hard to bear. A part of me still has difficulty believing I will never hear his voice again, or see him walk through the front door with a takeaway. Or hear him describe the Eiffel Tower as a giant axle stand, on a visit to Paris. But I also have a sense that the day will come when I won't think about him all the time. He will always be a part of my internal architecture. Even in the unlikely event that I meet someone new, Jamie will never disappear into the vapours. That's not how it works for me. But there are other people worth spending time with in this life, and I'm lucky enough to already have some of those.

I check my watch and leave the sanctuary of my car. Alfie and Mrs Lafleur are already inside the crematorium occupying two chairs on the front row. They wave me over, and I sit down beside them.

'Thanks for coming, Juliette,' Alfie says, already emotional. Mrs Lafleur has a tight hold of his hand and I let her take mine too, for a brief squeeze. 'You'll be coming back to mine after, for some lunch? It'll just be the three of us, but I'd like to raise a glass to Ivy with the people who cared about her.'

'Of course, I'd love to, Alfie, thanks for inviting me.'

He nods, satisfied, and we all face the front as the minister, Mr Wishaw, makes an appearance. He's one of the best, with a gentle manner, genuine warmth and empathy. Ivy could not have a better person to conduct the service. For a few moments, while the minister thanks us for coming today, I let my thoughts drift back to Ivy's flat and everything I learned about her. The bowler hats that greeted me in the hallway, the beautiful cabinets in the sitting room decorated with trailing ivy that wound itself into little hearts. I picture her neat and orderly kitchen, the recipes for cakes and her obvious love of baking. An image of the 1980s velour sofa comes to the fore, along with the study in pink that I found in her bedroom. The family photos, young Alfie in shorts, the box in the bathroom cupboard with a name tag from the hospital, Ivy's lost baby. I remember the photo of Ivy standing outside the haberdashery, when she was young and happy and full of life. I don't want to reimagine Ivy's life as a rock opera, or a 1940s musical. I want to remember her life as I found it, in a homely little flat in Starcross Crescent.

Just before Alfie gets up to deliver his eulogy, I hear the door at the back of the crematorium open and close, but I don't turn to see who has entered. There'll be time for that later.

Alfie takes his place at the front. He stands straight and smiles at me and Mrs Lafleur, with tears already rolling down his face, but his voice is steady.

'Ivy Edwards was my big sister. I can't remember a time when she wasn't there to hold my hand, when I fell and cut my knee, or to bail me out, when I was older, and so skint I couldn't pay the rent. She was always the practical one, our Ivy, but she had a big heart. She loved everyone who needed it, whether they deserved it or not. She was loyal. She didn't gossip about anyone, she always said it was unkind, that gossip only told you some of the facts and none of the messiness of the feelings behind things. You could go to her with any secret and she'd take it to the grave, she's taking some of mine with her today.' Alfie pauses, lowering his head, gathering himself together again. 'Ivy loved making clothes for people. She made this suit for one of my weddings that never quite happened, twenty-five years ago, and it's as good today as it was then. Ivy loved her husband, Stan, even when he did something daft like run over his own shoes with the lawnmower. He was a good man for all his mistaken ideas about Manchester United. He made her happy and she had a good life with him. They had a daughter, Sarah, who only lived for a few hours, but I know she'd want me to mention her today. Ivy had her fair share of heartbreak but she always found a reason to carry on, that was her way.'

He glances up at me and I can tell he's thinking about me and my loss. And I hold onto the second-date conker, sitting safely in my pocket, just for reassurance.

'We've had some great times together over the years, me and Ivy. I will miss her laugh and her voice on the end of the phone, asking me if I'd got my Christmas cards in the post on time. I never sent any, of course. I'll miss popping round to her flat every week for a cup of tea and a slice of sponge cake. I don't know how she did it, but nobody has ever made a better cake than Ivy, even when they used her recipes, which just proves it isn't all about the flour and butter. Ivy always said there was more to baking cakes than chemistry. I could talk about Ivy for hours and still be nowhere near done. I could tell you stories about her schooldays and courting days, but sadly, there isn't enough time. She would have loved to meet Juliette and Marina, and I'm sorry she never got the chance, as I've been lucky enough to do. I'll miss you Ivy, our Ivy, always one sock around her ankles when she was a little girl, and one sock pulled up to her knee. My sister, my best friend.'

And Alfie is done. He finds his way back to his seat as Mr Wishaw takes over again. He delivers the readings that Ivy chose for herself, saying the words that today, at least, offer some small comfort. And I don't allow myself to think about Jamie, this day belongs to Ivy and Alfie.

When the service is over, I turn to look at the person who entered the crematorium and give her a small nod. Abigail walks slowly up the centre aisle, as I try and prepare Alfie for what's about to happen.

'Alfie, I don't know if this is the right time or not,' I begin, hoping that today, of all days, I haven't misjudged things, 'but there's someone here who would like to meet you.'

Abigail stops just short of our little group, smiling anxiously. She's wearing a smart black dress and matching jacket, and she looks so much like Alfie I'm amazed he needs any introduction.

'Alfie, this is Abigail Armitage-Evans, your half-sister.'

Alfie gapes and it would be comical if it wasn't for the solemn occasion. Abigail extends her hand.

'I'm sorry for your loss. Juliette told me about the funeral, and I wanted to pay my respects. Ivy sounded like a wonderful sister.'

'You're my half-sister,' Alfie says, ignoring everything she's just said, looking at her like he's just discovered fairies are real, after all.

'It's lovely to meet you, Alfie. I hope you don't mind me coming here today?'

'Mind?' Alfie looks flabbergasted for a second, then he pulls her into a heartfelt hug, crinkling her dress. 'You're family. You've a right to be here. Ivy would have wanted you here.'

Abigail dabs her eyes with a tissue, when Alfie finally releases her, and for a few moments everyone is overcome by the occasion. But I can see the crematorium staff in the distance, checking their watches, glancing at the doors behind us where the next group of mourners is patiently waiting.

'Alfie, shall I bring Abigail round to your flat?' I suggest, so they can have some proper time together.

'That would be splendid, Juliette. I'll get the kettle on and we can all have some cake and a chat.'

Chat doesn't do justice to what's about to take place between Alfie and his half-sister. And Alfie looks so happy that I'm certain I made the right decision to contact Abigail about today. She puts a hand on my shoulder to thank me, as we leave the crematorium together, too emotional to form any words. I sense that our little group is about to expand again.

Jamie would have loved all of this. I wish I could tell him about Alfie's family reunion and the beautiful speech he made about his sister, about how much the words matter. But I can tell it to the snowglobe and the enamel box later. Just for now, there are other people who I need to be with, who I want to be with.

Tilda Carrow is the sole winner of the Carrow Award for Spectacular Writing (crafted by her husband from a yogurt carton) but she doesn't like to brag about it. Her expertise lies in observing her fellow human beings with a cake fork in one hand and a pen in the other – she only ever gets them mixed up occasionally – and in sharing some of her own difficult life issues through her writing. She doesn't have a social media *presence* because she suspects it's something you have to be born with.

Acknowledgements

I would like to thank my husband for his encouragement, support and insight, which has helped sustain me through all the highs and lows that writing inevitably brings. He has always had faith in me, and that knowledge has helped keep me going when things get tricky. I probably don't say it anywhere near enough, but thank you, I could not have written this book without you.

I would also like to thank my sister-in-law, and personal proo freader (not a typo). Her enthusiasm and support have been epic. She has helped me gain in confidence, when it's been lacking, and I'm so grateful for her belief in me.

Thank you both.
xxx

Printed in Great Britain
by Amazon